GLYN HARDWICKE

ACTING ON INFORMATION RECEIVED

Complete and Unabridged

ULVERSCROFT
Leicester

First published in Great Britain in 1986 by
Ross Anderson Publications,
London

First Large Print Edition
published February 1990

Copyright © 1986 by Glyn Hardwicke
All rights reserved

British Library CIP Data

Hardwicke, Glyn, *1921–*
    Acting on information received.—Large print ed.—
Ulverscroft large print series: mystery
I. Title
823'.914[F]

ISBN 0-7089-2191-4

Published by
F. A. Thorpe (Publishing) Ltd.
Anstey, Leicestershire
Set by Rowland Phototypesetting Ltd.
Bury St. Edmunds, Suffolk
Printed and bound in Great Britain by
T. J. Press (Padstow) Ltd., Padstow, Cornwall

Author's Note

LONDON'S dockland, presently so near a sad dereliction, existed precisely as described at the period of this story. The crime envisaged could certainly have happened but, being a composite of many, did not.

As for the characters—the heroes, police and legal, save for one or two affectionate portraits, are also composites. Anyone depicted as having the remotest tendency to villainy in any field of activity, is alas, wholly imaginary!

I am particularly indebted to my good friend Ian Alexander whose careful research and artistic skill have here combined to turn a maze of once mean streets into two little works of art.

GLYN HARDWICKE

THIS ONE FOR MIFF

Prologue

THE Royal Docks, Woolwich, London E 16. A soft, warm June night in the late 1960s.

There is something about a large and active dock complex in the small hours of a summer night which is intensely stirring —and not only to the romantic. The senses find a magic in the contrast between the sharp-cut pools of light and the extra darkness of the areas unlit. The colours of the lights are of a greater variety than a stranger might expect. White and yellow, of course, from street lights, deck lights and cabin lights. Red and green, naturally, in any situation involving port and starboard. But the jewels of light reflected in the placid water between the black-bulked sheds include, for some reason, sapphire, amethyst and opal.

Then, as one begins to assimilate the

patterns of light, one becomes aware of the sound—a sound that beats softly with a quiet, insistent throbbing. Each ship has a powerful generator deep inside its marine bowels which beats unceasingly. The cause is mundane. The spell remains.

A flicker of breeze—just enough to stir the still surface of the dock so that it reveals itself as water and not the black glass it had seemed to be—brings nearer the lumbering traffic sound that never leaves the streets of dockland quite alone, even in the smallest of hours. The overall impression is one of half-sleep. Of peace.

At No. 19 Gate in the south centre of the complex, the light from the window of the police box streams out across the entrance, supplemented tonight by that from the door which it is too warm for the duty constable to close. His trained ear picks up the sound of the approaching taxi as it bears left off the North Woolwich Road and up the slip road which is to bring it to the foreground of his attention. Probably a bunch of seamen returning from a night in the West End, if they have escaped the cheaper but more primitive attractions of dockland itself. He steps to the door as the cab pulls up, and then forward to the driver's window.

"'Evening, guv. Bunch of lads for some Portuguese boat. They keep repeating 'Eight/Ten Albert', which may make more sense to you than it does to me. Bit high, they are."

"Yes, the 'Algarve' is at that berth. She's Portuguese. You don't know the docks?"

"No, guv. Bit off my normal beat, you know, but they're paying over the odds from Piccadilly. Is it far from here?"

"About a mile. It's straight enough. Across there, look, and over to the right —right down the Centre Road which runs east between the sheds, with the Royal Albert on your left and the King George V on your right. The sheds are all marked with large numbers. The one you want is the last on the left before you get to the bridge over the cutting."

"Sounds clear enough. You on all night?"

"Yes. Look—they may ask you on board for a farewell drink. That's OK, but don't knock too much back, because this is your only way out again and I've got a trained nose."

"What—on the job? Not me, guv! Lemonade in a dirty glass is the strongest I'll take. My work depends on it. Now if there's any women . . . !"

"Not very likely. Scandinavian boats occasionally, they say, but not Portuguese. Anyway—suit yourself. No need to rush. I'll see you later—OK?"

"Thanks!"

The taxi glides forward. The policeman steps back and a muffled, drunken cheer sounds from the depths of the back. He watches impassively as it crosses over the junction and heads for the Centre Road. Then, stifling a yawn, he moves back into the police box.

In the taxi, the glass behind the driver's head slides back and the tension seeps through. Without turning, the driver's face creases into a grin.

"Easy, so far."

The face behind him is stern.

"Yeah. Now for the tricky bit. It's on the right, remember."

"I know—I know."

Steadily the cab moves like a large black beetle along the road between the pools of yellow light dripping from the street lamps which intensify the blackness of the giant sheds behind them on both sides. No. 20 on the left. 7/9 on the right. 16/14 on the left. The driver's eyes register the huge black figures painted in squares of white. Ahead now the headlights pick out the bridge across the cutting that links the two docks at their eastern end. He slows as they pass the gap between 8 and 10 sheds on the left, where the Portuguese ship rests in the Albert. Then he pulls across the road to the right, with only the railway line between the taxi and the high loading bank along the side of 3 shed. Half way along this, he slides quietly to a halt.

The order is whispered vehemently.

"Right! Everybody out—and quietly, for God's sake! Up on to that loading bank, the lot of you!"

The dark figures follow each other out of the passenger door, step gingerly across the deserted railway line, peering apprehensively to right and left as they pull themselves and each other up on to the concrete platform, four feet high. One man runs westward along it and disappears round the end of the shed. The other three cluster around a particular door. The leader taps softly four times in a set rhythm on the door. "God save the Queen". Tensely they wait for the planned response. Behind them on the road, the cab is softly turning round to head back for the Gate.

It is 10.30, the following morning. At 19 Gate, the predominant traffic flow has been into, rather than out of, the dock, but now a reverse pattern is beginning to predominate as lorries and trucks which arrived and have now unloaded are coming out, empty, while those which arrived empty to collect loads are beginning now to trundle towards the Gate, waiting patiently in a queue to have their papers checked by the Gate constable. There are actually two on duty, but PC Fredericks is at this moment busy directing in-comers to their destinations, while the outgoing queue is building up for the attention of PC Ellis.

He hands the driver of a huge articulated vehicle the papers he has checked as far as possible against the tarpaulin-covered load, pockets one copy for the moment, and waves him out on his way. Turning to the next in line, he hears the sound of a starter-motor being pressed again and again. Over-choked, probably. Good-humouredly he walks towards the driver of the big, square closed box-truck. It often happens.

Ahead, the articulated monster has cleared the Gate, turned left and vanished. There is some ten clear yards between the truck and the open Gate. Ellis can see the driver, red-faced and angry, and hear the whining rasp of the starter grinding again and again and again. The policeman is about two yards from the bonnet when, all of a sudden, the engine catches. Ellis smiles cheerfully at the driver, and is amazed to see neither relief nor an answering grin but grey, grim determination. As he registers the fact, the truck's doctored engine roars, the gear slams in, the clutch slides out. The whole thing seems to leap straight at him.

Twisting away instinctively, Ellis feels the agony as the truck's front corner shatters his shoulder, but not for more than a moment as his body flies up in a parabola. His helmet falls off. Then there is a sickening thud as the youngster's body smashes into the tarmac and a sharp crack as his head hits the kerb. Ellis is the only one near who doesn't hear it, as the truck speeds through the unobstructed Gate, slews to the right down the westward slip and roars away, heading for the North Woolwich Road and the Silvertown viaduct beyond.

The attention not only of his stunned colleague but of everyone nearby is understandably first on the crumpled figure. The whole incident has lasted no more than a few seconds. Nobody can begin to describe the truck, let alone its number-plate. Dashing to the police box to phone the ambulance, PC Fredericks feels that most of the time nowadays God seems to be on the side of the bloody criminals.

It is 4.30 p.m. In the Divisional Police Headquarters, Detective Superintendent David Gunn looks up from the papers on his desk and calls "Come in!" in response to the discreet tap on his office door.

"You wanted me, guv'nor?"

"Ah—yes, Jack. Sit down. What's the latest on young Ellis?"

"Still unconscious. Can't tell if there's brain damage yet."

"Bastards! It was the Berry gang, I presume?"

"All the hall-marks, yes. Left a man hidden in 3 shed at lock-up. He made all the preparations and let the rest in about 1 a.m."

"How did they come?"

"Taxi. Said they were pissed Portuguese seamen."

"What was the haul?"

"14 cartons—20,000 fags in each. Quarter of a million—give or take a few."

"No need to ask which brand, either. And I've no sympathy for them, Jack—none at all. We've told them time and time again. We've bloody begged them to package their export fags even slightly differently from their home-market ones but they won't do it. They don't seem able to appreciate that it's their packaging which makes their beastly fags unidentifiable as stolen anywhere in the world—and prime target material for every snotty-nosed tealeaf in the kingdom."

"Yeah. Not only that, guv'nor. They won't export them in plain cartons. They sit there in the lock-ups with their identity printed in large letters all over them. Doing the gang's work for them!"

"And it's just this one combine. All the others manage it. Why they can't, or won't, beats me!"

"I suspect it's something to do with insurance."

"Probably. Anyway, I don't give a twopenny damn for them, Jack. But this has led to the second gate-rushing job this year and this time they may have turned one of my most promising youngsters into a vegetable. I tell you privately, Jack, I'm right at the end of my tether. If we don't do something concrete about the Berry gang soon, something's going to snap. And if I lose my cool—"

"I know. Thank God, you never do."

"I never *have*. So far. But I've been thinking."

"About what we were discussing last week, you mean?"

"Yes. I've given up arguing. You're pushing an open door now, Jack. You still honestly believe you can infiltrate?"

"Given time, yes. Honestly."

"You know the risks."

"Nobody better. But they're calculated

ones. And if we can pull this off, we'll crack that lot wide open once and for all. It makes sense, guv'nor. All right, so we'll need a bit of luck, but God knows it's about time we had some, and I've got a feeling that we won't get it by sitting on our arses and trying to counter their moves. We've got to go out and *earn* our luck, if you like. I'm sure I can do this!"

"All right, Jack. I'm with you."

"Thanks. Very much. You won't regret it."

"I'd better bloody not, old lad! Now look—we discussed the means involved. As far as the Force is concerned, you are just about to be taken ill. Nothing dramatic at first—just 'flu. And then you won't come back. It'll be some rare and serious germ. You'll have been shifted to some obscure hospital for rare diseases in Scotland or somewhere—and you'll be much too infectious to be visited, anyway. Eventually you may recover and be posted off far away on a long, slow convalescence. As far as the Force knows, you will have vanished. 'Whatever happened to Jack Denny?', they'll ask in the canteen, and nobody will ever be quite sure. We'll put out a few well-chosen lies, and eventually they'll get used to your absence. They may suspect you of running off with the Chief Constable's wife, but in time you will be forgotten in the rush of work. Privately, on the other hand, you will not lose touch with me. If I have to make contact with you, we'll use the Personal column of the *Telegraph* as you suggested, but that'll be in emergencies only. You, though will contact me whenever you think it's safe and whenever you've got any news. Not otherwise. I'll straighten out the formalities at top level. There will be no questions asked up in Trap One, you can rely on that. We'll run it your way. We've just got to do something about those sods. And I'm not going to *ask* you not to take a single risk you can avoid—that's a bloody order—get it?"

"Got it, sir!"

The tall man grins, rises, goes to the door and then turns.

"Thanks, guv. Thanks a bundle!"

"Best of luck, Jack. You know—you've been overdoing it a bit, lately. You're looking a bit peeky. A touch of 'flu coming on, d'you think? You must take care of yourself, you know!"

1

CHARLES STRATTON, Prosecuting Solicitor of the Port of London Authority, walked with a hint of tiredness along the third floor corridor from the lift to his office. Reaching the door, he pushed it open and walked in, putting his heavy brief-case down on the corner of the desk.

Evan had heard him, of course. Stratton glimpsed the glass-panelled door leading to the smaller office as it opened and turned to get the mental relief he always did from his Personal Assistant's face. "Unflappable" was Evan Baunton's nickname, and with good reason. If things were going badly, the little man smiled. If there was a "Number One Flap" on about something, Evan never looked worse than solemn. He was grinning.

"Another redskin?"

"Ug," replied Stratton in the verbal shorthand they had developed over years of close association. This particular grammalogue had stemmed from his having remarked casually one day to Evan's query as to how a case had gone, "Another redskin bit the dust!"—a comment he had picked up from some source he could not remember.

"He didn't plead, then?"

"Not him!"

"This was the baby-food case, wasn't it?"

"Yes. Fourteen tins of it under the back seat of his car."

"I remember. Stubborn little sod. I suppose he said the Gate copper planted them there?"

"Rather to my surprise, no. Said one of his mates did."

"Well that's another standard. If one believed even a few of these excuses, life would be depressing. How did you get him?"

"He made a slip in cross-examination. Had to change his plea. Like taking candy from a baby."

"Was he represented?"

"No. He'd been to George Marshall and later to Mike Appleton. Both told him to plead but he wouldn't. He's happy enough. Feels he's had his little run for it."

"Take long?"

"No. Long wait to get started. Two hours sitting about waiting to start is more tiring than a three-hour case. I'm getting old."

"Aren't we all."

"Feels like a long day."

"Not over yet, either."

Something in Evan's tone made Stratton glance sharply at him. Behind that open grin was potential excitement. The solicitor walked round to the window side of the big desk, sat down in the high-backed black leather swivel chair and looked quizzically at his assistant. There had long been more than just a working partnership between Charles Stratton and Evan Baunton. Mutual respect, the necessity of knowing in each other's absence how he would react to a given situation—these were factors on the foundation of which they had built a relationship which had become almost telepathic.

"What's up, Evan?"

"Something at the Royals. 'Pop' wants you on the blower. Nobody's said anything but my big toe tells me something. Maybe . . ."

"Is he down at the Royals personally?"

"So it seems."

"Ask Vicki to get him for me, would you?"

"Sure."

Evan turned and walked over to the glass door, put his head into the little office and broadened his smile. It was all that was necessary. From inside, Stratton heard the voice of his secretary.

"Mr. Gunn at the Royals. I know."

Evan came back into the room, shutting the glass door quietly behind him. Stratton had only to glance at the big book-case against the wall and raise an eyebrow for the little man to take out a bunch of keys and fit one into the cupboard section below the book-shelves. From it he took two glasses and a litre bottle of a dry rosé. As he poured, the phone on the desk rang. Stratton picked it up.

"Thank you, Vicki." A click. "David? Charles here."

"Back from Grays? Good of you to ring, Charles. I have something I want to talk about—and not over this pesky machine."

Stratton wondered whether, if Evan had said nothing, he would have noticed for himself the trace of suppressed excitement in the voice of the newly promoted Detective Chief Superintendent and head of the Force CID.

"Fine. Out on the ground, are you? Want me down there?"

"No. Frankly, Charles, I—damn! Excuse me a moment."

Gunn's hand went over the receiver. Through it, Stratton could faintly hear orders being barked. He glanced up. Evan was carrying two glasses over, placing one on the blotter and raising the other in a silent toast. Stratton reached for his and they sipped together. As they did, David Gunn took his hand off the receiver, saying "—and shut that door, please!" Then he spoke into the mouthpiece again.

"Sorry about that, Charles."

"That's all right. You say you don't want me at the Royals?"

"No. I want somewhere more private. I'll be bringing someone with me. Are you in, this evening?"

"My flat, you mean? Yes."

"Ideal, if it's not awkward."

"Fine. I'd like Evan there, if he's free." Stratton raised his eyebrows as he spoke. Evan nodded.

"Of course," said Gunn at the same moment.

"He is. What time will you come? Want supper?"

"No thanks. Drink afterwards, perhaps. We'll come about nine."

"Good. You know the way in."

"I do. Till nine, then—and my apologies to Beth."

"She'll be delighted. Till nine, as you say."

He put the phone down and turned to Evan who was perched on the corner of the big desk.

"Sure it's not a nuisance for you?"

"Not a bit. Val's out this evening, anyway. It would have been a cold supper alone and a snooze in front of the telly. I'll tell her to expect me when she sees me."

"Great. Ask Vicki to get Beth, when she has a moment, so I can tell her we'll be three for supper."

"Thanks. I will."

"We'll walk over when we've finished

here. Meanwhile, what have you got to throw at me?"

"Not a lot. I'd like to run through the Garrett file with you. Jack Stewart's just rung about the Bullock job—he wants an adjournment from tomorrow at Thames Court. I've consented and had a word with the Clerk's office so there'll be no need for you to attend. We'll fix a day, later. So, with tomorrow in the office, I thought you'd like to get the Garrett brief dictated. It'll suit Vicki, too."

Stratton smiled agreement as he took another sip of wine. Sometimes he felt he was no more than a "front man" for his department, so efficient were Evan and Vicki. Still—even they could hardly run it without him to appear in court!

Evan disappeared into the little office as the phone on Stratton's desk rang again. He picked it up.

2

DAVID GUNN looked at his companion as he pressed the door phone at the western end of Thomas More House and waited for the reaction.

"They call Barbican 'The Fortress', I'm told. Small wonder!"

The tall man looked around him at the massive pillars of pock-marked concrete and shrugged.

"Built like one, certainly."

There was a click as Stratton picked up the door phone in the flat and said quietly, "David?"

"We're here."

"Pull!" Gunn grasped the metal block in front of him and the heavy door with steel-meshed glass swung towards him with another click.

"We're on our way!"

The two men stepped inside and, as the heavy door closed softly behind them, Gunn pressed the button of the lift.

Several floors above, Charles Stratton opened the front door of his flat and waited for the lift's arrival. When it came, he greeted the CID chief with an extended hand and a wide smile.

"Come in, David," he said, and looked interestedly at the tall, thin, bearded man behind Gunn's stocky frame. There was something familiar but not immediately recognisable about him. The two visitors came into the light of the spacious living room. Evan rose from the sofa and came across to take Gunn's hand. His eyes narrowed as the tall man looked around him in open surprise—the inevitable reaction of one who finds the welcome of a Barbican flat in happy contrast to the forbidding aspect of the estate's exterior. Then he uttered an exclamation.

"Good God—it's Jack Denny! I thought you were dead! How *are* you, you old villain?"

Stratton, who had been shutting the door, turned with a look of disbelief. The tall visitor was grinning widely. The beard was misleading of course—it altered the whole shape of the head, let alone the face, of the Detective Sergeant. The suit was old and shabby, the shirt collar slightly frayed and a little too large for the neck. The shoulders, slouched to fit the seediness of manner, looked narrow and skinny. Stratton took it all in and laughed.

"Marvellous, Jack! Really outstanding!"

"Thanks, guv'nor. Though the one thing I don't want to do is to stand out, if you know what I mean!"

Evan was shaking Denny's hand warmly before turning to exchange greetings with Gunn. Stratton walked over to a cupboard section of the big Ladderax unit which took up the whole length of the wall opposite the door, from the dining table in front of the hatch to the television set in the corner by the huge window—literally a wall of glass looking out onto the City with St. Paul's as a dramatic centrepiece. It was enough to make anybody gasp on seeing it for the first time. Waving his guests to sit comfortably, Stratton lowered a mirror-lined flap front and reached for bottles.

"Scotch and soda as usual, David? Evan, you're on claret with me—carafe's on the table so help yourself. Jack, what'll you have?"

"Beer if there's some handy, thanks."

"Lager in the fridge—all right?"

"Lovely, thanks."

"I'll get it," said a soft voice. The three men sitting rose as Beth Stratton came into the room. She had been crowned with rich auburn when she had married Charles nearly 25 years before. Now the natural waves were paler and there was a flick of white near her right ear, but this enhanced rather than detracted from a total effect that was altogether lovely rather than merely beautiful. It seemed that she had been born to smile. Her face smiled even in repose and now, as she came across the room to shake hands with Gunn, it was merry and welcoming.

"David—it's been too long! How's Dorothy?"

"Fine, thanks Beth. And if I may make so bold—you look prettier each time I see you."

"Thank you, David—how charming."

"No more than true, my dear. Er—I don't know if you've met Det. Sgt. Jack Denny. He doesn't normally look as scruffy as this, but he's on a job, just now."

Beth Stratton shook hands with the tall man. "Now sit down, all of you. Nice to meet you, Mr. Denny. No, I wouldn't say scruffy. A wee bit seedy, perhaps, but all in the cause, I'm sure. And dry—which is where I came in and something I will cure immediately. Lager, you said?"

She stepped lightly to the kitchen, emerging in what seemed but a few seconds with a cut-glass tumbler full of lager, which she put down on a small table near the sofa. Then she smiled round.

"I'll be in the kitchen with the hatch blind down, washing up, with the extractor fan on, which means I won't hear a word—and if that's not enough, David, I can easily do it all later and carry on with some sewing in the bedroom with my little radio, so do be frank."

"Beth, dear, I regard you as so much one with Charles that I wouldn't mind if you sat in here with us. It would probably have a good effect on my language, from which we should all benefit—and if you did make any remarks I bet they'd be intelligent and pertinent! Don't let us put you out at all. Treat us as if we weren't here!"

"And if you're not here, you can't help with the washing-up—I know what you mean! Not to worry. I'll be around if you want me."

She disappeared back through the sliding door into the kitchen. For a moment there was silence. Then Stratton said, "Right—what's it all about, then?"

Gunn lifted his glass and contemplated it.

"This," he said. "Only without soda."

"Raid on a lock-up, I suppose," said Evan. "Has it happened? Or, looking at Jack, here—maybe going to happen?"

Gunn looked at his sergeant. "Tell them, Jack."

"Right, sir. Well, it's not a lock-up raid. This one's a bit more spectacular."

"Don't tell me they're going to have a ship away!" said Stratton.

"No, guv, not up to that, quite. Though the way some of the big gangs are growing I shouldn't wonder if that might not actually happen one of these days. No—this is halfway between, as it were."

"A loaded container?" said Evan.

Denny nodded. For a moment there was silence as it sank in. Then Stratton said,

"That's a useful thing to know in advance. And yet it's quite simple, really. One set of well-forged documents and they can drive it away in the middle of the day—busier the better, indeed."

"Exactly," said Denny. "Next Thursday week, if their information is as precise as it seems."

"*Their* information? What about ours?"

"You mean you've managed a complete infiltration?" put in Evan.

The tall man nodded.

"Today's the first time I've seen Jack for two months," said Gunn. "I think I wouldn't have even now, but he wanted to pick up his pay!"

Evan frowned. "Marvellous, but very tricky! I hope you're looking after yourself, old lad. Those boys can be very distrustful, and if they clock on to you, they can be very nasty indeed. By the way —which lot is it? The Irish mob?"

"Not Irish, no. The whisky's Scotch and, by an odd coincidence, the No. 2 in the gang is Welsh."

Stratton swallowed.

"The only Welsh No. 2 I know is Harry

Williams. David, don't tell me Jack has managed to infiltrate the Berry gang?"

"He has. It's taken months and he's almost schizoid under the strain but yes, that's why I haven't seen Jack except very briefly for a very long time—and why I had to see you this evening."

"I see. Of course."

There was a pause for general assimilation. Then Evan coughed slightly. Stratton glanced at him and nodded minimally.

"Next Thursday week's June 14th," said Evan. "Is that the date the whisky's arriving, or the date they pull the job?"

"The job," said Denny. "I don't know the arrival date—day or so before, probably. Royals, for sure. My guess would be 'F' Shed, The Vic."

Evan looked at Stratton. "And out through 6 Gate. If we run this as it could possibly be run—"

"We could saturate the area, watch the job taking place, let it leave the dock and follow it all the way to the place we've been looking for for years. The place where their big loads are carved up into bits—the Berry 'slaughter'."

"Exactly!"

"Is that on, David?"

"Charles—as you say, we've suffered for years from not knowing just where the Berry gang take their gear before it's distributed, but it was impossible without good advance notice of a job coming off. Now, thanks to Jack, we've got that notice at last. It's a chance we couldn't pass up. On? You bet it's bloody on!"

"Fine!" said Stratton. "Jack—do you know what Scotch it will be? One of the big groups?"

Denny put his empty tumbler down on the small table beside him. "Funnily enough, I heard that only this morning. Not one of the big brands at all. Comes from a smaller distillery way up in the far north."

"What would life be without coincidence?" interposed Stratton. "I suppose it wouldn't be Invermuir?"

"It would indeed, guv'nor."

"You know it, Charles?"

"David, I not only know it—I've been all over it and stayed at the house of the owner. It's a small family company, actually. The head of it is an old chum of mine. Oh—and as a final touch—you're drinking it at this moment, David!"

"If you read it in a book you wouldn't believe it," said Evan.

"Then you could get all the facts about the order," said Gunn, regarding his glass intently. "And that's something that might save Jack risking his neck asking questions."

Denny grinned. "I'll drink to that!"

"Not until I've got you a re-fill," said Stratton, rising and pulling aside a corner of the blind that covered the hatch to the kitchen. "More lager in the fridge, Beth?"

Evidently there was. A moment later, Beth Stratton joined them from the kitchen, carrying a bottle of lager on a small tray which she held out to Denny who had risen and took it, thanking her.

"Evan, you and Charles have got your carafe. David—more Scotch?"

"No thanks—this one's enough for now."

"Darling—have you heard from Margaret McDonagh, lately?" asked Stratton.

"Not since that postcard from Italy last

week, you remember. They'll be home by now. It was sent from Milan airport."

"So it was—I remember. Fine, thanks."

Beth smiled round, tucked the tray under her arm and returned to the kitchen. Stratton smiled. "I hope that's a sign we're going to get all the luck," he said. "I'll ring Ian McDonagh shortly—but after Jack's gone. If he doesn't know the details, it'll be something he won't have to pretend he doesn't know."

"Thanks, that's thoughtful," said Denny. "And I don't want to break anything up but I'd better be slipping back. Is it as difficult getting out of these flats as it is getting in?"

"Balcony out there—easy jump!" grinned Evan.

"I'll show you down to the podium," said Gunn, rising. "One or two things which won't concern Mr. Stratton. Back in a few minutes."

Denny walked over to the kitchen door, slid it open and said thanks and goodnight to Beth. Then he shook hands with Stratton and Evan before following Gunn, who had pressed the lift button, out into the hall. Stratton said, "I'll leave the flat door unlatched, David. As long as you don't let the outer door click shut behind you, you can come back up and push this open—OK?"

The lift door opened and the tall, thin man followed the stockier one out of their sight. Stratton closed the flat door without latching it and came back in. He picked up the carafe and refilled the glasses.

"Very fine detective, Jack Denny," he said reflectively. "Has he any family, do you know?"

"Widower—no children," said Evan. "Good thing, really."

"Yes. I'll ring Ian McDonagh when David gets back. A really lucky break, eh?"

"Couldn't be luckier."

Stratton walked over to the section of the living room which formed the base of a backward "L" and which could be separated by a sliding wall if it was needed as a study. He began to riffle through an address book to find the number he would want.

3

DAVID GUNN arranged his briefing session for the middle of Wednesday afternoon. The main canteen at Royal Docks Police HQ was packed and smoke-filled. Each late-comer was greeted with cheerful ribaldry, men here and there finding themselves pleased but puzzled to see friends from other Divisions. Most were CID, but there were uniformed men here and there. At one end of the room was a small dais on which stood a table and three chairs. Conversation ranged from the excited to the blasé. Then a uniformed sergeant, who was keeping an eye on the stairs from the upper offices, through a pane of glass in the door, coughed loudly and held it open. Conversation stopped as though everyone had been struck dumb. They rose as a man, including Charles Stratton and Evan Baunton, who were at one end of the front row.

In dead silence, David Gunn strode in,

followed by Gerald Malone, the Divisional Superintendent, and George Bryan, the Det. Chief Inspector at present in charge of the Divisional CID. Gunn took the centre of the three chairs, putting a file of papers on the table, and sat down without ceremony, waving a hand in a gesture that released everyone else to sit, too. Bryan sat on his left. Malone remained standing on his right and cleared his throat.

"Right, gentlemen! Most of you have some idea of why we're here this afternoon. I won't waste time with preliminaries. I'll leave Mr. Gunn to tell you the details."

He sat down, turning his chair slightly towards Gunn as he did so. Just for a second the stocky figure who had everyone's full attention seemed lost in thought. Then he rose and looked at them with a half smile, the head moving a little from side to side as the eyes raked the rows of men—Stratton guessed there were about sixty altogether—from the straight-backed uniformed Inspectors in the front to the experienced CID men lolling, rather than sitting, on the window seat at the back.

"Thank you all for coming. I want to say this first. Really reliable information about a major criminal operation in advance is rare. All of you realise that total secrecy is vital to success. In this case, it's rather more. If anything in this caper goes wrong, the first and certain casualty is going to be one of your colleagues who is presently standing, so to speak, on a trapdoor. One slip, unintended and not apparently serious, and that trap will be sprung. If that happens, the fate of that very brave man and fine copper will remain on your conscience for the rest of your life. I am confident that he and I can rely totally on every man jack of you."

There was no murmur of assent—no sound at all. Gunn looked down and flicked open the file on the table. A glance at the top sheet and he looked up and drew a deep breath.

"Now—the central object of this operation is a container lying at this minute at 'F' Shed, Royal Victoria Dock. It is full of whisky which, I need not remind you, is a very marketable commodity the world over. Some of you watched this container arrive, the day before yesterday, when we were able to try out several observation points, some of which proved more effective than others. It was a useful dry run. Tomorrow's for real.

"At about 1.30 p.m., a long flat-bed empty lorry is expected to arrive at the Vic and to go directly to 'F' Shed. Its arrival may be preceded by a telephone call to that shed, telling those concerned that a mistake has been made. When the driver arrives, he will produce papers on the authority of which the container of whisky will be loaded on to the flat-bed and removed from the Royals, ostensibly headed for the India and Millwall Docks. A container will in due course turn up at those docks, though it will not be the one which left the Royals earlier, probably by 6 Gate. That one—the whisky one—will be driven straight from the Royals to a distribution point—a slaughter—somewhere in dockland, maybe not far away. That is what the Berry gang think. Some of us, gentlemen, think otherwise."

A half-smile showed again in his eyes as he raised his head and glanced to right and left. He expected, and got, no reaction. It was a pause for effect, to let that much sink in. Another deep breath.

"Now, there are one or two factors in this operation that make it unusual, perhaps even unique. First—the theft will appear to have succeeded. Checks will be made by the men in charge at 'F' Shed. All will appear to be in order. The whisky container will be loaded. At the Gate, the papers will again be carefully perused by the man on duty. I need not say that they will have been most expertly forged. The Gate officer, apparently deceived, will pass them as all in order. The lorry will leave the dock, no doubt watched, probably from the Viaduct above, by the gang. It will head straight for the 'slaughter', which we have been trying literally for years to locate. Unsuccessfully. Either there or on the way there, the driver's forged papers will be handed to the driver of a similar container which will head at once for the Indias, where it will be loaded on to a ship that evening. The Berry gang believe that not until that spoof container is unloaded in the Far East will any crime even be discovered, and the trail here will long since have grown cold.

"In fact, gentlemen, we are going to watch all this happen. We are going to follow that whisky wherever it goes, without being observed. When it reaches the slaughter, we shall all group there very quickly and we shall walk in—with any luck, catching them in mid-carve-up."

Again he paused, this time as if savouring the moment of capture. Again the room was as still as if he was the only man in it. Another deep breath.

"Now, gentlemen, let us look at the operation from our point of view. You will not concern yourselves with how, nor through whom, we got our advance information. Nor will you concern yourselves with the quiet negotiations that we have conducted with the producers and genuine buyers of that whisky, not to mention their insurers. It is enough for you to know that if anything back-fires, several of your superior officers, myself in the lead, will be for the proverbial high jump. The consequences of allowing a load to be stolen, even with the most worthy motive of finding the Berry gang's slaughter, are obvious. I am—correction—*we* are the stake in a gamble on the efficiency and integrity of this Force. I prefer to regard that gamble as a calculated risk. Of course we have contingency plans, with which those who are affected by them will be made familiar. But the end result should be the appearance of a bunch of right wrong 'uns at the Central Criminal Court. Any other result and—well . . ."

His shoulders moved upwards, effectively conveying what words might otherwise have done. Then his face creased into an expansive open smile.

"I might have said before what there is little need to say now—that the special circumstances of this case provide the explanation for the presence here today of members of both branches and all Divisions. Although the operation will be in and around the Royals here, it is one of such importance that it's only right that all our Divisions should be given a chance to shine. You have all been selected by your superiors. This job requires the cream of the Force, and though there are a few who cannot just now be spared from other commitments, this room basically contains exactly that. I hope you feel pretty chuffed about that, not least because those may be about the last amicable words you'll hear from me until this little party's over."

This time there was a hearty laugh from all over the room—partly appreciation, partly release of tension. The atmosphere was now one of considerable excitement. The old hands sprawled on the far window-seat gradually, so as not to make it obvious, began to move until they were sitting up straight. Gunn noticed it with an inner smile.

"Now for some details. There will actually be a great deal of radio work and our channel may well be monitored by the gang, so we must do our best to lull them away from the idea that we are on to them. So early tomorrow morning, sundry calculated messages will pass between Divisions to give any eavesdroppers the impression that we shall be undertaking a complicated training exercise during the middle day. But apart from this camouflage, everyone on this job will be a part of one of four separate teams, each with its basic task, and each with its own radio call-sign. The ordinary phonetic alphabet is useless here —it could cause confusion with routine messages, perhaps in other Forces. As you all know, personal radios can go funny, with messages being heard clearly at distances fifty times their normal maximum range. Being a simple copper, myself, and thus devoid of creative imagination, I asked our good friend Mr. Stratton to suggest some interesting call-signs."

He flashed a grin to his right, which Stratton returned with an artificial wince to accompany it.

"Those of you who know our solicitor will not be unduly surprised to learn that his first notion entailed the teams being labelled Claret, Burgundy, Alsace and Rhone, with my Headquarters, I say with some pride, being Champagne. But then we felt that wine was perhaps a little too near whisky as a topic, so we asked him to try again. The second lot consisted of Greek Gods, but here lay hidden difficulties into which we need not go. Mr. Stratton therefore handed the task over to his assistant Mr. Baunton who, straining into a world which he assures me he is not familiar with, came up with Matthew, Mark, Luke and John, which leaves HQ to shoulder the not inapt burden of patrolling the Damascus Road under the name of Paul who, you will remember, found it hard to kick against a lot of . . ."

A huge roar of laughter drowned the end of his sentence. A voice somewhere at the back of the room filled in the biblical blank with Rabelaisian gusto, thereby enabling those who didn't know, but felt they should, to laugh as heartily as the rest.

"At all events," resumed Gunn, "tomorrow I shall be known for the duration of this operation as Paul, which is probably about as near sainthood as I shall ever attain, as Mr. Baunton tactfully implies. My epistles, then, will certainly bring forth your gospels. And may God bless us, every one!"

He let the laughter die naturally. Then he turned over a page of the file on the table and looked up again, completely serious.

"Now to business, gentlemen—and right serious business it is. The sections of the operation which will concern our four teams are as follows. First, Matthew—charged with the saturation cover of the area *outside* the dock gates, with the object of spotting members or associates of the

Berry gang who may be engaged in the vital preliminary work of this crime. Associations of unknowns with gang members will naturally also be of great importance. So—identification, clear and correct, will be Matthew's primary function. This team will contain every member of this Force who has had occasion to make personal contact with any member of the Berry gang over the last three years.

"The job of Mark—the smallest of the three teams—will be simpler. Each member will go to a pre-set position, known only to his fellow members and to Headquarters. Anyone else might possibly give an instinctive casual glance to check the presence of a colleague, and such glances can be noticed by alert and cunning criminals. We cannot risk ruining this job. Enough to say that the arrival and movements of the flat-bed will be watched and plotted from first moment to last, within the dock gates. So much, then, for Mark.

"The fourth team—if I may mention it out of its proper order—will be code-named John. It will be the reserve squad, covering the provision of understudies and unforeseeable events.

"And this brings us to the team with the greatest responsibility of all—those who will be trailing the container from the Gate to the slaughter without themselves being spotted. You will all appreciate that, in a sense, everything in this whole operation is going to depend on Luke."

Stratton was not certain at first that Gunn's pause was intentional. But Evan's unquenchable sense of fun became apparent to everyone in that room at that moment. There was what sounded almost like a concerted hiccough as some sixty men suddenly all saw the same joke at the same second and choked back the guffaw it almost provoked. David Gunn was looking down at the file on the table without so much as a twitching muscle. But he had known in advance. He and Evan, both. His assistant was smiling broadly, blandly, to all appearances quite unaware that anything of significance had been said. Only because Stratton was so close could he see the corner of the small man's mouth twitch minimally.

"Cheeky bastard!" whispered Stratton. Evan might have been stone deaf.

The moment was past almost as soon as it had happened. In its calculated effect, it was typical of Evan. It was also typical of David Gunn to drop it casually at the end of a spoken paragraph so as to get the maximum fun from it. Both knew that it would dawn upon everyone that a disrespectful reference had been made to the Chief Constable of the Force which, provided it was made wholly without overt reaction, could be recalled with high delight for years to come, though it was too subtle to be bandied about and so have its effect reduced. For everyone was aware that the Chief Constable, William Bath, was a nice, decent, worthy but sadly ineffective leader. There were good reasons for this, known to very few. But the Chief had a nickname which derived from a casual reference by some Force wag to "Bath being no more than lukewarm". The reference was so personal, so "in", that it was never mentioned, though there was not a man who did not know it and recognise it at this moment. The simple fact was that not merely the success but the existence of this whole operation depended on its remaining outside the personal knowledge of the Chief Constable, who could never have brought himself to approve it. And since this could not be stated in terms, it was better that it should be acknowledged in the form of a tactful joke. Much better, thought Stratton.

Following his brief but carefully calculated pause, David Gunn raised his head and concentrated hard on an invisible point roughly in the centre of the room and about five feet above the heads of his audience.

"Some details will be enough to put you generally in the picture," he said, and began to outline the pattern on which he had worked so carefully and so hard.

4

IT was as though nature had wanted to get in on Gunn's act. For three weeks it had scarcely stopped raining. Occasionally it had slowed its force to a drizzle, but most of the time it had poured solidly. Floods spread all over the country. Race meetings everywhere were abandoned without even the formality of daily inspections. Cricket was out of all question. Dockland had merely shrugged its shoulders and plodded damply about its business.

Then on the Wednesday afternoon, actually while the briefing was taking place, the rain had stopped—really stopped. There was even a momentary glimpse or two of a pale, watery blue sky, high above scudding clouds. Londoners looked up cynically, prepared to find that it was only a pause in a record wet summer —a breather while nature gathered fresh strength for downpours to come. Yet Thursday dawned without so much as a trace of cloud. The sun rose amazedly into a clear blue sky. All over England, people turned, outside their front doors, and put their macks back on their hall-stands before re-emerging with beaming smiles into a glorious mid-June day. At suburban stations, even jackets were beginning to be discarded and commuters, who had withdrawn defensively into themselves for weeks, now reverted to being at least slightly sociable to acquaintances.

Charles Stratton and Evan Baunton drove down to the Royals together in Stratton's car, sliding off Silvertown Way down to and then east along Victoria Road, swinging right over the level crossing, past the "Connaught" and left into No. 9 Gate, bumping over the railway lines and round to the big car park behind Divisional Police HQ. There, Stratton locked the Citroen and they walked round to the main entrance. The wall clock facing the door stood at 9.30, which explained the apparent lack of activity. Everyone on Matthew had been somewhere out on the ground in plain clothes since 8 o'clock. There was an amiable giant in uniform by the door. Stratton smiled a greeting.

"Have you seen Mr. Gunn?" he asked.

"In Radio Control Centre upstairs, sir. He said you were both to go straight up when you arrived."

With a word of thanks, Stratton led the way up the stairs and along the corridor. He tapped quietly on the last door on the right, opening it as he did so.

The room was large. It had originally been two, and the light wall had been knocked down many years ago. The end furthest from the door was dominated by the vast radio console—an apparatus which always reminded Stratton of those huge Wurlitzer organs which used to be regular features of cinema programmes, emerging from what would have been the orchestra pit in a theatre, and descending back into it ten minutes later leaving the auditorium full of colour and sound. The radio console's face was banked with rows of small coloured lights—red, green and yellow—some of which winked busily. Above its width was a newly constructed attachment in the form of a very large scale plan showing in detail not only the Royals with its miles of quays and blocks of sheds but the streets of dockland north and south of it. In front of this plan, which had been made under the seal of strict security by two Head Office draughtsmen working deep into several nights, was a clear sheet of glass in a wooden frame. Around its edges rested a collection of counters—round, square and triangular—each attached to a rubber suction-button. A small amplifier at one end of the console top was twittering messages in unemotional voices from all over the area.

A tall grey-haired sergeant, chain-smoking, and an eager young constable, restless with excitement, seemed capable of deciphering these as if they were accompanied by none of the heavy static which rendered most of them unintelligible to the new arrivals. Small green circular counters were beginning to appear here and there on the upper part of the plan showing the streets to the north of the docks.

David Gunn was sitting in the corner by the window in a chair upholstered in a rather garish blue PVC with arms which looked too small for him to be comfortable. He waved them to two upright chairs beside him, taking a clipboard and a stop-watch off the seat of the one nearest to him.

As they sat watching, Stratton and Baunton began to distinguish the messages from the crackling background given out by the amplifier. "Mark—27—9—16" caught Stratton's ear, and at once the young constable reached for a small blue triangle and fixed it to the north side of the dock. A few moments later he heard "Mark Benign 16" and a similar triangle was attached over a shed on the north side of the Royal Victoria Dock. Then it dawned on him and he turned to Gunn who was watching him with a half-smile.

"Simple, as you see," said Gunn quietly.

"It was 'Benign' that threw me at first."

"Me too," said Evan. "Until I realised that the triangle went up over B Shed and I saw it must have been 'B9'."

"I had the same thought," said Stratton. "And then I realised that the 9th letter of the alphabet is 'I' and the 16th is 'P'—"

"Making it almost certain that '9—16' meant 'In Position'."

"Exactly. And then I remembered that the first message started 'Mark 27' and there's the triangle on 27 Shed for confirmation."

"All I hope is that the Berry gang haven't got anyone monitoring the operation as bright as you two!" said Gunn.

"No—knowing the significance of 'Mark' and looking at the plan and the counters made it soluble," said Evan.

There was a tap on the door and Gunn turned. The pink face of Gerry Malone appeared, eyebrows lifted in unspoken query. David Gunn was out of his chair and out through the door at once, with a speed unexpected for one of his bulk.

When he came back, five minutes later, there were at least a dozen blue triangles on the plan. Whichever way the lorry approached, it was going to be under observation all the way to "F" Shed. Stratton wondered what each man was doing at that moment. Probably munching sandwiches or sipping coffee, he thought. Gunn resumed his chair, peering across at the map.

"Everything all right?" asked Stratton quietly.

"Yes. Tricky moment. It was Luke. Could I see him this afternoon about something? I said I had a series of meetings down here which would take all day and he said tomorrow would do. I thought for an awful moment he was going to suggest coming down and combining our chat with a look around the Division, but it was probably only my guilty conscience!"

He consulted his clip-board. "Ah! Only the key man to come, and he's due to report in—"

The amplifier crackled and the PC picked up the last little blue triangle. "Marquis 9—16" it sounded like, and down went the triangle on "S" block, directly opposite the shed where the container lay.

"Who?" whispered Stratton.

"Bill Brewer," said Gunn. Stratton nodded. If he had hand-picked the team, the rangy, cool-headed Det. Sgt. Brewer would have been his choice, too.

The sergeant at the console turned. "Mark all in position, sir."

"Right. Acknowledge, please," said Gunn, and the sergeant switched on the desk microphone. "Paul to Mark. All set.

Paul to Mark. All set. Out." Gunn glanced at Stratton.

"Nothing more now till Luke gets set—depending on what comes in from Matthew, of course," he said, putting his clip-board down. "You two care for a cup of coffee in Gerry's office?"

5

IT was shortly after 12.30 when the Jaguar was spotted. They were back in the control room with cans of beer and thick cheese sandwiches beside them. The breakthrough, when it came, was conveyed in a tone so devoid of apparent excitement that, if Stratton hadn't been looking at Gunn at that moment, he would have missed its significance.

"Hello Paul—this is Matthew 6. I have a green Jaguar under observation. Stationary on the north side of Gresham Road at its eastern end, near Shipman Road. It has been there for three minutes. Standing on the pavement beside it now is Harry Williams. He is looking at his watch, repeatedly. The driver is, I think, Paul Burney. Front seat passenger believed to be Lucky Delafield. The registration number is VLC 167 F. Repeat—VLC 167 F. I think this is it. Over."

The mention of Williams had brought Gunn out of his chair and across the room to the console. Now he took the mike and snapped the switch on, his voice as steady as his movement had been agitated.

"Matthew 6—this is Paul. Reading you. Hold on. Over."

The young PC had already moved. Just off Prince Regent Lane, at the eastern end of Gresham Road, was a black rectangle on its suction button. Gunn's eyes scanned the area around it. He snapped the switch on again.

"Paul to all Gospellers. We're under way. There is a green Jaguar VLC 167 F —repeat, VLC 167 F—waiting in Gresham Road, eastern end, north side. Driver probably Paul Burney. In car, Lucky Delafield. Beside it and getting the twitch is Harry Williams himself. Stand by for action." He paused for long enough for facts to be scribbled in note-books. Then he took a deep breath.

"Now—everyone stand by, with the following exceptions. Matthew 10 will go east along Victoria Dock Road, turn left into Throckmorton Road and then second right into Berwick Road. Rendezvous on foot nearby with Matthew 6 on north-west corner of church, vehicle staying ready to

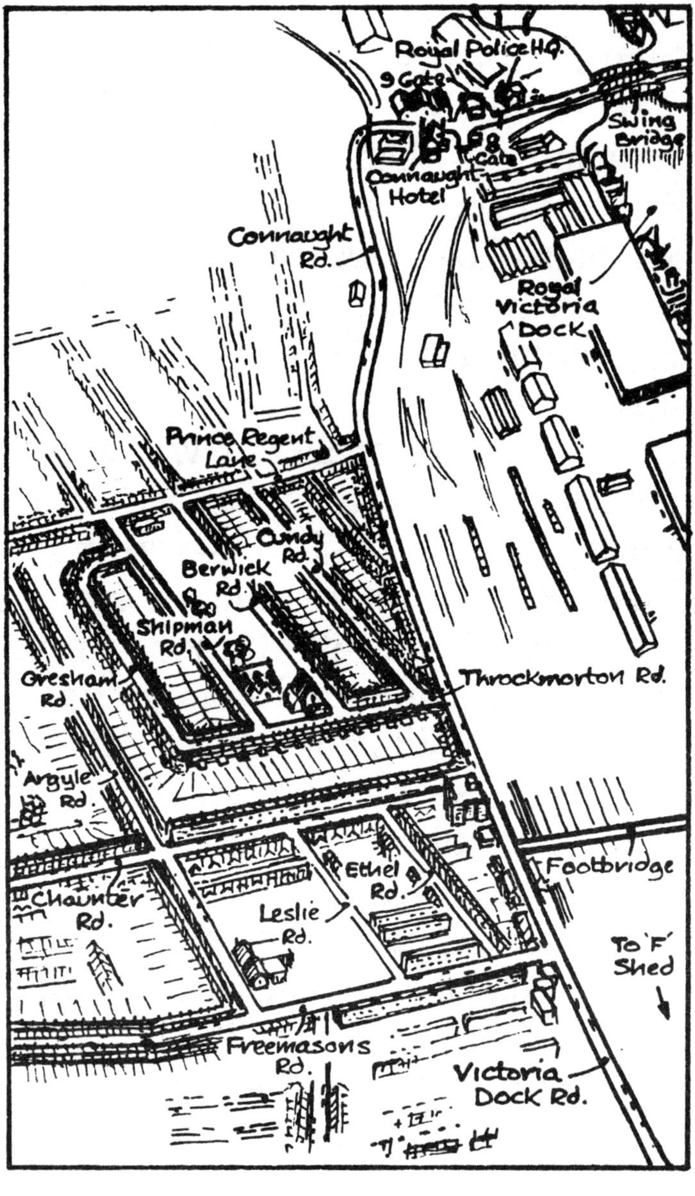

Royal Police H.Q.
9 Gate
8 Gate
Swing Bridge
Connaught Hotel
Connaught Rd.
Royal Victoria Dock
Prince Regent Lane
Cundy Rd.
Berwick Rd.
Shipman Rd.
Gresham Rd.
Throckmorton Rd.
Argyle Rd.
Ethel Rd.
Footbridge
Chaunter Rd.
Leslie Rd.
To 'F' Shed
Freemasons Rd.
Victoria Dock Rd.

go in Berwick Road. Next—Matthew 4—pedal along Shipman Road to its east end, and make a fake call at some house on the south side from where you can see the Jaguar in Gresham Road. The rest of you—all stations—double your vigilance. That lorry must be near, now. Report when spotted. Out."

He snapped the switch off and gestured to Stratton. "Clip-board, please, Charles." Stratton grabbed it and handed it across. Gunn studied it intensely for a moment, then turned over a page, then two more. Then he resumed his study of the wall-plan, on which the PC had placed a green square in Berwick Road to the south of the church. There were two green circles on its north-west corner, now. At the other end of Shipman Road there was a green circle on the southern side, opposite the gap.

The silence in the room was broken unexpectedly by Evan Baunton's voice. At some stage he had quietly got up and walked over to the window. The room, which was at the west end of the building, looked out over the car park to the swing-bridge which crossed the cutting that joined the Albert to the Victoria Docks.

"Guv'nor—here, a minute. It just could be . . ."

Stratton was beside him at the window in a moment and Gunn not more than a second or two later. Rumbling steadily northwards over the swing-bridge was a long, flat-bedded empty lorry.

"I know there's thousands of the things," said Evan, "but I thought—it's heading the right way, after all."

"It could be, Evan—it could be!" Gunn's excitement was obvious. "We assumed it was coming from the north. Suppose it's been sitting in the Albert Lorry Park till rendezvous time! Keep watching!"

He moved back to the console and grabbed the microphone.

"Paul to all Gospellers. There is just such a lorry as we're waiting for, on the swing-bridge between the Vic and the Albert, heading north. No means of knowing whether it's our target but it *could* be. Can't see number-plate from here. If it does not turn left into 8 Gate or right into 9 Gate, it should soon be in sight of Matthew 2. Keep your eyes peeled, lad, and report what it does. Over."

Half turning to the window, Gunn grinned at Stratton's raised eyebrows and pointed at a green circle at the northern end of the old footbridge linking the north side of Victoria Dock with Victoria Dock Road at No. 7 pedestrian gate and both of them with the old Custom House Station. Stratton nodded, picturing the man on the bridge staring east towards the level crossing about three-quarters of a mile away. From the window, Evan spoke again.

"Just a glimpse, but he's past the Connaught. Went into neither dock. Fingers crossed!"

Tension mounted in the silence that followed. Then at last the amplifier crackled.

"Matthew 2. Got him, sir! He's—heading west—wait a bit—no, he's turning right into Prince Regent Lane, I can see his winker. Yes, there he goes! Over."

"Paul to Gospellers. We think we may have the lorry now moving north along Prince Regent Lane. Matthew 4, you could be nearest. Report the moment you see it. Over."

A brief pause. Then again the crackle of the amplifier.

"Matthew 4 to Paul. Got him, sir! He just passed the east end of Shipman Road, going north but slowing. I moved to the corner, unnoticed by the Jag, and saw him pull left into Argyle Road. Driver is wearing tartan cap with bobble on top. I think I'm going to have a puncture. Over."

"Paul to everyone. This is it. Remember —any suspicion that they are being watched and the whole thing's blown. Now—Matthew 6—move very cautiously one street further north, with Matthew 10. See if you can watch the Jag without being noticed. Over."

The PC moved the circles. The villains had chosen their meeting-place carefully. Throckmorton Road went no further north than Gresham Road, so it was not possible for anyone to carry on northwards until they could look along Argyle Road and check the position of the lorry. For the moment the lorry didn't matter, but it soon would. Gunn spoke almost as if he had read Stratton's mind.

"Paul to Matthew 3. Drive cautiously south along Freemasons Road. Get to where you can see east along Argyle Road. When the lorry moves, try and follow him to the Docks, but first I'd like confirmation that he is in Argyle Road—it's only an assumption, so far."

A full minute went by. Stratton began to wonder if anything had gone wrong. He glanced at Evan, who had returned to his chair and was now placidly munching on a sandwich. Evan winked. Stratton felt that any food just now would choke him. He picked up his can and took a sip of lager. Then at last the speaker crackled again.

"Matthew 4 to Paul. The lorry driver's just walked into Shipman Road from Prince Regent Lane. He's approaching the Jag in Gresham Road. Harry Williams is obviously relieved. Lucky started to get out but Harry waved him back inside. I don't know the lorry driver—woolly cap as mentioned, black leather jacket and jeans. I am now tinkering with my back wheel with my back to them, but I have a

61

small mirror. Harry and the lorry driver are talking now. I can't see any papers. The car's blocking my view. Harry's giving him some instructions. The driver's putting something into his inside pocket—could be papers but I can't see. Now he's off back the way he came. Harry's back in the Jaguar. Excuse me—over!"

It sounded like someone making excuses on leaving a party. Stratton saw the grin that was never far from Evan's eyes. Then more crackling.

"Matthew 6 to Paul. Papers were handed over all right. We could see them from here. They were roughly the size and shape of delivery notes. The Jag's gone, now. Unless it's swung back down Shipman Road. I'm moving south as I speak. No, it's not in Shipman Road. I can see Matthew 4—he's pedalling off eastwards—I can see him now turning north into Prince Regent Lane. Over."

"Paul to Matthew 3. Come in please. Over."

"Matthew 3 here, sir. I'm on Freemasons Road, watching the lorry at the far eastern end of Argyle Road. I didn't want to interrupt, before. Here comes the driver

62

now, from Prince Regent Lane, on foot. He's getting into his cab. I'm ready when he moves. Over."

Gunn said quietly to Stratton, "We've lost the Jaguar, of course. But that's not serious. It'll turn up later. I would hazard a guess that that lorry won't actually move off for ten minutes or so. About 1 o'clock, I expect."

6

GUNN was right on both points. At exactly 1 o'clock the lorry moved off. Matthew 3 had spotted the driver's movements in the cab and quietly started, turning right into Coolfin Road and quickly rounding Murray Square, until only the bonnet of his van would have been visible to the lorry as it passed down Freemasons Road and paused at the junction, right opposite Matthew 2 on the foot-bridge, who reported it turning east along Victoria Dock Road. Behind it, the scruffy little van with the specially souped-up engine that was Matthew 3 followed the same route, but with two cars between them.

Once over the level crossing and past the Connaught Hotel, the empty flat-bed turned right, entering Victoria Dock by 8 Gate, waved in by the duty PC, for checks were made of all vehicles leaving but very rarely of those entering the docks. Matthew 3 had pulled off the road inside the Gate, a moment later. His job was for the moment done.

Slowly along the north side of the dock rumbled the lorry, followed now by the eyes of the men placed discreetly on the roofs of the sheds and office blocks—the "Mark" team. The last of these to report was Bill Brewer, opposite "F" Shed, and when the lorry turned in there and went out of his sight, there was nothing to do but wait. In the near future, as Gunn had observed at the briefing, everything was going to depend literally on Luke.

Gunn had decided not to re-check all the Luke team yet. He made sure that "John" —the reserve squad—was standing by in case they were required. Then he sat restlessly at the console, clip-board and can of Heineken in front of him. It was the worst bit, for him. The next move was with the Berry gang.

Action, when it came, surprised Stratton.

"Paul from Luke 9. Here comes the green Jag—VLC 167 F—heading along Silverton Way southwards, approaching the viaduct. He's passed the slip road to 6

Gate. He's pulling in to the pavement just beyond it. Lucky Delafield's getting out. Funny, I can't see anyone in the back. Lucky's crossed the pavement. He's leaning on the parapet as if he's waiting for someone. He can see the last fifty yards of the stretch the lorry will cover before it reaches 6 Gate. Luke 10 and I are strolling south along the west pavement, chatting casually, me with my deaf-aid. We are opposite Luke 5, now. He's crouched down, fiddling with the engine of his bike. He gave me a quiet thumbs-up. Neither Paul Burney nor Lucky seem to be taking a blind bit of notice of anyone around them. Burney's got a fag on. Lucky's concentrating on the view. I can see Luke 7 about 200 yards ahead facing this way, apparently having one hell of a row with Luke 8, his fare. Luke 7 looks as real as if he earned his living as a cabbie! All according to plan, here. Over."

"Thank you Luke 9. Listening out."

Gunn's voice was deeper, gruffer than usual as he consciously avoided the higher pitch that marks excitement in the voice. Stratton sat impassively, his mind racing, his eyes on the plan above the radio console. It couldn't be long now, he thought.

7

JOSEPH PELHAM was having one of those days when everything seemed to be going wrong. The unexpected contrast between the rain of the past three weeks and the steamy heat of the morning had brightened him only until he had gone down to the bottom of the garden before breakfast and seen the appalling effect of the downpour on his vegetables. His peas were battered almost to the ground, his broad beans were limp and lifeless, his lettuces were slimy, his carrots a soggy mess. He had closed his eyes and shaken his head as if that would somehow exorcise the disaster. It had not. Gritting his teeth, he had retraced his steps to the house, to the tea and toast that his dismal, slatternly wife was preparing—in her sleep, to look at her!

His car had taken an age to start, and when he had got it going it had kept stalling, causing him to over-choke the engine. When he had finally got it running properly, the road to the docks had been one long traffic-jam. With infuriating slowness, moving a yard or two at a time, he had crawled wearily along the Beckton Road, through the ghastly tangle of the Silvertown roundabout, and finally wheeled at a fair lick over the last 300 yards before the slip road and 6 Gate.

Then when he had got down to work, it seemed as if nobody else proposed to do so. Most of his men were just standing around in the sun, as if it would steam the memory of three weeks of rain out of their bodies. He had had to exert his authority —raise his voice. That had had the effect of making them even more indolent and surly. Joe Pelham sometimes felt he was the only honest bugger on "F" Shed. Everyone else seemed to be on some fiddle or other. He shuffled through his papers. Why, for example, was that big container stacked on top of the one underneath it, when it was the one underneath that was scheduled for the bottom of the ship's hold? Who'd authorised that? Questions of the men had brought nothing more informative than the expected universal "Dunno."

The morning wore on, small error piling on small error until all the errors merged in Pelham's mind into "one bloody great mogador". The tea-break, when those supposed to be under his supervision were immune from his censure, came and went. And then, just before the lunch break was due to start, there came this curious message from a hurrying man he didn't know even by sight, that he was wanted at the other end of the Shed, where the Senior Traffic Officer needed to discuss something not specified but clearly within Pelham's province. Relieved at the prospect of being useful—possibly even of being noticed as efficient and knowledgeable, he left his little cubicle of an office and strode purposefully down the Shed, threading his way between huge piles of waiting cargo, past areas of deserted calm and pockets of straining, frenetic activity.

The only trouble was that nobody knew just where the Senior Traffic Officer was, when he got to the far end. He had been there—several men had seen him bustling about with papers in his hand and a worried look on his face, not five minutes before. But now he seemed almost to have vanished off the face of the earth. No, he hadn't left any message with anyone the foreman could find. Pelham curbed his frustration. He reminded himself that this sort of thing could happen with the best will in the world. The STO's disappearance could be explained in any one of a dozen ways. And anyway there were obvious priorities before he could deal with some problem which might be both local and unimportant, soluble by a few brief words. Finally, after about ten minutes' fruitless search, he gave up, left a message with an ignorant and bewildered docker that he was going back to his own pitch but would stand by to help as required, and strode self-importantly back, trying hard not to feel a fool. Reaching his office, he perched on a corner of the table, wondering just how it was that what had once been a pleasant, lively job had degenerated into this eternal bloody grind.

Things were always going wrong—mucking up his carefully planned schedules—but in such a way that he could never lay the blame tidily and directly at anyone's feet. For example, he asked himself—what the hell was that long flat-bed lorry doing over *there?* He checked his plans. There was no reason at all for its presence that he could find. He looked out again at the pitch. Christ! Now someone had got that bloody crane working! Who the hell was supposed to be giving orders around here, anyway?

He was on his way to vent his anger when he saw the driver of the lorry talking to someone who was just out of his, Pelham's, sight behind the containers. The driver had papers of some kind—he was shoving them forward, pointing at something on them. Then he was pointing at the big container on top of the pile. It occurred to Pelham that it was the big one in the wrong position that was apparently going to be moved. Might as well leave the matter then, he thought. Perhaps it had dawned on somebody after all that the one underneath should have been the one on top of that pile—or beside it, at any rate.

When he looked out again, he saw that the crane had slung the big container up, but now it looked as if it was going to load the bloody thing on to the flat-bed. What the. . . ? And just what was Ian Willow, of all people, directing the operation for?

That sodding lout was always throwing his weight about! The trouble was, the men seemed to be willing to do whatever Willow told them to. There was that simple-minded sod, Lane. He would always do anything Willow ordered. No initiative! Good God—if Willow told Teddy Lane to jump into the dock water from a crane he really believed the silly sod would just shrug his shoulders and do it!

Pelham was still fumbling angrily through his papers when it dawned on him that the flat-bed was now standing loaded with the big container and apparently ready to move off. But this was incredible! That big one held whisky. It was due to leave on the "Lightning" at eleven, on the tide! He saw Willow gesture thanks to the crane driver, high up in his cabin, and then he saw him wave the lorry off. It couldn't be true! He couldn't believe his eyes! He'd been told nothing about this. He'd had no papers—no phone call—and now part of the ship's cargo was being bloody hi-jacked! And it was him, Joe Pelham, who would be held responsible!

It was a flaming conspiracy, that's what it was!

In a frenzy born of anger and fear, Pelham ran from his little office, through the shed and out on to the pitch. Wildly he looked all around. Suddenly, all of the men seemed to have melted into thin air. No sign of Lane—of Willow—of anyone. He peered up. He couldn't see anyone in the crane cabin—not that it would have done him much good if he had. And there was the lorry, just turning the corner of the shed and heading for 6 Gate!

If he had thought about it, it would have been far better to have gone back to his office in the Shed, to have grabbed the phone and rung the copper on the Gate. Within thirty yards he saw he was only exhausting himself, and he was that much further from a phone. He struggled on round the end of the Shed and up the side of "Z" Shed. He could see the lorry ahead, now. Perhaps there would be lorries ahead of it at the Gate! At this time of day, it might even expect to have to wait five minutes in a queue to get past the Gate copper and out. The hope gave him fresh impulse. Wildly he ran on, staggering across the railway lines without so much as a thought that there might be a train coming.

He was about 200 yards from 6 Gate when he was hit by an intolerable stab of pain in his left side. He buckled and fell. From the ground, he looked ahead. The flat-bed with the whisky was next-but-one to the Gate. He saw the copper with the papers of the lorry in front, asking the driver something. Somehow Pelham struggled to his feet. It was only a stitch, he told himself. But it made more than an agonised totter physically not on.

He began to swear, now. Not the "dockology" that came automatically to anyone working at the docks. Out of his mouth now came streams of meaningless filth that he had heard others make use of—phrases he had never used in his life—words he scarcely knew. The Almighty, perhaps because He wouldn't answer back, became the principal target for the ugly, irrelevant, pointless blasphemy. His cries were not intelligible—they were a string of agonised croaks. But somehow, with their help, he kept going, beginning even to beat the stitch, to make progress despite it. He was within shouting distance of the Gate, now.

Ahead, he saw the young copper hand the papers back and the front lorry move slowly off. Then he turned to the flat-bed bearing the big container. Joseph Pelham stopped and then, with a dreadful retching noise, scooped the steamy dockland air deep into what was left of his lungs.

8

POLICE CONSTABLE JOHN MICHAEL ABBOTT, PLA. Police, six foot four inches of eagerness, had been specially briefed by David Gunn personally. When he reported for duty that morning, his sergeant had passed on instructions for him to go straight up to the Super's office, where the CID Chief was waiting to see him. His stomach turned over.

"Have I done something wrong, skipper?"

"No, son—I think you're specially picked."

Tapping the office door, he had heard Malone's fruity "Come!", but saw as he entered that it was Gunn behind the desk, while the Superintendent riffled through a file on one side.

"Ah! Abbott!" said Malone.

Taking this as sufficient introduction for his purpose, Gunn had quickly outlined the operation which had already begun, in which the young PC was to play a small but key role. He would be given sufficient information when it became available to enable him to recognise a long flat-bed lorry carrying a container, as it approached 6 Gate shortly before 2 p.m. He was not to exhibit the slightest interest in it. The driver would hand him a set of papers which he would formally inspect. Whether or not he noticed anything at all unusual about them—which was unlikely as they would be most expertly forged—he was to give no sign at all that they were other than in perfect order. They would appear to authorise the transfer of a container which the lorry would have picked up at "F" Shed and would be taking to West India Dock where its ship and destination would have been varied. He was to give the papers a cursory glance, then a more careful perusal, and finally he was to pronounce them correct. He was to check that the driver knew his route to the Indias and then wave him out through the Gate. He was not in any way to concern himself with what followed. Any questions?

Unquestioning, PC Abbott had gone back down to the Muster Room feeling not six foot four but about nine foot six tall, nursing his personal assignment proudly to his breast.

"Wipe that stupid grin off your face, Abbott!" from the sergeant had in no wise deflated him, though it had reminded him of the essential secrecy of his mission.

The morning—sunshine all around him balancing the sunshine within him—had gone by with unusual dispatch. He took his lunch break early, and before 1 o'clock he was back on the Gate. A motor-cycle colleague had come up to him at 1.15 and handed him a slip of paper with a make, model and registration number on it, as well as another number which he took to be that stamped on the container load. He had acknowledged the note with a gravity which he hoped concealed the thumping of his heart, though the messenger had shown interest neither in the message nor in him.

He was checking through an articulated refrigerated combine carrying umpteen carcases of lamb when he spotted the whisky container on the flat-bed crossing the railway line about 100 yards away. Checking the papers of the meat lorry, he placed himself where he could get a good look at the "bent" job as it pulled up just behind. The driver was a little rat-faced fellow wearing a black leather jacket and a Scottish tartan cap with a scarlet bobble on top. He waved the meat lorry on its way and turned as the flat-bed moved forward to the gate beside him.

"'Morning," said rat-face, handing him the usual papers. He acknowledged the greeting and examined them casually. They were certainly well forged. If he had not been told in advance, he would not have queried their authenticity for a moment. He looked through them again. They were all there. He detached the one to be kept by him. Then, as he looked up to the cab, he was vaguely conscious of some unusual movement out of the corner of his eye.

"Yes, that's OK. D'you know your way from here to the Indias? The Main Gate will be the one you want there."

"Yus, fanks," came the reply in broad Cockney. "Spent all me life round these parts."

"Oh—I thought by the titfer you were from Scotland."

Down the left side of the immense container he caught again a flash of movement. A man had appeared behind it, his face red, almost purple with effort, gasping for breath, a man who had plainly run himself into the ground. Abbott's hand paused on its way up to the cab, still holding the forged notes he was about to hand back up to the driver. At that moment the man made an agonised, wheezing intake of breath and shouted, "Don't let it go! Container stolen!"

Desperation had given Pelham a final volume he had not thought he could muster. The cry travelled not only to PC Abbott but to the driver directly above him in the cab. For a second the young constable was mentally stunned. What was he to do now? He had been told to let this bent load out, being apparently satisfied with the papers. The one thing he could not do was to turn to the breathless foreman and say, "Shut up, mate! I know!"

For a moment, time, as it can do when attacked by acute tension, seemed to slow down enough to allow Abbott to think, if not slowly, then at least logically. Then he looked back up at the driver.

"These were all OK. There's a bloke back here upset about something or other. I'll see what he wants. You carry on."

It sounded reasonable, he thought, as he saw the driver's hand move from the cab window down towards the papers. Then he saw that it was reaching not for the papers at all but for the outside handle of the door. It twisted down and the door swung quickly open. Abbott had to duck to avoid it cracking him on the side of the head. As he did so, he was knocked clean off his feet by the flying arm of the driver as rat-face leaped from the cab to the ground.

Hitting the road surface, Abbott was momentarily conscious that all the careful planning had gone disastrously wrong. He rolled sideways as he had been taught, pitching on to his shoulder. As he did so, he caught a glimpse of Jenkins' back in pursuit of the fleeing driver.

PC Hugh Jenkins had finished his sandwiches and had come to the door of the police box for a breath of air and sunshine before taking half the load off his friend and colleague Mike Abbott. This happened to be the exact moment that Pelham hurled his unintended verbal spanner so unerringly into the oiled and measured works. Jenkins knew nothing of the plans now wrecked. He knew only that a rat-faced little bastard, at the wheel of that big container job that Mike had been checking, was leaping from his cab, knocking Mike flying, and was now "taking it on his toes".

It was enough. To emergencies, policemen are trained to react. When the particular policeman is not only very bright but happens to be the fastest wing-threequarter that the PLA rugger team has enjoyed for more than a decade, the effect might reasonably have been expected to be spectacular.

Hugh Jenkins took off after the fleeing driver as if it was his last chance to save an almost certain try by the All Blacks at Cardiff Arms Park. The driver could not have been a more direct target if he had had a ball tucked under his arm. Before his quarry was level with the back of the container, and as Abbott was still rolling over against the front wheel, Hugh Jenkins had left the ground altogether, launching himself through the dockland air with arms outstretched forward. For a moment, he was a human ground-to-air missile, guided by years of breeding, training and experience. His hands overtook and closed about the driver's thighs, and his shoulder slammed with all his twelve and a half stone momentum into the smaller man's legs just above the back of the knee. Both men hit the ground hard, locked together, scraping the gravel until stopped by sheer friction.

Jenkins heard his tunic rip and swore, mentally. The driver, whose face hit the ground at the same moment, heard nothing. He was to take more than an hour to recover consciousness.

9

UP by the parapet of the viaduct, 100 yards from 6 Gate, Albert "Lucky" Delafield was too far away from the action to hear voices and he was blocked by the container from any sight of Pelham. Consequently, he could hardly believe his eyes. It had, he thought, been going fine. The gate copper showed no signs of suspicion over the papers and was actually handing them back when it was as if time itself hiccoughed. When it re-started, a second later, it was working on a totally different scenario. For no reason at all that Lucky could descry, Rogers the lorry driver flung open the door of his cab, leaped to the ground and took off into the dock as fast as his legs could carry him. He was pursued by a copper who came from nowhere that Lucky could see but who flung himself at Rogers and brought him crashing to the ground with a flying rugger tackle.

Totally bewildered, Lucky turned his

back on the scene and faced the Jaguar, his mouth opening and shutting like a goldfish in a glass bowl. Eventually words filtered out of it like bubbles, bursting when they reached the open window of the car.

"Jesus! It's blown!"

Paul Burney at the wheel was still trying to relate these words to the situation in which he found himself when he heard a single forceful syllable from behind him in a tone of absolute and unquestioning command.

"Move!" roared Harry Williams.

Burney moved. The Jaguar engine sprang to life, in went the gear, out came the clutch and the tyres screamed as the back wheels spun, slithered, then gripped the road. They leaped forward.

Standing open-mouthed first beside and then behind it, Lucky Delafield's world continued to pursue a path that defied both logic and familiarity. He gawked, he blinked, he shook his head. He had acquired his nick-name years ago in the same way that a man of outstanding size will sometimes be known as "Tiny". For Albert had come stumbling into the adult world in that curious state definable as accident prone. Generally well-liked, he was as generally avoided by all operating crooks for without doing a thing he seemed to attract trouble just by being there. He was recruited to this particular job only because the tall seedy-looking man engaged by the gang had suddenly developed 'flu the previous evening, and there had been no-one else available and no time to send for a more adequate substitute. Harry Williams had enlisted Lucky perforce, just as a look-out, with an unspoken determination to jettison the little jinx the moment anything went wrong, whatever the consequences.

Quite unable to comprehend any of this, the mystified Delafield was not even conscious of the noise as the greasy looking lout who had been tinkering with his motor-bike had at last got it going, flung himself across it and lit off after the Jaguar with a deafening roar, doing the first twenty yards on the back wheel only, handlebars rearing up dangerously. Nor, of course, was he aware that the taxi-driver who had been arguing loudly with a fare on the other side of the road about thirty yards away had received a signal from his colleague Luke 5—Peter Wilson to his friends—as the speeding bike passed the taxi still accelerating after the fleeing Jaguar.

Poor, bemused Lucky didn't even register the fact that taxis do not normally sound something like Formula III racing cars. All he knew was the feel of the hand on his shoulder, firm and not notably gentle, when the cab had swung right across Silvertown Way, had jerked to a stop beside him, and the fare had jumped out and grabbed him. The words he used, by contrast, did mean something. Lucky had heard them before. Lots of times.

"All right, Lucky—you're nicked!"

Meanwhile, out of sight over the crest of the viaduct, Peter Wilson was lying flat along the tank of his machine to lessen wind resistance as the distance between the bike and the green Jaguar lessened yard by yard. For some reason which Wilson could not understand but registered with relief, there was almost no traffic either way, as they hurtled down the slope into North Woolwich Road and began to curve gently round to the left. He wondered where the

Jaguar would try and make for. He knew Paul Burney well as a top-flight "wheels man", and the Jaguar had doubtless been most carefully selected and expertly tuned, but then Wilson's machine was also rather special and unusual. Burney could but have realised already that he had no hope of getting away unless he, Wilson, fell off or crashed. He wondered if Burney would try doubling in and out of the complex of streets ahead on his left, which he reckoned he was more familiar with than the Jaguar driver.

The bike was now near enough to the back of the car to get the benefit of its slipstream. But that was not enough for Wilson. It wasn't a matter of tailing it. He had to stop it. He gulped air and flung the machine out along the car's off-side, leaning as far as he dared to his left as though threatening to nudge the Jaguar into the curb. Suddenly he found himself shooting ahead of its bonnet as Burney slammed on the brakes. Tyres screaming like a TV movie chase, the Jaguar swung into Boxley Road.

Wilson's first reaction—it was instinctive but he was to reflect later that it may have saved his life—was to accelerate. Had he not done so, the off-side tail of the Jaguar might well have side-swiped him as it swung crazily out and round. Then he was braking as hard as he could and leaning over to the left as he aimed for the mouth of Fort Street. The manoeuvre was impossible. He was too near it and travelling much too fast. But there was a street further on, beyond Fort Street and parallel with it—Mill Road. Into this, still at high speed but one slightly more controllable, Wilson turned.

Tearing along it he recollected Pirie Street ahead, a little one linking Mill Road and Fort Street, at right angles to them both. Once off the main road he did not accelerate again, but his mind saw the situation as clearly as if he was looking down from a helicopter hovering directly above the little complex of streets. Once into Boxley Road, Burley would find himself heading for an apparent dead end at Evelyn Road, but on nearing this, he would see that he was really facing an alternative pair of hair-pins, right and left. The left one would take him along Evelyn Road, but he might not be sure that there

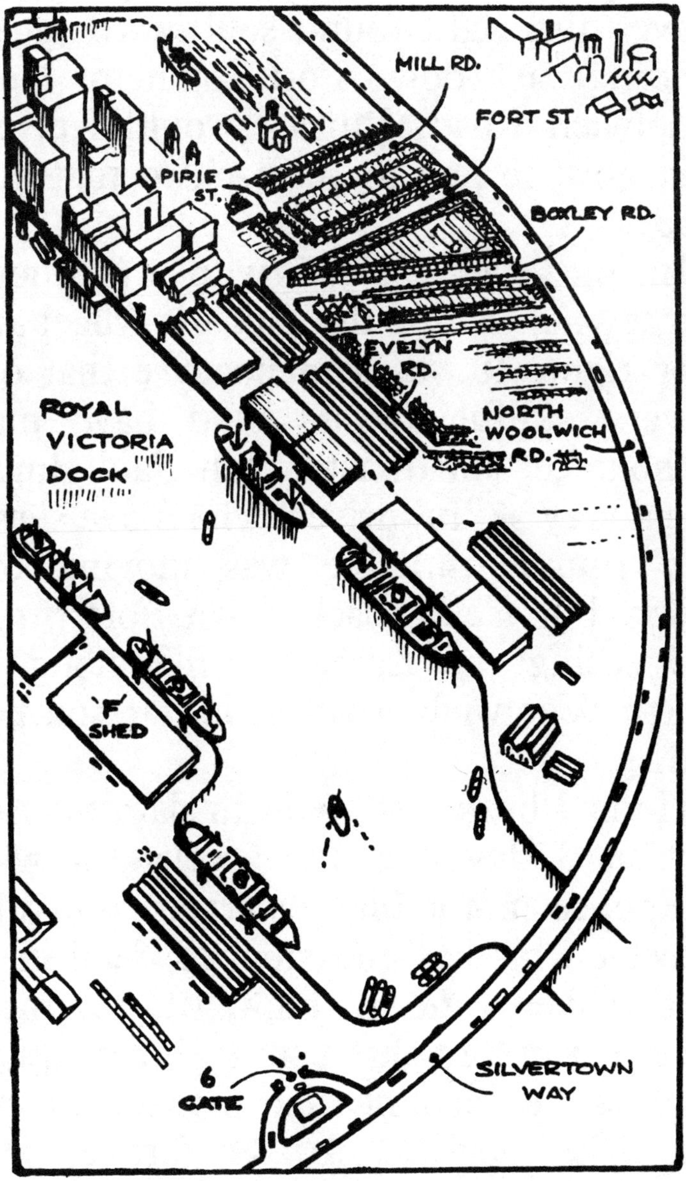

MILL RD.
FORT ST
PIRIE ST.
BOXLEY RD.
EVELYN RD.
ROYAL VICTORIA DOCK
NORTH WOOLWICH RD.
'F' SHED
6 GATE
SILVERTOWN WAY

was a way out of it, although in fact there was. But the hair-pin to the right would swivel him right round southwards again, heading back down Fort Street for North Woolwich Road. Burney would feel that somehow he had to get back to that main road.

In the event, faced with the choice, Burney had swung the Jaguar's wheel hard over right. It was a manoeuvre that only a very skilful driver could have made without certain disaster, but Paul Burney was a very skilful driver. The move slewed him round until he was moving only slowly but facing back down Fort Street, and seeing the traffic passing along the North Woolwich Road at its far southern end.

He had been just about to slam his right foot hard down on the accelerator when the police motor bike emerged from Pirie Street on his left and stopped dead in his path. Given time to think, Burney might have driven straight at him. But there was time only for instinct and instinct directed Burney's foot on to the brake pedal instead. Slam down. Something Burney had once heard went unexpectedly through his mind. This is the way the world ends —not with a bang but a skid-mark.

There was a thud behind him and to his left as Harry Williams' body left the special bucket seat installed in the back which allowed him to sit in comfort but sufficiently low down to be unnoticed by a passing eye. The Welshman's head hit the side pillar. He was not knocked right out, but completely dazed.

As the Jaguar came to rest not more than three feet from his right knee, Peter Wilson exhaled slowly and then dismounted, snapping his foot-rest down as he did so. He went to the driver's door of the Jaguar and opened it. Paul Burney's head turned and looked up at the young officer dressed like a "rocker" in jeans and studded sleeveless leather jacket.

"Fair play, copper—you can ride!" said Burney.

For a moment, Wilson knew the cameraderie that great skill can bring to all its exponents. That, rather than his mind, widened his mouth into a grin.

"You could have made a great police driver," he said—then changed his tone as he heard a groan and saw Williams clutching a badly bruised temple. "Here you—out of it! This side!" he snapped, opening the rear door. "Now—both of you—on your feet!"

Out of the back pocket of the greasy jeans came the neat, grey personal radio, and he pressed the button that sent the tiny aerial shooting out and up. He flicked the switch on with his thumb.

"Luke 5 to Paul. I am at the junction of Fort Street and Pirie Road, off the North Woolwich Road, I have stopped Jaguar VLC 167 F and I have arrested Paul Burney and Harry Williams. Please assist. Over."

10

IN the radio control room, the pieces of information that together made up the jig-saw puzzle of the position had come through out of chronological order and, for a time, those who had planned in such detail could only wait until the dust had settled.

The effect of the unpredictable appearance on the scene of Pelham—a hefty spanner hurled into the works just when everything was running so smoothly—was to put them into a state of stunned shock. Then, as if to confuse matters further, the next message related to the arrest of Delafield up on the viaduct, which in isolation made no sense at all. But once the precipitate flight and almost immediate capture of Rogers was learned, and some general outline had been provided by Luke 9, some order began to prevail over the initial chaos.

Shortly before the drama began, they had been joined by Det. Chief Inspector

George Bryan. It had been clear from the start that whatever resulted from the planning and leadership of David Gunn—the sowing and cultivation, as it were—the control of the harvest, good or bad, would lie in the capable hands of George Bryan.

Stratton was glad. There were few men with whom he was more delighted to work. Together, he and George had enjoyed the sweetness of success and the bitterness of failure many times in the past. Bryan had been no more than a Detective Sergeant when Stratton had first worked with him, and over the years they had developed an accord which, though it could not match the rapport between Stratton and Baunton, had held great advantage, personal and professional, for them both.

Built rather along the same stocky lines as David Gunn, George Bryan had what might have been an unruly shock of red hair, had he not kept it closely cropped and firmly damped down. Similarly, over a natural excitability the policeman had imposed a rigid control of absolute calm, as he sublimated the energy that accumulated into an unrelenting drive. He was in a sense the archetype of the "thinking policeman". He had not only thought much—he felt and cared deeply, being conscious, as each case progressed, of the technical details it involved but only as part of the ethical strategy related to the crime as a whole. Stratton would never cease to enjoy the ebullience and admire the skill of David Gunn, to whom every case was an exhilarating battle. But for a working partner, there was no-one in the Force whom Stratton would have chosen in preference to George Bryan.

When the message about the arrest of Williams and Burney came in, Gunn shot a glance across the room at his junior colleague.

"That's it, then, George. All right?"

"You round it off, sir."

"Paul to Luke 5. Message received. Congratulations. Arranging immediate assistance. Luke 8—where's that cab of yours?"

"Luke 8, sir. Right by 6 Gate."

"OK. Put Lucky in charge of the Gate Officer and belt off with your mate to help Luke 5 at Pirie Street. Know it?"

"Yessir! Wilco at once. Over."

Gunn took one of his long, deep breaths.

"Paul to all Gospellers. From now on, your control will be Det. Chief Inspector George Bryan, to whom I am now handing over. To everyone, my hearty thanks. Well done! Paul—out!"

He snapped the desk microphone switch off and turned with his open smile to Bryan.

"You have the ship now, George. Bring me in as much or as little as you wish. If there are any flaws in the case so far, they're down to me, of course. I'm ready to help or advise but only if required. The decisions are all yours. Clear?"

"Understood, thanks, sir."

"Well, it didn't turn out quite as we planned, though it's not over yet by any means. But at least we've got four of them bang to bloody rights so far—and they include Harry Williams, which I confess makes me feel very chuffed. What's ahead?"

"Well, subject to Mr. Stratton's views, I'd say the prospects of potting the lorry driver are strong. He can never explain why he bolted after the PC had passed him through, unless he knew his papers were phoney. Lucky is in it up to the neck, of course—he's as good as gone. And I'm cautiously optimistic about Williams and Burney. Of course they will say they thought they were being pursued by a thug, rather than a cop, but the weight of evidence is against them when we add what we had seen earlier. They'll deny that wholesale, of course. They may even try alibis. But we've four in the can so far and it doesn't look all that dull." He looked at Stratton. "How do you see it?"

"It's a bit early yet, George, but I like it too. What rather interests me is the foreman who clobbered the whole show, probably in an excess of zeal. He *should* be able to lead us to the one man—possibly men—who were PLA staff and who were in on this job. True we've missed the Berry slaughter which was the prime objective. But spotting a traitor in our own camp is excellent compensation, wouldn't you say?"

"I would, yes. Like to sit in on my chat with the foreman?"

"Very tempting, George, but I'd better not. It could lead to allegations in court that the prosecuting solicitor is really a witness avoiding cross-examination. I've always wanted to sit in but I've never found it safe to, thanks all the same."

"Understood. But when it comes to interrogating suspects in the presence of their solicitors, I've never seen the logic in not being able to have mine along!"

"That's an interesting ethical argument we'll pursue together another time, George. Perhaps you and I are just a couple of old fashioned idiots."

"Well, what's your idiocy going to do first, then?" asked Gunn.

Bryan grinned. "Check that Williams and Burney are really in the bag, and then send for that foreman Pelham."

"Be nice to him now, George," came from Evan Baunton. "He didn't realise that he was wrecking your biggest operation for years!"

"Aren't I always lovely to people I hate?" smiled Bryan as he walked over to the console and picked up the microphone.

Gunn winked at Stratton. "Let's get out

of his way, Charles," he said. "Can I give you a lift back to Trap One?"

"Got my car here, round the back, thanks. Come on, Evan. We're on our way."

11

GEORGE BRYAN'S session with the conscientious, unhappy Joseph Pelham was a long and harrowing one. Pelham considered himself the only man at "F" Shed whom nobody liked or respected, simply because everyone else was engaged on his own private fiddle. The old standards of integrity had waned to vanishing point. And once the quiet policeman, with a discreet application of sympathy, had got Pelham talking freely, the man's bitterness fairly poured out.

Bryan let him rant on. The occasional question was enough to bring him slowly to the container incident. He named the simple-minded Teddy Lane and the dangerously bent Ian Willow. As he listened patiently, making no notes which might have dried up the flow by inhibiting the lonely, bitter man who clung to his standards because he had nothing and no-one else to cling to, George Bryan decided just what he had to do. Gently he began to round the session off and finally he called for a sergeant on his staff to whom he handed Pelham over for a formal statement to be committed to writing. Then Bryan had a word with Colin Haines, a very bright young aide in whom he had spotted potential detective skill, combined with a level-headedness which did not always accompany it.

The discussion over, Haines took the small blue van to the western end of Victoria Dock, where he parked it round the corner from "F" Shed at an unused loading bay. He strolled inconspicuously over to the shed office where he had a word with the Traffic Officer, who was as discreet as those officials almost always are. The Traffic Officer ambled off along the shed and came back with Teddy Lane. When, some minutes later, Haines returned to the van alone, Lane followed casually and joined him shortly after. Few would be likely to have noticed anything. Haines waved his thanks to the Traffic Officer as he drove back to the Albert, where he parked the van and showed Teddy Lane up to Bryan's office.

Lane was a weedy little fellow who

looked frightened to death even when he wasn't. Bryan sent Haines for three cups of tea and chatted about soccer in general and West Ham in particular until he returned. Slowly the built-in terror began to thaw as he came to see that these were not authoritarian monsters bent on putting people away, but ordinary blokes who led ordinary lives off duty. Bryan judged exactly the moment when he should bring up the subject of the container.

Lane was frank about it from the start. He had acted, he said, on direct orders from "Tits". For a moment, Bryan and Haines were completely nonplussed.

"Sorry, Teddy—didn't catch. Who?"

"Willow. Ian Willow. You must know him. He's known as 'Tits'. Some song, or something—by Ian Mikardo, would it be? I never asked. I don't use it to him direct, myself, though some do. He's always spoken about as 'Tits'."

"You had us fooled there for a moment, Teddy," laughed Haines. "No, it's not by Ian Mikardo. It's from a musical play called 'The Mikado', in which there's a famous song about a bird—the feathered kind—who sits on a tree and sings

'Willow, tit willow, tit willow'. That'll be the origin of that, for sure!"

"Oh ah," said Lane, not comprehending.

"Anyway, it was Willow who told you to do something with this container, was it?" said Bryan. "Does he often give you direct orders?"

"Yes. Well he is the ganger, isn't he."

"Sure. But were there any others in on this?"

"No. Only Tits and me. If he needs one bloke, it's always bloody me he picks on."

"What about Pelham the foreman? Didn't he know about this?"

"Nah! Tits don't tell Pelham nothing he don't want him to know. Anyway—Pelham wasn't there."

"Not there?"

"Nah. Not when the lorry arrived. He wasn't meant to be there, anyway. Tits said something about it—I forget exactly what, now. But Pelham wasn't around. Didn't know a thing about it, he didn't. Wise move. Pelham would have gone ringing people up if he'd got instructions not like what he had before, you know."

George Bryan exchanged a glance with

Haines and scribbled a note to ask Pelham just how he'd been got out of the way. Then he turned back to Lane, who had been waiting patiently in silence ever since he saw the policeman's attention was off him.

"Sorry, Teddy. Carry on. You're being most helpful."

"Where was I, then? Oh yes—well the flat-bed arrived, and Tits handled the whole thing. I think he'd fixed something in advance with the crane operator. Not the usual one, see—he was off having his lunch. Well, this big container was there and this flat-bed arrived like I said, and Tits told me to get the slinging chains under it at each end and fasten them when the hook came down because it had to go on the lorry, like. So that's what I did then, isn't it."

"Did you know what was in the container?"

"Nah. Nothing to do with me, was it. I do what I'm told and keep my nose clean—that's all."

"You didn't see the driver's papers, then?"

"Papers? Not me—no. Tits saw to all

that side of it. The driver had a set of them, like, and I saw him show them to Tits, you know. But I knew nothing about it."

"I believe you, Teddy," said Bryan. "Trouble is, I'm sure that when I see Tits, he'll drag you in with him. And if so, I'm going to have to charge you with being in on the whole job. But I'll give you my honest opinion—if the jury believes you, as I do, then you'll be cleared—acquitted—found not guilty. And I'll help as far as I can by telling the court I believe you. Indeed, I won't charge you at all unless Tits Willow won't let you out of it when we see him."

"You think that's what he'll do? Yes, I shouldn't be surprised. It means a trial, does it? Won't my record help? Never been in trouble, you know. Always kept my nose clean, I have."

"I know. So has Willow, as far as convictions go."

"Yeah. Crafty bastard!"

"I'll tell you this, Teddy. If the court believes you, Tits is going to be in big trouble, even with a clean record. So between you and me, Teddy, you stick to the truth and maybe he won't be around to bother you for quite a time."

"Yes, well if you believe me, why charge me?"

"Because if Tits swears that you were in on it and brought him into it, there will be *some* evidence against you that a court ought to hear. He's going to be charged. I'll tell you that now. But sometimes we have to charge people even when we believe them. People don't understand that. But charging someone doesn't mean they'll be convicted. So if you stick to the truth and tell the jury it was all down to Tits and you were only doing what he told you to do, you won't be. And he will!"

"So you say, Mr. Bryan."

"And so I mean, Teddy. If there's any way of keeping you out, I'll take it. But think for a moment. Suppose we charge Tits and not you. You now become the key prosecution witness against him, don't you. And he's on bail pending the trial. What sort of a life's he going to lead you till then, eh? But if you're charged too, he's bound to be sympathetic, see? Think about it from that angle."

"Yes, I can see that," said Lane, after

a pause. Then he shrugged. "But he's a sod, is Tits. Honest!"

"Push you around, does he?"

"Not physical, like—no. But if he wants someone to blame when anything goes wrong on the pitch, who does he always pick on? Yours bloody truly, that's who!"

"What's he got against you, Teddy?"

"Dunno. Just his idea of a relationship."

"Well, just between us, Teddy—if it gets a bit much and you think we might help—have a quiet word with Mr. Haines here, or me. No favours, mind. If you've done something wrong, we'll put you straight on for it. Right down the middle. But we like you, and we don't like big bullying sods like Tits Willow throwing their weight about on our patch, see? And we're not afraid of anyone. Well, we don't have to be. You've heard the expression 'without fear or favour'? Well, that's us!"

"OK. What happens now, then?"

"Mr. Haines will run you quietly back to somewhere near 'F' Shed and then bring Tits back here officially. And I tell you, Teddy—he's not going to get pushed around, but he's not going to get any favours, either!"

Lane looked up. For a moment, a half-smile flickered across his face. Then he stood up.

"And thanks for the tea, guv."

12

SITTING in the same chair that Lane had occupied, Ian "Tits" Willow looked a very different proposition. Self-confident to the point of arrogance, he sat, big and burly, square and wary, determined not to give an inch to the enemy—his basic view of all police. Not that it made any difference to the attitude of Bryan and Haines, except that the sympathy they had shown to Lane was now replaced by a cool formality.

According to Willow, he had been discussing a job with some of his men when he was handed a set of papers by the driver of a large flat-bed lorry which had just arrived at the Shed. The papers referred to the big numbered container which had been delivered from Scotland two days before. These showed a change of plan. This container was to be shifted on this flat-bed over to the Indias and put aboard a different ship. None of his business. There was nothing apparently wrong with the papers. He had given them back to the driver and had called to a nearby crane-driver who he could see was having his sandwiches up in his cab. Lane had got the chains in position, the crane had swung over, and Lane had hooked up. He'd even given a hand himself. He didn't know what the hell all the fuss was about. Were the papers dodgy, then?

"Yes, Mr. Willow. Very dodgy. Forged, in fact. The whole bundle. The container and its contents were, with your kind assistance, stolen."

"What do you mean 'with my kind assistance'? Are you suggesting I knew about any theft? Because if you are, chum, you'd better watch it! I've got a clean criminal record, you know. Never been in trouble in my life, I haven't. Kept my nose dead clean, I have. And if anyone dares put me on for something there'll be big trouble all right. Malicious arrest—false imprisonment—the lot!"

He stopped when he saw that these threats were having as much effect upon the two policemen as on the walls of the room. They were looking at him placidly, faces quite blank, waiting for him to stop.

Then there was a long silence, during which the sound of Willow's bluster reverberated through the air and through his own head. It seemed to sound less effective—indeed, unnecessary and, after a while, a bit silly. Finally the silence itself grew oppressive. Someone had to break it. There was no sign that either policeman intended to do so. They seemed content to sit and regard him politely, incuriously and silently.

"Yes, well you say they were forged, then—those papers. Well they fooled me. No crime in that, is there?"

Another long pause. Then Bryan took a deep breath.

"No."

It wasn't really much of a contribution. Again the silence began to oppress Willow. He wasn't used to it. Always his bluster could be relied on to provoke anger or apology, leaving him to get the best out of whatever followed. But this was like hitting a ball of cotton wool. His determination not to be the one to break silence wavered, then fell.

"All right, then—what are you saying I did?"

"We haven't said you did anything, Mr. Willow. Indeed, we haven't yet even asked what you did. I was just about to when you made your little speech, just now, which my colleague and I felt was a trifle uncalled for. Perhaps we ought to forget you said anything, eh? Now, where were we? Oh yes—I had just informed you that the container was removed from the shed by means of forged papers. That was an operation which the lorry driver could scarcely perform unaided. He therefore asked the assistance of the staff at the shed —yourself and Mr. Lane plus, you have told us, a kindly crane driver. So far so good. You have implied that you had no advance warning of this operation."

"Advance knowledge? You mean did I know the lorry was coming before it came, like?"

"I couldn't have put it better myself."

"Well, your answer's no. I'd never seen the lorry or the driver before in my life— and you can't prove I had!"

Again a long silence followed, making Willow first conscious and then resentful that he had been tempted into raising his voice. He stuck it for a bit, then again broke it himself.

"I didn't know anything about any of it."

It sounded sulky—like a small child who had done wrong. He had never had this silent treatment before. It was leaving him worried and confused. This time, Bryan relented.

"I see. Tell me—you're the ganger, aren't you?"

"Yes."

"Did you pick Lane especially for this job?"

"Did I pick Teddy Lane? You've got to be joking! That little runt is about the stupidest, duffest bloody docker that ever got a place in dockland. No—he was there. He'd seen the driver—brought me the papers, hadn't he. They looked OK to me. I turned to Lane and told him to get the slings ready for the lift. I didn't stop and think over all the gang and then select Lane. I'm not that daft!"

"I see. Lane happened to be handy, so he got the job of preparing the slinging chains."

"That's right."

"It never occurred to you that Lane might be one of the gang engaged in the theft of the container?"

"Teddy Lane? You don't know the man, obviously. Lane wouldn't have the brain to be bent! He's the most useless bugger of the lot, is Lane. No brains, and as for physical strength—he wouldn't last five rounds with a geriatric gerbil!"

"You don't know him well outside work, then?"

"Know him well? Look, mate—I wouldn't say I lead a jet-set existence outside the docks but by God it's a cut above that idiot! I bet it is! No—if it wasn't for the job, I wouldn't be seen dead with the little sod!"

"I understand. And you mentioned you'd never seen the driver of the lorry before. Just let me check the others quickly. Are you at all friendly with Lucky Delafield?"

"Who? Never 'eard of him!"

Bryan consulted his notebook and turned over a page. Then he looked up again.

"Paul Burney?"

"Burney? Burney? Don't think I've ever

even heard the name. No, I can't help you there, I'm sorry."

"Very well. Oh, there was one other name—Harry Williams. Do you know Harry?"

Willow's face was a real study. His brow furrowed, he looked up to the ceiling mouthing "Williams, Williams" in a reflective way. Then he slowly shook his head from side to side.

"No. No. Harry Williams I do not know."

"Well I'm sure you know *of* him," said Bryan encouragingly. "You know—the Berry gang. He's their No. 2, nowadays."

Only the closest observation would have detected the momentary constriction in Willow's throat. Only a very suspicious mind could attach significance to a swallow that looked so natural. Perhaps it was unlucky for Willow that George Bryan had the mind and was in the position to make the observation. Colin Haines didn't catch either. But he noticed that Willow indicated his total ignorance by means of another head-shake, as if he didn't quite trust his voice to deny it convincingly enough. Neither detective gave any sign at all of pressing the point.

"Oh well—it really doesn't appear that Mr. Willow is in a position to help us very much, does it Haines?"

"No, guv'nor."

"Oh—what was the driver's name, by the way? The Berry gang driver? I've forgotten it."

Haines began to riffle busily through the pages of his notebook. Willow grinned contemptuously. Some detective! Can't even remember the name of the gang he's supposed to be chasing! Bryan was showing signs of impatience with his junior, now—snapping his fingers and saying "Driver—driver!" under his breath as Haines went on turning page after page.

"Burney, you said," volunteered Willow, finally, demonstrating his superior memory.

Instantly he could have cut his tongue out. Both detectives were looking straight at him, grinning broadly.

"No, Mr. Willow—I meant the lorry driver. Ah! Rogers—that was it! Paul Burney was indeed driving the getaway car as always for the Berry gang. But then, you said you'd never heard of the Berry gang, didn't you, Mr. Willow? Or at least you shook your head. I know you said you'd never heard Paul Burney's name. I remember that very clearly."

"Nor I have, then!"

"No—no, of course. The only thing is —when I was trying to remember the name of the driver just now—wasn't it odd that you should be so kind as to remind Mr. Haines and myself that it was Paul Burney—the man whose name you said you had never heard—whose—er— vocation it is to be about the finest wheels man in the business of crime today. Can you explain such a singular little lapse on your part, Mr. Willow?"

"I don't know what the hell you're talking about!"

"No?"

"No I don't, then! And you can't trap me into saying things I don't mean like that, you crummy, underhanded bloody copper, so stuff it!" He rose angrily, towering over them. "And I haven't bloody got to stay here answering your bloody questions, neither! I know my rights! Either you charge me or I'm off!

I'm not 'helping the police with their enquiries' as your filthy jargon goes. So you can piss off, coppers—see?"

To George Bryan, this tirade was not merely predictable—it was most gratifying, marking the complete success of the tactic which he had not seriously expected to succeed, establishing Willow's direct involvement with the Berry gang to some extent. Neither he nor Haines moved. They sat politely smiling without a word—the treatment that Bryan always used with angry men. Occasionally it provoked them to the violent speech he was ready to listen to with equanimity. More often it left them, as it had earlier left Willow, suspended and helpless. For the second time in ten minutes, Ian Willow began to know the feeling of cotton wool. This time he could hold out no longer. He had to push his luck.

"Well? Well? Are you going to charge me or do I walk out?"

"Oh do sit down again, Mr. Willow. I really think you are a little previous, don't you? I mean—up till a minute ago I was asking you a few general questions seeking information abut what went on at F Shed when a container of whisky was stolen. But in the light of your replies, I have some reason to believe that you are to some extent personally involved. Therefore in your interest—as indeed you would expect, knowing your rights as you said you did—don't you think you ought to be given a formal caution? You must have heard it before. Seen it on telly, perhaps? I'm sure you'll find it familiar. It consists of my saying 'Ian Willow, you are not obliged to say anything unless you wish to do so, but if you do wish to say anything, it will be taken down in writing and may be given in evidence.' Now—is there anything you wish to say at this stage?"

For all Bryan's gentle tone, Willow felt as though his stomach had suddenly emptied itself. He experienced what might be described as a "cold flush". His mouth opened and shut several times. His knees began to wobble. He sat down—rather more quickly than he meant to.

"I'm saying nothing!" he said, his voice a full tone higher than normal. George Bryan smiled encouragingly.

"Oh, very wise of you I'm sure. Mr. Haines will note the fact."

"You're not going to get away with this, you know!" said Willow, trying hard to whip himself back into his normal arrogance. "I told you—I've got a clean record. I've never been charged before this."

"You haven't been charged now, Mr. Willow. Only cautioned. All that is is a reminder that nobody can force you to talk but that if you choose to it will be on the record, so to speak. That's what's known as the Judges' Rules."

Willow's tongue flicked out, passed over dry lips and then disappeared almost with the speed of a snake's. He said nothing.

"There are in fact a number of formalities to be observed before you are formally arrested and charged," went on Bryan, patiently. "It's a nervous time for you I'm sure, but we'll try and make it all as simple as possible. For example—when you are formally charged, one little piece of procedure involves your emptying your pockets on to some surface like a table so that an inventory can be made, and it's all put into a polythene bag and you sign the list certifying it's correct, so that one day you may have every single item safely and correctly returned to you—well, those that are yours, anyway! Well, part of that routine can be shortened quite a bit. If we run through the examination here, in private, informally, instead of examining each one before it is described and listed in the charge room—you understand? There's not the slightest obligation on you to do this at all, of course. But I have noticed that our—clients, shall we say?—often appreciate all the privacy they can get. So I just wondered—would you like to have an informal run-through of your pockets up here in private before we do all the arrest-and-charge procedure downstairs? Entirely up to you, of course."

Willow found himself swallowing repeatedly. His throat had gone dry. His mind was racing. There was nothing remotely incriminating on him, was there? If he could afford to co-operate, all this might really be just a con trick. They mightn't go through with a charge at all. And if he was going to be searched, then better in private up here than down in the charge room with some ham-handed idiot in uniform.

"I've got nothing on me I need to hide.

You want to examine my hankie, or something?"

"Bless you no! You may or may not be a thief, Mr. Willow. Nobody's suggested you might be a flasher! Cheer up! No—what I had in mind is a pocket diary or note-book. You know the sort of thing. It takes a bit of looking through downstairs."

"I've got a pocket diary. Nothing unusual in that," said Willow. He fished it out and tossed it with a gesture intended to look casual on to Bryan's desk. "Help yourself."

"Thank you indeed. That's the kind of co-operation we value. Make a note of that, Haines—Mr. Willow made an entirely voluntary disclosure of his pocket diary. I'll flick through it, shall I?"

As he picked it up, George Bryan was suddenly conscious of something he had experienced only rarely before—an almost imperceptible feeling that this was important. He wondered if it could be something to do with telepathy. Was it Willow's apprehension that he was receiving like a radio wave in his mind? He opened the diary and flicked through the pages with his thumb. Nothing of obvious significance. A note or two in the dated section that followed the printed information which is in all such diaries. He paused here and there at a squiggle. Nothing remotely incriminating. Nothing unduly legible. And still this curious response in the back of his head. After the dated section came a few blank pages for memoranda. Nothing there. Spaces for names, addresses, telephone numbers—all blank—wait—what was that? He flicked back to where a small scribble had caught his eye. There it was! He stared at it for a long moment, unable to believe his eyes.

He shot a glance at Willow, who was assuming so obvious a nonchalance that Bryan actually raised his head and grinned. Nobody innocent could feel quite so carefree at such a moment. He received what Willow intended to be a reciprocal grin, but it was confined to the mouth alone.

"Now *there*'s a funny thing!" he said lightly, as if excited by no more than a passing curiosity. "There's a little note at the bottom of this page which says 'HARRY—246 8071.' It's probably just a coincidence but somehow it recalls to my mind the sound of your voice only a matter of minutes ago, Mr. Willow. Your voice saying 'Harry Williams? Harry Williams I do not know!' Do you remember that?"

Willow's mouth opened and shut three times. No sound emerged. The fourth time, a voice only vaguely reminiscent of its owner squeaked, then coughed and said, "Er—Harry Wilson. Friend of mine. Not Williams. Wilson."

George Bryan smiled genially.

"Really, now! *What* an interesting coincidence! That you should have a friend not only whose name is Harry but whose surname begins with a W, although there's no W here in the diary—or had you forgotten that, Mr. Willow? But the really big coincidence is that your friend Harry Wilson should possess the exact registered telephone number of that very same Harry Williams that we were chatting amicably about just now—you know—the Berry gang one! Isn't that fascinating, Mr. Willow?"

Willow gaped. Bryan pressed gently on.

"Of course I'm sure there's a perfectly innocent explanation for it. I mean—if it did refer to the Berry gang, you would hardly have shown such admirable co-operation as to let us find it, now would you? Unless, of course, you had completely forgotten you'd got Harry Williams' number down here at all. That *might* be one explanation, I suppose. What do you think, Mr. Willow?"

"I'm saying nothing!" croaked Willow. "I'm not obliged to. You told me that yourself! Well you're not getting one word out of me. Not now nor any other bloody time you're not! No-one bloody is!"

"No-one? Oh come, Mr. Willow! You'll have to give your lawyer instructions, won't you? And when we get to the Old Bailey and the nice gentleman asks you how do you plead, you'll want to say 'Not Guilty', won't you? Or even 'Guilty', of course. Who knows?"

Willow's lips pursed with the effort of ignoring the gently mocking provocation.

"Well, I think we'd better adjourn downstairs to the Charge Room, don't you? Mr. Haines will ring them first and make the arrangements, will you please, Haines?"

"Of course, guv'nor—right away!" said Haines, as he rose from his chair. He saw no valid reason to wipe the broad grin off his face.

13

VICKI BECK completed her routine by putting Stratton's glass of rosé beside him on the blotter and taking her own half-glass back to the far corner of the big desk, where she perched herself on her chair in that curious side-saddle often adopted by secretaries who listen to everything said at meetings, record those remarks which the makers would like to be recorded, omit those which they would not, and edit the resulting whole into a comprehensive report containing a balance, a perspective and even a literary quality which the original would almost certainly have lacked. Few secretaries achieve this consistently. Miss Beck was one of the few. As Evan said regularly—"Not just a pretty face, our Vicki." And as the lady in question was indeed dazzlingly pretty, the comment was not merely gallant but accurate.

Stratton looked across the desk on which the glasses found a place among the papers of his colleagues and friends who sat facing him—David Gunn and George Bryan. Gunn was the more overtly cheerful, with exuberance in every movement and gesture. Bryan was the more reflective—just a reservation or two behind the smile. At Stratton's right elbow sat the indomitable Evan Baunton, of course.

"Well, Charles," said Gunn—"it's a mob-hander all right. Six in the can. We set 'em up, you knock 'em down!"

"If I may, guv'nor," put in Bryan, "it's really only five. Teddy Lane's on the sheet purely to give us what we need against Willow. I'm sure he wasn't part of the original plan and I'm sure we won't pot him—nor do we want to. There's only five real targets."

"Quite right, George. Still—a happy little fistful for you, Charles."

"And don't think I don't appreciate it, David. You chaps have done a marvellous job. But you know—this is the exact moment when your average telly play, even the average crime novel, ends, with the villains all neatly caught and charged. The audience, or the reader, knows they've done it and they switch off, or close the book, happy and contented. In life, as you don't need reminding, it hasn't finished at all. Evan's and my part of the exercise hasn't even begun. We've got a container which we might not have had on its way to its right destination and five villains bang to rights. Now we've got to arrange matters in accordance with strict rules so as to get those five their come-uppance at the end of a trial which is concerned not with truth but with proof. I know that's a hobby-horse of mine and I won't go on. But it's still a two-part exercise, in which you lads have done your part with honours. Now let's face *our* problems. Evan—how about a summary from you to kick around?"

"Right. Well, we've won weaker cases than this. We can afford to be reasonably confident. Let's eliminate Teddy Lane first. We want five in and one out. Against Harry Williams our first strength is the surprise he's going to get when he sees our committal evidence—it'll give him a nasty turn, that will. He's getting all set to swear he was driving along Silvertown Way in his Jaguar with his chum Paul Burney at the wheel when they found themselves being chased by a greasy looking Hell's Angel on a high-powered bike. After trying, and failing, to escape, they found to their amazement that said thug was a copper, albeit a member of a scruffy, unimportant and little-known force which is not really meant to go chasing innocent people all over the roads and streets outside the docks. He will open his eyes very wide and be ready to ask how on earth he could be tied up with a large container which happened to be about to emerge from 6 Gate as he passed by and about which he knows nothing. And when he gets our statements he will know that we can indeed tie him up with that container for he was observed handing the driver of the lorry which bore it a bundle of papers which were forged authority to take it out of the dock."

Stratton lifted a hand.

"Pause a moment there, Evan. We can't prove that the forged notes tendered by Rogers to the gate copper were the same bits of paper handed him by Harry two hours before. I'd hoped Harry might have left dabs on them, but whether he was gloved or they've been wiped, or it's our bad luck, there was nothing liftable from them, as you know. So I expect Harry to claim mistaken identity in Gresham Road —probably having a nice firm alibi for 12.30 to 1.30 all set and ready. Because unless the jury are sure it was him and his Jaguar in Gresham Road, Harry's going to be laughing. And with the public's idea of dockland, I bet the jury will think that fleeing from a wheeled thug's an everyday event round here!"

"Steady, Charles," put in Gunn. "Now you're going too far the other way. Assuming only that our evidence is believed, we've got witnesses to show that the Jaguar wasn't passing—it was waiting on the viaduct overlooking that gate and it moved off fast *before* the bike started chasing it, leaving Lucky gawping on the pavement."

"I think they'll brazen that out, David —allege our evidence is all fabricated— that they were passing, not waiting. And I know Lucky is a gormless, accident-prone ass but he does know which side his bread is buttered on. He'll swear blind that he was standing by this parapet when he heard a sound behind him and there was this green Jaguar he'd never seen before in his life, being chased out of sight by a thug on a bike."

George Bryan nodded agreement. "While Paul Burney will corroborate Harry. Granted that Wilson did look like a thug, too! No, I think Burney will share Harry's alibi between 12.30 and 1.30. But it's not going to be easy for them, any more than it is for us. Remember, we know what happened. The jury don't. And they're only going to be told a limited amount."

Stratton was conscious of a movement to his left. Vicki Beck had twisted herself round and was hesitating with a pair of elegantly pencilled eyebrows half raised. He smiled at her. There had been more than one case in which she had made a useful if unacknowledged contribution to the planning. "What's troubling you, Vicki?"

"Well, when Mr. Bryan mentioned the jury—don't we have some taped or written record of all the radio messages to and from the control room? If we could get a transcript out and play the tape in court they'd know everything."

David Gunn smiled. "If I may, Charles—you're quite right, Vicki my dear. Except that if the worst came to the worst, I'd sooner lose the case completely than reveal the sort of operation we can mount if we wish. You're right in the short term but it would be at the cost of future success. We'd be monitored to extinction."

Crestfallen, Vicki nodded. "Of course. Sorry I shoved a useless oar in."

Stratton shook his head. "Not useless at all. Very perspicacious. And don't be sorry. If you think of anything that might be relevant, you say so. We're all so deeply involved that someone in a position slightly more outside might spot what we're too close to notice."

There was a general murmur of agreement. Evan picked up his glass and raised it to Vicki in silent salute. The others copied his gesture. She smiled appreciation and sipped. Stratton cleared his throat.

"Against Rogers the lorry driver we have the strongest case. His panic at the gate *after* the PC had accepted the papers was fatal. Only a guilty man would take it on his toes when told to go by a copper, just because some clot came up yelling 'Stop, thief!' or words to that effect. Sure he will say he didn't know the papers were forged. He will deny ever having been near Gresham Road, let alone having met Harry Williams there. But since the original notes were given him in Scotland he surely can't explain how it was he handed forged ones in at the Gate."

"He will say," observed Evan, "that they were switched without his knowledge en route, probably in a pub. No, not even an English jury could be daft enough to accept that. You're right. Rogers is a push-over."

Gunn was on to the point at once. "Charles, is there some way in which we can make Rogers the centrepiece of the whole case, so that when he falls he brings the rest down with him?"

"David Gunn—as a criminal lawyer you make a first class copper! Perry Mason might have managed it, but then he worked by Californian rules which are much more elastic than ours. And he never prosecuted!"

George Bryan put his glass down. "To me the trickiest of the lot is Willow. The most important, too—he's the traitor in our own camp. We'll be fighting the Berry gang for years yet—we may never finally smash them—they re-group like blobs of mercury, these types. We know them. Only now have we actually infiltrated them for the first time. But how often have they infiltrated us? How many Willows are there in every dock? The question makes me feel very uncomfortable. But if we get Willow and get him good, then some others, currently 'sleeping', might just back out when their turn comes. I'd like to consider the case against him."

"Right, George, let's do that," said Stratton. "First—we'll have the help of Lane, though it will be modified by warnings about accomplices' evidence and so forth. Still, I think Teddy will stick to his assertion that it was Willow who ordered him to put the slings on the container. To counter that, Willow will say 'Your Gate copper was fooled by the forgery—so was I.' And that's where we're in a spot, because if we say we weren't fooled we will be scuppered for letting a crime take place for our own purposes, which is unforgivable. So the case against Willow isn't going to depend on that. It will stand or fall on interrogation. He must now go on saying that he didn't know Harry Williams. And we show Harry's phone number was there in his personal diary."

"Which Willow will insist was a frame-up," said Evan. "He'll say George faked the story and planted the evidence."

"All right, Evan," said George. "But he'll have to be pretty careful, because I made sure I returned the diary to him before we all went down to the charge room where he produced it from his own pocket *and* signed its inclusion on the list of *his* property."

David Gunn grinned. "And without knowing, I'd take a large bet that on the way downstairs he asked to go to the loo where he could have torn out that page and flushed it away."

"You'd win, guv'nor. He asked. I refused."

"What did I tell you?" said Evan. "Police brutality! No—seriously though—he will deny all mention of the entry, admit the diary was his and allege the entry was written by us after he was charged."

"I think he'll have to take that line," said George.

Gunn, determined to stay cheerful, added, "Mind, we've got young Haines to corroborate the interview. Nor was that Willow's only slip. He named Paul Burney as the gang's driver though he had said earlier than he'd never heard Burney's name."

"No, Pop, that target's easier for him," said Evan. "He'll deny making the slip altogether, claiming it was dreamed up by George and Haines and added to their notes. Our word against his, and he gets the benefit of any doubt, apart from the fact that the jury don't know that George and Colin are saints and Willow's a liar and a crook. Too many jurors today are ready to believe that coppers will bend any evidence in order to pot those they believe to be guilty. Added to which, there's the adage of the criminal Bar—'If you have no defence, then allege corruption and brutality against police witnesses.'"

"Get away with you!" said Gunn. "All that means is that George and young

Haines are going to face a hot time in the witness box at the Bailey. They have before—well, George has, anyway—and they'll have to again and again. It's not worth dwelling on—just part of our job. No, I think the strongest evidence against Willow will be Willow himself. I just do not believe any jury will see him and hear him and then believe him. And I bet our counsel will tickle him up till he doesn't know which way he's facing!"

George Bryan smiled sadly. "True, guv'nor, and consoling. What saddens me is that all the chivalry has gone out of it. Crooks didn't used to throw their hands in—they fought like hell and always will, and quite right too. But these young barristers today—they used to show some professional regret when they had to go for a copper's integrity. Now they believe in what they're suggesting and grab every chance they get. But it's part of the job, as you say, of course."

"Well don't let's get bloody maudlin about it, anyway," said Gunn. "Damn it, if anyone had told me last month that by today we'd have nicked four members of the Berry gang red-handed, saved a container and got one of our own villains as well, I'd have laughed him to scorn. OK—so there'll be problems. Always will be. Lots of them. But we can't go into a fight ready to lose! Tell me, Charles—who'll be running this? I assume you'll get to the Bailey—I wouldn't be happy about some branch of London Sessions off the lingerie department of Harrods!"

"No problem there. I expect a Section 1 committal to the Bailey. And once there —it's a job for Oliver Rickler, surely."

"I agree. Nobody better. He knows our Force and admires it, he'll fight like a tiger and hit like a steam-hammer for it. Rickler's our man."

"Vicki—how about a drop more wine all round?" added Stratton.

The elegant Miss Beck rose to her feet.

14

"RIGHT then, Vicki. I'd like those to go this afternoon, if you can manage it."

Stratton had finished half an hour's dictation—mostly letters, with a memo or two. Now there was time to make final arrangements for tomorrow. He glanced up as his secretary reached the glass door.

"Ask Evan to come in when he's free, will you? I want to tie up the big committal."

"Coming now!" came Evan's voice. Stratton, whose hearing was by no means what it had been, relied increasingly on Evan's keen ear, rather to his own annoyance. Now, as Vicki vanished, the little man appeared in the doorway, a large bundle of folders under his arm. These he began to arrange on the far side of the big desk.

"Separate folder for each of the six," he explained, laying them out in a line. "Defendant—solicitor—counsel—on the outside of each. Then our Court File, with police reports and statements, etc. Lastly, our office file."

Stratton was not sure whether this comprehensive neatness was Evan's own nature or his pandering to his chief's inordinately tidy mind, of which Stratton was conscious and a little ashamed. He had now reached the stage when, unless everything was clearly ordered, he had doubts about his efficiency in dealing with it. Was he getting finicky, he wondered?

"Right. That's fine, as usual. Now—forms and papers served?"

"Yes. No problems. It will be a Section 1 Committal. About ten minutes the lot. Our phone bill's going up all the time, though! Trouble with a mob-hander like this, there are so many cross-references that can't wait for the post. The picture's clear now, you'll be glad to know. The trouble was Willow—surprise surprise!"

"In the case, yes. But in the handling too?"

"Aye. Trust that sod to be awkward! He's gone to some firm nobody's ever heard of. All the others are regulars we know. Tits had to be the odd man out, of course! Still all clear now."

"Good. Now—who do we face, down the line?"

Evan turned to the end folder. "Harry Williams is with Brooks, of Stepney—they handle all the Berry gang primaries as you know."

"Sure. Will that be Mike Norden? Or will he put up counsel at Newham tomorrow?"

"He'll have Peter Dennis at the Bailey but Norden himself will handle tomorrow's committal."

"I've always been surprised that a man as nice and honest as Norden can go on taking the work of the Berry gang. It makes our life more pleasant, I know, but I'm surprised."

"I agree. Now their second-string brief is a character much more naturally suited to the job, if you know what I mean."

"Dickie Horton? I agree. I suppose it will be Burney lumbered with him."

"Right. Happily, Dickie always knows when he's on a loser. He won't bother with Newham. Junior clerk and counsel for him. He'll use Jim Smith at the Bailey—

he's a youngster cutting his teeth in Dennis's chambers. Cheers me up, that. If Dickie was bustling about, it'd mean he was confident and I'd be anxious."

"Good. How about Lucky Delafield?"

"Poor old sod—the gang aren't even looking after him. I expect they'll pay his bill in the end, but Lucky's had to see to things himself. He's gone to Overton and Elkins of Leyton. Reliable lot. Elkins will be there tomorrow. He's booked a bright up-and-comer for the trial. Name of Derek Morgan."

"So far so good," said Stratton. "That brings us to Rogers."

"Vic Everett, New Cross."

"Everett? Nice man, Vic. Always like him around. Clever too, but without playing dirty."

"Yes. He handled that Paxton job very well—took it clean off us, if you remember. He'll be there tomorrow, unless he's bunged with a case which doesn't finish today. He's briefing Alec Glossop for the trial—that ten foot Scottish guy in Marsham's chambers, you know?"

"Ah! The tartan cap!"

"No—just coincidence. Rogers is New Cross born and bred. Got half a sheet of form, too."

"The Berry gang will probably cover his bill eventually, too. They recruited the chap, although they can't be too pleased about his panicking. Anyway, that's four sorted out, leaving our strange bed-fellows Lane and Willow. Who's Teddy gone to?"

"Neil Tomlinson, from Norman Henry's firm in Hackney, I'm pleased to say. One of the best. I've put Neil in the picture. He's on legal aid, of course. He'll get his acquittal in the end and we'll get full co-operation. His counsel's name is Charles Osborne, not known to me. Neil will be there tomorrow. Very discreet. A wine lover, of course."

"Yes, we meet often at Solicitors Wine Society meetings. But I was afraid Teddy Lane's man would want to make a submission—I'm pleased about that, Evan. Who's the odd-ball you mentioned, though, for Willow?"

"Firm named Edwin Poulter of Loughton."

"You mean Leyton."

"I mean Loughton."

"Mistake, old son. Loughton's a very smart, respectable residential suburb out the far side of Epping Forest. I doubt they've ever heard of criminal work unless it's motoring, or riding up a wrong path in the Forest. Fraud, I suppose, possibly. But blagging in the docks—no."

"Odd, isn't it. The firm is entirely conveyancing—old man Poulter and one other. But they've got this bird with them. She rang up. I gather one of their clerks is personally related to Willow or something—hence Loughton. Bird's name is Erica Drew, will you believe."

"Erica Drew? Sounds as if it would suit in lights on Broadway—and I don't mean Stratford Broadway! A bit too unsuitable for a solicitor. I smell trouble."

"*Do* you now?" said Evan, serious at once. "I had the same instinct. It's that toe of mine. It twitches. I'll try and get some gen on the inviting Erica when I have time. But we'll sight her tomorrow. Her counsel will be John Jackson. Mere pupil, I gather—stand in for someone not yet finalised. I asked her who she was planning to use and she snapped that she would tell me when it was fixed and not before! She sounds *almost* out of her depth on the phone. I get the impression that she's quite experienced but the elastic's at full stretch—know what I mean?"

"If you're referring to her nerves and not her knickers, yes I know just what you mean. Tried a bit of jargon on her, have you?"

"Exactly. She knows all the simple stuff. She rang me—well, rang you, actually—last Friday. 'Erica Drew here,' she said—very twee. 'Mr. Ian Willow has consulted me.' Not 'my firm', let alone 'the firm I work for'. I took details without comment and then she said 'I presume you're seeking a Section 1,' ever so very casual, like."

"What did you say?"

"I said yes, I hadn't expected anything else in a case this strong. Then I asked her if she had anything for me under Section 10 and I felt her boggle for a moment. I think she had the Criminal Justice Act on the desk—I swear I heard the pages flipping over! Then she said 'Admission of facts, you mean? Well not until I've considered your written evidence anyway.'

The right answer, of course. But my toe twitched again. I may be doing the girl an injustice, of course. One shouldn't base one's views, let alone one's tactics, on hunches. But my toe's not usually wrong."

"We'll play her very carefully, Evan. Of course she may turn out to be some old bag, retired after decades of unsung service with the DPP, for all we know! Voices can mislead. But there should be no complications tomorrow. Newham is impeccable, of course."

"Of course. 'Himself' is away on his hols at the moment, in fact. Paul Cantley's in charge. I've given him all the gen and he's approved the statements. Court One, as you'd expect with this mob. Charlie Gleed the one-armed wonder in the Chair, and two others not yet settled. I've done your special forms—Vicki's running them off now. The whole thing shouldn't take more than fifteen minutes. Thank God for a really efficient Magistrates' Court, as I never stop saying."

"We're lucky all the way round, you know. Thames is one of the best Stipendiary's Courts in London—that covers the

Indias and the upper River. Newham covers the Royals and the main court at Grays is another absolute binger. Aren't we lucky, though!"

15

THE summer which had begun so dramatically on the day of the container theft was now firmly established. Charles and Evan chose to make their usual journey to Newham by tube, with a half-mile walk to the old East Ham Town Hall, which gave them exercise and a chance of a final reflection on the coming work.

The long corridor off which the principal court lay to the right at the far end was cool and almost inviting as they turned in at the swing doors. Evan disappeared into the Clerk's office to check on the final details of the case with Paul Cantley, while Stratton went on through to the little office under the stairs to have a word with Walter Rees the Court Inspector, and his staff—asking for information on the day's list and to tell them anything they wanted to know about the big committal. Emerging, he found George Bryan arriving with Sgt. Brewer. The police were not personally concerned with this modern-style committal but they always attended as a courtesy and in case they could be of help.

When the court doors were unlocked and while the heavyweight sergeant called the roll in ringing tones, Stratton went in and took his favourite place at the far left-hand end of the front row, putting his briefcase on the pew immediately behind him so that Evan could sit there and arrange his papers. Then, leafing once more through the file which he now knew almost by heart, he waited for his opponents to arrive.

Nick Elkins was first—a small man with a grey Vandyke beard, hair plastered firmly with something in the Brylcreem family if the smell was anything to go by. He smiled a welcome.

"Charles Stratton, PLA. You're for Lucky, aren't you?"

"That's right. I'm Nick Elkins. We've met—here, I think."

"Yes—that curious South African affair. You pleaded—most eloquently too, I recall."

"You're very kind—and you were very helpful."

"Pleasure. Not much I can do for you here, I'm afraid."

"No. My man's accident-prone, I fear. Even on his own story he hasn't a chance, poor little sod!"

Stratton smiled sympathetically as the court door opened to admit Victor Everett from New Cross and Neil Tomlinson for Teddy Lane. They were all mutual friends of long standing. Neil was stout, young, cheery with a brown full-set beard and a deep, rich voice. Victor, by contrast, was tall and slim, grey hair thinning now, and a soft voice—a man of great charm and as upright professionally as he was in figure. They pushed into the front pew with affectionate rudery about Stratton's weight and then, sitting side by side and opening cases, they teased one another as old friends will. Stratton checked that they both met Elkins.

Next into court was Mike Norden— short, dark and very Jewish—the No. 1 solicitor used by the Berry gang. He called good-hearted greetings as he stepped over Elkins and sat on his left. With him, and preceding him into the centre of the pew, was a young man with a fringe of brown hair which gave him a curiously anachronistic appearance, as if he was a Roman who had swopped his toga for a Burton suit. Introduced by Norden as James Smith, Counsel for Burney, he turned out to have a nervous, high-pitched voice. They were followed by a nondescript clerk from Dickie Horton's office who slipped into the back pew to sit directly behind Smith. At the same moment, Stratton caught sight of George Bryan and Bill Brewer slipping across to the bench immediately below the high raked public gallery. He glanced at his watch. A few minutes to 10.30. Newham was always on the dot. Evan would be here in a moment, he thought.

Just then the door opened and his assistant could be seen holding it for a young lady who could only be the mysterious Miss Drew. Stratton took in the petite well-groomed frame, the blonde hair, short, not obviously tinted and expensively cut, the smart barathea black jacket and skirt, the white wide-collared blouse. Too much bust for her height, thought Stratton, a bit clinically—in ten years time she'll begin to be blowsy. But for the moment, he conceded, she was highly presentable, with a touch of the pouter pigeon. Her smile at Evan was a combination of self-confidence and physical suggestion. Well, he thought—Evan's about her size, and he can look after himself! He half rose as they came along behind the second pew, in front of the large, empty dock with its high front rail.

"Miss Drew—my chief, Mr. Stratton," said Evan, carefully avoiding both facial and vocal expression.

Stratton greeted her formally—just her name. She smiled at him very directly, her eyes demanding his attention, questioning, assessing. He thought she'd overdone the lipstick slightly—and it was the glossy kind he disliked. There was no sign of individual personality yet. She entered the back pew and moved along to its centre. Evan was about to take his corner behind Stratton when a tall, thin, gangling man with metal framed bi-focals hurried across from the door and Evan moved out to let him in. He sat on Miss Drew's left. Her glance as he did so was distinctly cool and unappreciative. She spoke across him as he opened his briefcase.

"Mr. Stratton—my counsel, Mr. Jackson. Mr. Stratton is the PLA prosecuting solicitor, John."

Oh—first name and open contempt, is it, thought Stratton. Interesting. Out of the side of his mouth and over his shoulder he whispered, "Any problems?" Evan bent slightly forward and spoke quietly but clearly into Stratton's right ear—the better of the two—with a volume that was exactly right. He never missed a word of Evan's in such a context, and yet no-one else had ever caught anything not meant for them.

"None. All ready to go. David Elbrow, local undertaker, of all things, sitting with Charlie, plus jolly Mrs. Cornock. Here they come!"

The court sergeant bawled, "Rise, please," as from the corner above the far end of the bench the door opened to admit the rubicund Charles Gleed, retired businessman, his empty sleeve tucked inconspicuously into the left-hand pocket of his jacket. The large, chubby Joan Cornock passed behind him as he took the centre chair, taking that on Stratton's side of the court. Third came the quiet fair-haired Elbrow, whose sombre black suiting was the only indication of his calling and contrasted with his ready smile. Finally, shutting the door behind him and carrying a thick ledger under his arm, came Paul Cantley—dark, bushy hair and heavy moustache, neither of which hid his enjoyment of his work. He stepped through the little gate in the bench and down two steps to his own raised desk, where he opened his tome. Then he looked round the court briefly, sitting only when all three magistrates had done so. Everyone else then sat, except the huge court sergeant, to whom Cantley said, "One to six, please," checking with the list on his desk.

"Williams—Burney—Delafield—Rogers—Willow—Lane!"

Some were up with friends in the public seats. Two were in the corridor and were now hustled in. They lined up in the dock. Stratton made sure for the umpteenth time that his papers were in order on his clipboard and glanced round. Six assorted faces stared glumly from the dock. He rose. Gleed smiled.

"Yes, Mr. Stratton."

"May it please your Worships, I appear to prosecute in this case. Of the six men in the dock, Williams, on your left, is represented by my friend Mr. Norden, Burney by Mr. James Smith of Counsel, Delafield by my friend Mr. Elkins of Leyton, Rogers by my friend Mr. Everett of New Cross, Willow by Mr. John Jackson of Counsel and Lane by my friend Mr. Tomlinson on my immediate right."

As each advocate was named, he half-rose, bowed and resumed his seat. Stratton devoted his attention exclusively to the front and spoke clearly, without emphasis, fairly quickly, running through a routine with which he knew his hearers were fully familiar.

"Your Worships will not be troubled long this morning, this being a committal under the provisions of Section 1 of the Criminal Justice Act 1967 under which, as you know, each of the defendants through his advocate acknowledges that there is a *prima facie* case established by those parts of the Crown evidence that have been

THE COMMITTAL HEARING

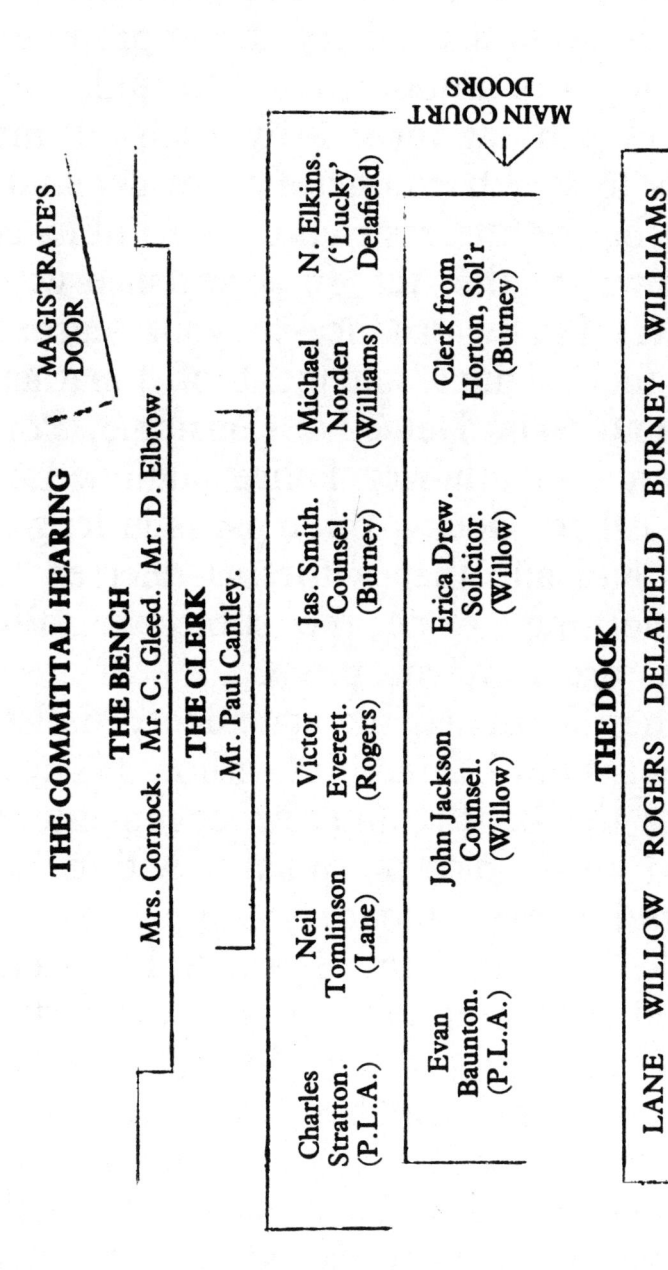

THE BENCH
Mrs. Cornock. Mr. C. Gleed. Mr. D. Elbrow.

MAGISTRATE'S DOOR

THE CLERK
Mr. Paul Cantley.

Charles Stratton. (P.L.A.)	Neil Tomlinson (Lane)	Victor Everett. (Rogers)	Jas. Smith. Counsel. (Burney)	Michael Norden (Williams)	N. Elkins. ('Lucky' Delafield)
Evan Baunton. (P.L.A.)	John Jackson Counsel. (Willow)		Erica Drew. Solicitor. (Willow)		Clerk from Horton, Sol'r (Burney)

MAIN COURT DOORS

THE DOCK

LANE   WILLOW   ROGERS   DELAFIELD   BURNEY   WILLIAMS

PUBLIC SEATS, etc.

submitted to each of them in statements of evidence accompanied by the appropriate statutory documentation, through my office. I am authorised by each of my friends to say that none of them demands the lifting of the restrictions on publicity laid down by the Act. In accordance with that Act I now produce to your learned clerk the original statement of Jonathan Raymond Ball, Detective Constable, Port of London Authority Police stationed at Royal Albert Dock—three pages in length—this and all other witnesses referred to this morning to be the subject of full witness orders if you please."

As he mentioned the statement, his left hand went out behind him without his eyes leaving the bench, and the document he needed was placed quietly within it. Continuing his sentence without a pause, he held it out in front of him and a black-gowned usher stepped forward, took it and laid it on Cantley's desk. By the time the sentence was finished, Cantley had checked the identity of the deponent, the fact that each page was correctly signed and the number of pages involved. He scribbled "FWO" on the top corner of the front page and nodded to Stratton as the sentence finished. Stratton's left hand went once more silently out behind him for Evan to act as before with the second statement recorded on Stratton's clip-board on the specially designed form. It was a routine that he and Evan had operated dozens of times since the Act came into operation and when it was properly done, as it was in all courts handling PLA cases, it was neat, smooth, undramatic, clear and precise.

In little more than five minutes, Stratton had produced in this way eight selected statements, copies of all of which had been sent well in advance to each defending solicitor as well as to the Clerk's office. Evan had seen to all this, as well as speaking with each on the phone, "ironing out any bugs in advance" as he put it. These statements were not the only ones to be used at the trial—they were only those which provided a complete outline— making together a case which, had there been no contest from any defendant, would have established guilt. None of this clear and speedy procedure had been possible before the 1967 Act, when each witness would have had to appear in person and be led slowly through every word of their evidence while the Clerk wrote down every word by hand, the defence lawyers remaining ignorant in advance of every one and reserving all cross-examination. Then each statement would have to be read back to the witness who would sign it before it went away to be typed over the weeks following and sent by the court to everyone concerned, the whole entitled "Depositions". The present system had revealed the old ways as the archaic rubbish they were.

Once the statements were all in, Stratton ran quickly through the remaining formalities, asking finally for the committal of all six by consent and on continuing bail to the Central Criminal Court, Old Bailey. When he resumed his seat, the Clerk passed Gleed a small card from which the statutory formulae were read out—in particular the direction that details of any alibi that any defendant might wish to advance should be sent to Stratton's office in proper form at least eight days before trial. Then all six defendants were directed to stand and each advocate in turn rose briefly to confirm his consent to committal, all defences being reserved.

Charles Gleed then pronounced the formal committal, granting the applications for bail on behalf of each of the defendants and extending the Legal Aid certificates already granted so as to cover the trial. Stratton was granted one in respect of prosecution costs from public funds—in fact he merely said, "And a Form D please, your Worships," in response to which Mr. Gleed murmured, "Certainly," and nodded. And it was all over.

Stratton glanced at his watch. Exactly 10.45. Under the bad old system, the same result would have caused an entire court to be occupied for at least a whole day, even disregarding the hours and hours of copying and checking in the Clerk's office, all of which had been done in advance and in Stratton's office.

There were a few minutes now in which everyone involved sorted out their papers and moved out, with bows to the bench, into the long corridor. Stratton waited without moving until he heard Evan's whispered, "Right!" before he rose, exchanged smiles of goodwill with Paul Cantley and the bench, and moved over to the door.

Outside, chatting with George Bryan, Stratton caught a glimpse of the petite Miss Drew disappearing along the corridor in animated conversation with Jackson— she doing all the talking. Behind him, Evan noticed his glance and spoke softly.

"A mite top-heavy but good legs. *Very* self-confident and correct procedurally on all counts. But my bloody toe is still twitching like mad. That damned woman is trouble with a capital T. I don't know how or why but I'm dead certain of it. We are going to have to watch her like a hawk!"

"Not inappropriate," murmured Stratton. "There's a trace of the pigeon about her build, don't you think?"

"It's the bra, actually," grinned the impish Mr. Baunton. "I'm an expert in these things!"

16

THE tall young man—well over six feet and with a stride of appropriate length—swung round the corner from his home and approached his office, squinting contentedly as he turned right into the morning sun streaming out of a cloudless sky. Another hot one, he thought.

The first thing that struck most people on meeting Joe Dickenson was how different he was from everybody's idea of a "private eye". Still in his early thirties, fresh-faced, bright and distinctly contemporary in appearance—unless the job he was on required otherwise—with fair, wavy hair which would never lie flat. Such was the reality behind the formal brass plate reading "J. DICKENSON—ENQUIRY AGENT".

Certainly he did not look at all like a retired Metropolitan Police Detective Sergeant with two years on C1 (popularly but not adequately known as "The Murder

Squad")—retired, moreover, with honour and for personal reasons just as a highly promising career was about to come to full bloom. Nor, for that matter, did he exhibit any sign of the grief and strain that a beautiful young wife's being smitten with multiple sclerosis in her twenties can only have meant to them both.

Things were much easier now that his sister Emma had moved into their little house off George Lane, South Woodford. Emma and Joyce were deeply fond of each other and had been since long before Joyce had begun to drop things around the house so consistently that she had finally gone to the doctor about it, to receive not teasing but deep concern and a series of tests which had ended in the diagnosis that meant slow and certain death after increasing incapability had gradually affected every part of her young body.

Together Joyce and Joe had kept the facts from everyone else until they had themselves fully assimilated, if not mastered, the prospects. It had taken Joe many months to conquer fully those odd moments when he had to be apart—totally alone, for a spell. Looking back on it now, he thought how easy it would have been for him to have taken to drink, had he not kept himself constantly aware that he was the single life-line on which Joyce depended for her survival. Even now there were a few times when he would drive to a quiet corner of Epping Forest and sit clenching his hands, until the nails of the long fingers drew blood from the palms of the big hands, while the tears poured uncontrollably down his face and he railed with every foul expression he had ever heard, but in silence, against the bloody-minded deity who had allowed as fine a person as Joyce to contract this unspeakably awful and incurable disease—above all for depriving her of being the ideal mother she so wanted to have been and so clearly could have been. Then he would return, spent, and Joyce would never mention, though she guessed, his private agony that was so much less than her own.

Joe had resigned from the Yard without anyone having an inkling of the reasons why he had chosen to pack it all in just when everything was beginning to move for him. Joyce—then still happily and fully active—had come with him to his farewell party, accepting the traditional huge bouquet with a glow and giving no sign of the pain she knew in her heart for the career that she was so unwillingly blighting. His mates had put it down to an unconquerable desire to be his own master. His brilliance had led them to assume that he could not fit into a team, even as a leader. The pathetic truth was that Joe's basic insecurity had made him essentially a team man. No-one had known or even suspected the truth. Now even the memory of him at the Yard must be fading rapidly, he thought, except in the memories of a few particular friends.

The little office near the station was small and cheap but not at all bare. Joyce had insisted on that. Curtains, a few pictures, even the occasional flowers in a little vase on the top of the filing cabinet in the corner—all these helped clients to correct the image that Marlowe, Spade and Frank Marker had created in the minds of the general public. Now he was gradually becoming more widely known, mainly to solicitors with crime work centring on the nearby Crown Court at Snaresbrook, within walking distance of his home and office. And more work was bringing more still, as satisfied clients mentioned his name to others who might have been in need of a discreet, trustworthy, uncontaminated retired policeman. Even some of his old colleagues had brought him a few cases. Just how his latest client had got on to him, however, he had no idea. Just a phone call out of the blue, some days before.

"Mr. Dickenson? My name is Erica Drew, of Edwin Poulter & Co., solicitors of Loughton. I understand you undertake enquiries in criminal cases."

"Certainly I do, Miss Drew. How can I help you?"

"I am defending a docks foreman by the name of Ian Willow. He is charged with theft, alternatively handling. The subject of the charge is whisky. The PLA Police are running it. There are others also charged and I anticipate that a conspiracy charge will be added following a committal by consent to the Old Bailey."

"I see. Very roughly, what would be the nature of the enquiries? I presume he says he didn't do it?"

"Vehemently. There are several lines of

enquiry I have in mind. If you will accept instructions generally I will write to you about the case. What are your terms?"

He told her. She seemed surprised, though whether she found them higher or lower than she expected she gave no indication. One thing did surprise him—it was not a legal aid case, she said. Docks foreman? He could surely have got it automatically, especially at the Old Bailey. Still that wasn't his business. The girl sounded young—pushing the sexy voice a bit strongly, he felt—probably so used to it as a come-on that she was barely conscious of it now. Well, so long as her instructions were clear and legal and she paid her bill, what did it matter? He'd turned down one or two jobs as disreputable but not from solicitors. Poulters of Loughton, she'd said. Never heard of them.

He reached the white door, fitted the key, turned it and went in. Shutting it on the latch behind him, he turned to open the wire basket below the letter slot. Quite a handful this morning. He took them, remembering weeks when there were none at all and little hope of any—smiled to himself and made his way up the stairs, unlocked the half-glass door with his name painted a little too expensively on it, and went in to the typist's room, equipped with a desk and a machine against the day when he could afford not to be his own typist and so into the inner office—smaller but lighter and brighter. He dropped the handful of letters on the desk, took his jacket off and hung it neatly on the hanger on the door.

He opened the window. With the room door open, cool air tempered the hot sunshine and stirred the papers on the desk. He riffled through the pile. Two for next door for a start! He'd take them in when he'd read his own. Electricity bill —less than he'd expected—nice surprise. Two cheques in settlement of accounts— things were looking up indeed! And this, he thought noticing the Loughton postmark, would be the slightly breathy Miss Drew and her new instructions.

He slit it open. Yes—Edwin Poulter of Loughton. Respectable address. Good quality paper. Embossed heading, not printed. No mention of Drew among the principals. She was probably an Assistant Solicitor, perhaps with prospects. Two pages, single-spaced, neatly typed—impression of efficiency. A phrase or two caught his eye—legal jargon a-plenty. He flicked over the page. There it was—"Erica Drew". Large round hand—feminine—a bit brassy? No indication of her position. Might even be modesty! He recollected the voice and smiled. No, nothing modest there, let alone coy. *Very* confident. He turned back to the start and began to read. When he had got right through to the bold signature, his smile had been replaced with a worried frown. Hoping he might have misread it, he began again. Then a third time. After that he let it lie on his blotter and threw himself back in his chair, stroking his chin thoughtfully.

PLA Police. When he was at the Yard he'd paid a couple of visits to their HQ. Proud little Force, delighted to co-operate —did, too, most usefully. What was the name of that DI with the red hair, known as "Ginger", naturally? They'd been an exceptionally jolly bunch in the bar. He looked back at the letter. Yes—the very name—Bryan. George Bryan. The chap he'd worked with. He sat up and reached across the desk for the slim Police Almanac. PLA Police—there it was.

He pulled the telephone towards him and began to dial.

17

SERGEANT ALBERT HOBBS, the corpulent old-stager who ran the Divisional Office at the Royal Albert Dock, was in no two minds about her. He had been at his usual position against the front desk and had noticed the scarlet Mini-Clubman shoot past the door heading for the car park. Now he was upstairs reporting to George Bryan, who was so far managing to conceal his amusement at the big man's outrage.

"A couple of minutes later, sir, and here she comes up the steps and into the entrance, looking around her as if she'd just bought the place. Bold as brass! Busty little bitch!" he exploded, alliteratively.

"I'm sure you were as properly respectful to her as you would be to any member of the public, Sergeant Hobbs."

"Who—me, sir? Indeed I was, sir! 'Good morning madam,' I says, very cool and polite. 'Can I assist you?' Stuck her nose in the air. 'My name is Erica Drew,' she says, 'and I wish to see Detective Chief Inspector George Bryan'—just like that, sir—as if she expected me to serve you up on a plate with bloody parsley round you!"

"I rather think my head on a charger would have done," remarked Bryan drily.

"Anyway, I looked her full in the face, sir, and I said, 'Have you an appointment, madam?' She drew herself up to her full height—about five feet two—and she says, 'Are you suggesting that it is necessary to have one before I can see your superior officer?' 'No, Madam', I said. 'It's just that since I have no record of an appointment, I am not sure where Mr. Bryan is and what he is engaged upon at this particular moment.' Polite but firm, sir."

"Exactly, Sgt. Hobbs. Firm, as you say, but polite. And how did the—er—'busty little bitch' react to your polite firmness?"

"She put her executive briefcase on the counter with a bump and snaps, 'Then I suggest you should find out, sergeant!'"

"Whereupon, Sgt. Hobbs—no doubt suiting the action to the word—you left her standing there and came to find out exactly what I was doing, I venture to suppose."

"Well you could hardly expect me to fetch a chair out of the canteen for her to sit on while she waited, sir!"

"No, no of course," said Bryan, smothering a laugh. "And anyway, she had the counter to lean on."

"Exactly, sir. I might add for your information that on my way here I took the opportunity to call on Inspector Graham, he being on leave, sir, and use his telephone to call 9 Gate and ask what Miss Drew said when she came through on her way here. They told me she had asked her way to this Headquarters, stating that she had an appointment with you, sir."

"Ah! Well done indeed, Sergeant. And I am pleased to confirm that the little lady is a little liar on the point."

"As I had expected, sir."

"Quite. On the other hand, I have met her and I know of her quite well. I was even expecting some such approach. You know the big container case?"

"Yes, sir."

"She is the solicitor acting for Willow."

The big sergeant's heavy eyebrows

almost disappeared under his hair line. "The devil she is, sir!"

"There I think you over-estimate her villainy, Hobbs. A cool, calculating little bitch, certainly. Busty if you say so. But the devil—apart from somehow always thinking of him as male—I would stake my life she is not! I'll be happy to see her in a few minutes. Tell me—is Sgt. Brewer in?"

"Yes—in the CID office, sir."

"Stick your head in there as you go down, sergeant, and ask him if he'd pop in here right away. I want a few words with him and then I'll ring down for Miss Drew. I suggest she should be escorted up, for all our sakes, rather than just given directions."

"I shall bring her myself, personally," said Hobbs, with such tautological emphasis that he did not have to add, "because I wouldn't trust the damned woman out of my sight."

"Good. Then, thank you Sergeant Hobbs."

Hobbs swung round and out into the corridor. Once Bryan was sure he was out of earshot, he let out his laughter in a gust.

He was still chortling quietly when, with a quick tap on the door, Brewer arrived.

"Come in, Bill. You've seen the outraged Hobbs?"

"Aye. Called on spec, has she, sir?"

"It would seem so, yes. Trying to catch us unready, no doubt. In which she is happily wrong. We are always ready. Hand me that file, will you? Thanks."

Brewer passed over the big folder from the top of the filing cabinet in the corner. Bryan opened it and found the little diary from Willow's pocket, in its polythene bag. Then he picked up the phone.

In a minute or two they heard the ponderous footsteps approaching. Albert Hobbs was not nick-named "PC Plod", by his colleagues for nothing. The thuds stopped, presumably to allow the sergeant's "busty little bitch" to catch up. Then came the authoritative brace of bangs with the sergeantine knuckles on the door, which quivered.

"Come in!" called Bryan, rising, as did Brewer.

Hobbs threw the door wide and made an appropriately lordly gesture. "Miss Drew, sir!" he thundered as if he was wearing not blue uniform but scarlet tails. And the lady appeared.

Do her credit, thought Bryan—she was a pretty little piece. Almost elegant. The costume was still barathea but this time bottle-green. The blouse was cream. The smile as she entered was natural and charming, betraying amusement at the old sergeant's pomposity. But when the door shut and she was alone with two men of different quality, it changed to a different smile—inviting, sexual even, yet not so exaggerated as to be obvious. Bryan felt his stomach react. He did not, he hoped, betray his extreme wariness.

"We met at Newham, Miss Drew. This is Det. Sgt. Brewer, who was with me but was not, I think, lucky enough to get a personal introduction."

Her eyes acknowledged the graceful compliment. Then the modest Brewer found himself the object of her smile. A word came into George Bryan's mind as he watched her. Predatory.

Brewer stepped forward and pulled a chair nearer the desk for her. She thanked him without taking her eyes off him. Then the beam seemed to be switched off as she sat down and opened her briefcase.

"Now, Mr. Bryan—obviously the thing I want to do first is to have a good look at the diary you contend you found on my client."

"Contend, Miss Drew?"

"Assert—insist—call it what you like. I did not say swear, as you have not yet had to do that."

"If it makes you any happier, Miss Drew, I am quite prepared to do it at any time. You do not perhaps carry a testament in your case?"

"I do not. And that, at least, you have no right to search."

"Really, Miss Drew—whatever gave you the idea that I would be interested in searching anything belonging to you? I do not associate a solicitor with the actions of his client. You could not afford to break the law. I am concerned only with those who do."

"And with those you *think* have done, even though they may not have!" she snapped with sudden venom.

"One moment, ma'am—we seen to have strayed from the point. You want to see the diary found on your client. To that you have every right. I have it here."

He picked up the little polythene package and held it across the desk toward her. She took it, turned it over and then back.

"I need to open it."

"Naturally. Please do. The polythene bag is merely to keep it separate from other exhibits and free of dust. We have a stock of bags. Tear it open, do."

About to do so, she paused and flicked up her eyes to meet his. He noticed that they were grey—the colour and temper of steel, he thought. He had the impression when she came in that they were blue. They showed clearly her lack of trust in his integrity. The knowledge shook him, for a second. Suddenly she dug a sharp-pointed finger-nail into the polythene, slit it and ripped. It tore open. She took the diary out and opened it.

"Without wishing to influence you in your examination at all, Miss Drew, I might mention that the relevant point in my evidence relates to an item which you will find among the pages provided for addresses and phone numbers which follow the dated pages and are headed 'Memoranda'. But you may look at whatever you wish."

She made no reply, flicked the dated pages through with her thumb, once and then again more slowly, then let the memoranda pages through singly until she came to the address pages. Then she changed her grip on the book, turning over single pages, concentrating on each in turn. Finally she reached the page with the "Harry" entry at the foot of the right-hand page. She gave it a moment's concentrated attention.

"This is the actual entry you claim was made by my client?" she said again, looking up with those steely eyes.

Bryan could not resist it. "No."

"No?"

"Since I did not see him make it, I cannot claim it was made by your client. I claim only that I found it as you see it and that since it was in Willow's pocket, it is a reasonable presumption that either he made it or someone did on his direction. But in fact Mr. Willow admitted making the entry. His explanation was that it referred to a different man—a Mr.

Wilson. He conceded the coincidence, too. The sample is too small for there to be any reasonable chance of the expert reaching a firm conclusion about its authorship. Its significance, as you will appreciate, is that the phone number is that of Harry Williams, one of the operative heads of the Berry gang and co-defendant of Willow."

"It was too easy," he thought. "Must be a facer for her, seeing damning evidence like that under her nose." But she was plainly thinking furiously. Bryan decided to stoke the fire a little.

"A remarkable coincidence, seeing that moments before Willow had denied all knowledge of Harry Williams' existence."

"Remarkable only if this is Willow's diary, and that you or one of your colleagues didn't make this entry after he had produced it to you."

"Miss Drew, this is a personal chat, which I am sure you don't wish to be made the subject of a record. But both those allegations are about the most serious and provocative that you could make about a policeman. Faking evidence. Framing an innocent man. They would involve perjury at the trial. Of course I understand your discomfiture at seeing this evidence for the first time. Under the circumstances I am prepared to forget your unfounded and unfortunate remark."

That'll teach you, he thought. Her reaction shook him more. "Forget it if you like, Mr. Bryan. It is one which will be made again—at the Old Bailey!"

"That, madam, is a matter wholly for you."

"And while we're on the point, Mr. Bryan," she said, snapping the diary shut and putting it back in the torn polythene bag, "I shall be sending an enquiry agent round to have a really good look at this diary in the next week or so. I take it there will be no objection to his seeing it?"

"None, Miss Drew. You've got another one, then?"

As the words left his mouth, he wished them unsaid. He saw their import dawn on her. Her eyes, which he had been watching with amusement, now revealed first surprise and then triumph. One stupid six-word casual remark and the entire situation between them had reversed. Instant peripeteia. Now she was studying how best to exploit the situation to her advantage. He drew no more than a crumb of consolation from the knowledge that at least the trap was not one that she had laid. Her triumph and his disaster were purely fortuitous. That made them no less devastating.

"*Another* one, Mr. Bryan?" It was reminiscent of 'A *hand* bag?' by Dame Edith Evans in all her glory. "Another *what?*"

"Another shot in your locker," said Bryan, desperately.

"That's not what you meant, is it? You slipped, Mr. Bryan! You did not mean me to know that you have been in touch with Mr. Dickenson."

"Dickenson?"

"Yes, Dickenson. How else would you know that I had to get myself another Enquiry Agent when that hypocrite declined my instructions? I choose my words, too. He had the cheek to give me a little lecture on ethics. In *this* game! And what does he do, the moment I turn my back? He rings you up and gives details of all my tactics to the enemy!"

"Is that how you think of the police service, Miss Drew?"

"Certainly. You and I are engaged in a

personal war, Mr. Bryan. Your job is to get a conviction of six men. Mine is to get one of them acquitted."

"Wouldn't you rather say that the motives of both of us amount to justice? I know you believe your client is innocent. I know you think I framed him. I did nothing of the sort, in fact. I never have. I never will—and I believe you know that, whatever Willow told you."

"My private opinions, Mr. Bryan, are nothing to do with the case. I am not Willow's judge. I am his advocate—his 'mouthpiece'. He says he is innocent. My duty is to secure his acquittal."

"Even if you find he was lying to you?"

"More strongly, if I think he was lying to me."

"Forgive me, Miss Drew—it is not my place to discuss ethics with you. I am not fighting the system of criminal justice. I am fighting crime and criminals. I am here to see that everybody on my patch obeyes the law, whoever he or she may be."

"Mr. Bryan, however skilfully you try, you will not sidetrack me from the unarguable fact that Mr. Dickenson either wrote or phoned or perhaps called on you, but anyway gave you the details of my private professional instructions to him. We shall see what a Judge at the Old Bailey says about *that!* I promise you only that he will be told about it. In public. By me. And you will not be able to allege that you were taken by surprise—I warn you now."

"I hear what you say, Miss Drew."

"If you are wise, you will take careful note of it. You may even consider withdrawing the charges against Willow. And thank you for this unexpected but handsome weapon in my armoury with which you have accidentally provided me! I wish you good morning, Mr. Bryan!"

She snapped her briefcase shut and rose to her feet. For a moment she glared, her mind searching for a particularly devastating parting shot. Then, deciding that she could not improve the situation, she turned. Brewer quickly opened the door for her. She flashed a glance at him, returning even in that second to her role of seductress. One nod and she was gone, leaving Brewer looking after her as she disappeared down the corridor.

He closed the door and turned. George Bryan had sunk into his chair and was resting his chin in his hand, his elbow on the blotter before him. He looked pole-axed.

"Holy Mary Mother of God!" he muttered disconsolately.

"Bad luck, guv'nor. It could happen to anyone."

"Thank you, Bill, but in fact it happened to me. I let myself right into it. She had nothing to do with it. I got too bloody cocky. And now I've wrecked the whole bloody case! If I'm shown up in the witness box, they'll all get away. And think of our reputation as a Force! Oh, the proverbial you-know-what has hit the proverbial fan all right, Bill, and I am the silly bugger that threw it! David Gunn will go a damned sight more than 'pop' when he hears about this, and I will be his target —and he'll be dead right! Let this be a warning to you, Bill, and never forget what you have learned. Never! Because I'm afraid I shan't be here to remind and advise you. This could mean my job."

18

THE only trace of cheerfulness among the four men who sat in a corner of the hall of the Chambers in 2, China Court, Temple—the floor which estate agents always call "lower ground"—was attributable to Evan Baunton, who was carrying on a mock flirtation with Angela, the bright little typist in the tiny office which led from the hall. He and David Gunn were drinking tea, thoughtfully provided for them, as clients of special standing, by Henry Rayne, the slim, dapper little senior clerk who combined efficiency with a light charm, contriving to look younger by ten years at least than his age must have been, and thereby hiding the vast experience he possessed. Stratton did not like tea and never touched it, while the unhappy George Bryan sat swamped in his personal misery, unable to participate in even the mildest form of companionship.

Henry—his surname was painted on the

outer door but few noticed it and many did not even know it, for he was never spoken or referred to as anything other than "Henry"—seized a moment between the stream of phone calls that made up the greater part of his function, at 4.30 p.m., to pop his head out of the office and ask, "More tea, anyone?" Getting a string of negative replies, he added, "Mr. Rickler will be off the phone in a moment and we'll have you in right away."

Stratton tried to cheer himself up with recollections of how he and Oliver Rickler between them had pulled many chestnuts from the fire. Solicitor and barrister had discovered a level of thought that was almost empathic. On this was founded, and quickly grew, a close and happy personal friendship which both valued highly. This had broadened in time to include Evan Baunton and several of the younger members of Oliver's chambers and it had long been rare for the PLA crime work to be sent anywhere else. By a combination of diplomacy and expertise, Henry had proved almost always able to provide them with whatever was needed, from his "flock", even in emergencies.

Oliver Rickler, meanwhile, who was comparatively junior when he and Stratton first met, had gradually risen by merit to a position so senior that it was not often, nowadays, that Henry could make him available. This container job, however, was one in which Stratton had forewarned Henry as soon as it occurred. Tom Alexander, Rickler's star pupil and now a full member of chambers, was also briefed for the case, in which Rickler, though not a "silk", was being treated virtually as if he were.

From the inner office came a "ting", followed by Henry's appearance in the hall and then up the passage with an aside of "Now in a minute!" He popped into the room at the far end of the corridor like a rabbit into its hole, emerging a moment later having checked that the right papers were in the right place and that there were enough chairs round the small desk in the window bay which Oliver used. Evan and David Gunn put their cups down as the dapper little clerk now waved them along.

Tom Alexander was holding the door open for them as they trooped in. He was beaming happily—part of the close relationship which had met with triumph and disaster over the years but never with bitterness nor the lessening of the mutual trust that bound them. Rickler was standing behind his desk, hand outstretched to greet Stratton as he led the group in.

"Charles—you *are* looking well! Come and sit down!"

"Oliver. Good to see you. Let me see—you know David Gunn, the head of our CID of course. I think you probably also know George Bryan, the DCI at the Royals. And Evan, of course."

They settled themselves and Rickler, when everyone was ready, leaned forward.

"Well, I gather that this was to have been a straight pre-trial con, but something awkward has come up. Then let me just say first what a splendid job you pulled off here, Mr. Gunn. I'm sure a few of your team—Wilson the motor-cyclist for one and that Welsh lad for another—will end up with compliments in open court irrespective of the result. The facts are clear—we caught them almost red-handed and we turned what looked like a disaster into an outstanding success. By 'we' I mean all four of you in different ways. Now let's see what our end can do. It's not exactly a push-over by any means. But let's salute the job as a whole."

"Very kind of you," said Gunn. "And coming from someone who knows our Force and its problems, we value that most highly."

"It's my honest opinion—which Tom, here, shares. Now—how do you want to deal with things, Charles? Are there any small points we can usefully clear out of the way before we turn to the major one?"

"Yes. There's one in particular which is causing me a little concern. It's Willow's counsel."

"Ah. I was going to ask you. Do we know who it's going to be, now?"

"We found out this morning. Phone call from his solicitor. And it's a name I've never heard of, which makes me unhappy because I know all the regulars at the Bailey and I like to know who I'm working with or against. You may know him, of course. His name is Everett Crane."

The effect of the name on Rickler was marked. For a moment his eyes opened wide, then closed, and his lips pursed.

Slowly he exhaled with the suggestion of a whistle. Stratton glanced at Tom Alexander, to find the young man looking as baffled as himself.

"Everett Crane," said Rickler, softly.

"Doesn't strike a chord with me. Should it?"

The barrister brought his mind back from what looked like a contemplation of the distant past. He listened as if in retrospect to Stratton's question.

"No. Tell me, Charles—how long have you been with the Port? When did you start with them?"

"Early 1961."

"And before that you were in the Provinces, weren't you?"

"I was, yes."

"And you, Tom?"

"I was at school, I'm afraid!" said Alexander.

"I was in Hong Kong," said Evan, brightly. "And you?"

"Oh I was here, but a very junior member of Chambers. Which is why, if you don't mind, I'll get Henry to pop in for a moment. His memory would be much more accurate than mine."

Stratton nodded and Rickler picked up the phone on the corner of the desk. "Henry—could you pop in a moment? Thanks."

As they waited his arrival, Rickler smiled reflectively and said, "Tell you one thing—no, two things, though neither's really relevant. He's in Reg Abbott's chambers, and he's an elderly man with a limp."

"Still means sweet nothing to me," said Stratton.

There was a tap on the door and Henry's head popped round it as it opened.

"Ah! Come in, Henry. I want you to tell us all what you know about Everett Crane."

Henry closed the door behind him and came into the centre of the room. They all looked at him.

"Everett Crane? Well, that's not a name I expected to hear in Chambers again. Has he died, possibly?"

"I hope not," smiled Rickler. "I've appeared against some pretty shady characters in my time, but never a ghost!"

"You mean Crane is back at the Bailey?"

"In this case. Briefed for Willow."

"Well, Mr. Rickler, you do surprise me!"

"I am surprised myself. The others are not. Would you tell them why we two are? Your memory's better than mine."

"Not really—only a little longer, perhaps. Well, gentlemen, Everett Crane used to be one of the brightest men at the criminal bar. Always at the Old Bailey. Briefed in all the big cases. Heading straight for the top. And then overnight, he lost it all. That's an exaggeration, of course, but in a short time everyone knew that Everett Crane had hit the bottle. He went from a man who had scarcely more than an occasional social drink to someone who got through two bottles of Scotch a day. He turned into an alcoholic almost overnight."

"Was there a known reason?" asked Stratton.

"There was. Very tragic, too. He had a beautiful wife, who was a solicitor, somewhere in the City. Big commercial practice. She didn't call herself Crane—she used her maiden name, though I can't recall what it was. Anyway, one day the Fraud Squad turned up—this was about nine years ago now. There had been one of those huge complicated frauds—you know the sort—network of companies, each dependent on the other, all interlinked, and some of them phoney. And it was thought that this woman was the brains of the whole shebang. I've no idea if she was innocent or guilty. I guess the Squad were probably leaning on her pretty heavily. Anyway, she died. Bottleful of pills—notes for the Coroner and so forth. The scandal was restricted to a fairly small circle and even there it was a bit of a nine-day-wonder. But the effect on Crane, as I said, was immediate and devastating. Even when he got over the first burst, the slightest strain and he'd be gone again. Old friends among solicitors threw him little cases from time to time, but he couldn't even manage those reliably. I've seen him very occasionally in the distance, limping about the Temple, but I'm afraid I've usually turned quickly into someone's doorway until he's gone by. Tragic, really. One of life's casualties, poor Crane. But how on earth does he come into this six-hander?"

"Unknown firm out at Loughton," said Stratton. "Girl trying to build up a criminal practice. But how on earth she picked Crane passes my comprehension."

"By the way, Henry," said Rickler. "Am I right in thinking the limp's got nothing to do with it?"

"Quite right. Some accident, I think. He used to laugh about it—said it was a good identification point. It was, too. Fancy! I never thought I'd hear his name again within these walls unless it was to hear he'd been found dead, or as a warning to someone. Everett Crane, back on the job. Well well!"

"That was the name the Drew bird gave me," said Evan. "And she wasn't joking, that I swear. I showed no surprise, of course, never having heard of the fellow."

There was a long pause, broken only as Rickler turned to his clerk with a shrug.

"Well thanks anyway, Henry. We'll play this one by ear. I hope it won't be difficult. Maybe he's managed a cure—it's not unheard of. But of all times to try and come back, when the criminal law has just gone through the biggest upheaval in substance and procedure it's had for 120 years—not the easiest time, I'd say. I hope he has found a cure, though. I hate people going that way, especially if they're good."

"Oh he was better than good, was Crane," said Henry musingly. "He was outstanding." He jerked into movement. "Ah well—lots to do. Was there anything else, Mr. Rickler?"

"Nothing at all, thank you, Henry."

The clerk switched on his beaming smile and was gone in a flash. The door closed softly behind him. It was the unhappy George Bryan who broke the silence.

"Well, I knew that bitch would grab every chance she could to make it awkward for me, but I never thought of that one!"

"You don't exactly care for Miss Drew, it seems, Mr. Bryan."

"You can say that again, Mr. Rickler!"

"And then double it—in spades!" added Evan.

"That's what we wanted especially to discuss, Oliver," said Stratton. "We've hit a bit of a bump."

"Correction sir," said Bryan. "*I've* hit

one. Or I am the blasted bump, if you like!"

"I've told you, George, it could have happened to anyone."

"I know, guv'nor—but in fact it happened to me."

"Well, let's hear about it. These things sometimes look worse than they turn out to be," smiled Rickler.

"Well, it relates only to Willow," said Stratton.

"I expected as much," said Rickler. "The Berry gang are like the poor—always with us. But Willow's the traitor, as you mention in the brief, Charles. He's sure to be the source of any trouble. By the way —this Loughton firm. I've not come across them before, have I?"

"Exactly," said Evan. "'Who's this bird?' he asks. And there's the rub. Though Shakespeare never knew our Erica, alas."

"And who's 'our Erica?'" smiled Rickler.

"Oh I don't know, though," went on Evan as if Rickler had not spoken at all. "Lady Macbeth must have been based on someone."

This raised a smile even from George Bryan. Only Evan himself affected to look bemused, as was his customary pleasure.

"Our concern," said Stratton, "centres on a young lady by the name of Erica Drew, apparently employed by a small conveyancing firm in Loughton, of all respectable places. It seems she is developing the criminal side of the practice. And she would seem to have been studying the telly rather than the textbook. She recently decided to enlist the services of an Enquiry Agent and by chance she got hold of a most upright young man who had recently set up his plate at South Woodford. Used to be at the Yard, I think you said, George?"

"Yes, sir. C1. Doing very well. I worked with him once or twice. He resigned for personal reasons but with full honours. No trace of a cloud over him."

"His name's Dickenson," said Stratton. "It seems that when the Drew girl wrote to him with instructions, she more or less told him to dig up perjured evidence of some kind. We didn't see the letter, of course, but we do know that he was told to get hold of—to fake, if necessary—any evidence on which she could mount a powerful attack on George Bryan's credibility. There's more to it than that, but to young Dickenson's credit he rang George and told him."

"What a silly little baggage!" said Rickler. "And what did you tell him, Mr. Bryan?"

"Well, sir, I told him he could refuse her instructions if he wished."

"Entirely right and proper."

"Yes, sir, but unfortunately the woman came to my office to inspect the diary which she alleges I planted or forged an entry in after it was found on Willow. She's a pert little madam, and I stupidly went and trampled on her a bit. Only verbally, of course," he added quickly as Rickler's eyebrows went up. "It was too easy to take her down a peg and I got cocky. I let slip that I knew Dickenson had refused to act for her. Immediately she alleged corruption, saying that I had suborned her witness, as well as faking the original evidence. And she left, saying she's going to bring it all out at the trial. Oh she's blowing it up—we can cut her down to size I'm sure. But you know what a little smoke can do with a jury when it's accompanied by suggestions of police corruption. It can cast a dirty great cloud over the whole case and our whole Force."

"Yes, I see," said Rickler, thoughtfully. "And six separate defence closing speeches to follow. Not an easy one at first sight."

"It's all my fault, sir. The trouble is, the bitch needled me into it. I've got no excuse at all."

"As I see it," said Stratton, "if Willow starts up a bandwagon like this, we can't expect the other counsel not to hop on to it just because they're decent chaps. They've a duty to their clients, after all."

"Which makes it more relevant that Willow's counsel will be the unpredictable Everett Crane," said Rickler.

For a long moment there was silence. Evan broke it.

"Anyone join my new club? I'm founder, chairman and secretary, but there's room for a few carefully selected members. I'm calling it the 'Screw Drew Society'."

When the laugh died down, Rickler smiled across at George Bryan.

"Mr. Bryan, I'm going to suggest that

you put this specific problem in my hands and then forget it. I don't want to give you a snap answer at the moment—I want to think about it very carefully. But I am confident that we can iron out this little bump completely. Of course you can expect to be attacked in the box—but you're used to that. I'll let you know how I propose to tackle this particular point about Dickenson, before we go into court. And I know you'll go on worrying about it meanwhile. But try and think of it this way—you, through the Authority, have hired me to do your worrying for you. That's my job. It's not yours. You're too close to it, anyway, to be able to see it in its true perspective. But from my position, I can see its importance in relation to all the other points in the case. So I know how much worry to allocate to it, if you see what I mean. And I'll go so far as to say that I don't think it's as serious as you naturally do at present. Will you leave it for me for now?"

"Gladly, Mr. Rickler, thank you," said Bryan, the relief already showing on his face.

"Good! Now—any other preliminary points, Charles?"

"None I want to bring up, anyway," said Stratton.

"Right! Then let's get down to the details of presentation—the order of the witnesses, the production of the exhibits and so forth."

He opened the brief on his desk and pulled out of it the large lined foolscap notebook in which he had already made his written preparations.

Evan Baunton began taking a number of folders out of the bigger of his two briefcases. He handed the first one to Stratton.

19

OLIVER RICKLER'S opening had begun along strictly traditional lines. Smooth, courteous introductions, first of himself and Tom Alexander, then of each professional opponent in turn, followed by a concise outline of the counts in the indictment—conspiracy, theft and handling stolen goods. The conspiracy charge had been added once it was clear that the evidence justified its inclusion in the indictment. All the defence counsel had anticipated this.

Rickler had gone on to stress firmly to the jury that it was on the shoulders of the Crown that the burden of proof primarily lay—that each accused man was not guilty at that moment and would remain so until the contrary was proved beyond reasonable doubt. On all matters of law, he had said, they must listen to no-one except the Judge. The concern of the advocates was solely with fact.

Oliver Rickler was a born communicator. Gifted with a voice that was soft but clear—proving repeatedly that clarity of sound is never a matter merely of volume—he had the rarer gift of putting even the most complicated matters into terms that the ordinary listener could at once fully understand. The occasional picturesque phrase served to highlight a point here and there—always the point that the mind unfamiliar with the context needed by way of a peg on which to hang the mental picture.

As he spoke, his hands rested lightly on the sides of the little folding stand which Henry always checked was on the desk in court before him when he arrived. It raised the effective working surface from thigh-height to waist-height, enabling him to stand straight-backed and to refer with no more than a downward glance to his papers. This eliminated the necessity of constantly bending down to refer to them or else of juggling with them in his hands, making the turning of a page a small but distracting balancing act. Judges, too, liked the upright but relaxed stance which Rickler found it no effort to maintain, if necessary for hours. His gestures were few, restricted to those points which demanded a movement if emphasis was to be made.

When it came to cross-examination, Rickler's style was less formal, the stand now becoming something on which he leaned, menacingly or confidentially, towards his target in the witness box. But all he said in court was delivered with a restraint which commanded attention, as the soft voice spoke smoothly but never monotonously. Stratton, who knew him well, could never make up his mind whether this was nature, or art become second nature.

The formalities of the case past, the prosecutor was free to turn to the background against which he would later paint the individual defendants in primary colours, each clearly distinguishable from the others. He knew that the average juryman would be unable to comprehend the sheer bulk of seven hundred cases of whisky. So—if one drank a dozen bottles a week, he told them, it would amount to nearly fourteen years drinking—assuming anyone lived to complete it! It would entail vast storage problems and it was target material for any big gang, provided they could arrange its distribution.

"And at this point, members of the jury, I am going to ask you to think back some years to the time, after the Second World War, when the immediate impact of peace had worn off, and we were all turning to the future. Many things had changed, never to return to their pre-war form. Among these was crime. Also, the whole face of dockland had radically altered. You see—when you have hundreds of millions of tons of all kinds of goods, resting in hundreds of sheds and warehouses in the docks, you have a ready-made target area. And for the man whose life and work lies among those goods, there is constant and considerable temptation.

"I'm sure it won't surprise you to be told that the dominant crime in dockland has always been theft of one form or another. But until the early fifties, it was almost entirely individual and what I might describe as 'opportunist theft'. A docker—and here I use the word to cover all the many varieties of work with goods in the docks—would often find himself face to face with some item which he could, with small chance of being noticed, slip into his pocket or under his jacket. True, there were the coppers at the gates. One docker really did observe to a member of the PLA police—'If it wasn't for you lot, I'd work for half a quid a week—and all I could carry home!' But let's face it, members of the jury—if you leave the docks on foot at the end of a shift, through one of the main gates, in the middle of a crowd of several hundred, the chance of being spotted carrying something stolen in the inside of your jacket is frankly small. This is known as pilfering. Owners have long recognised its nuisance value—they insure against it—indeed, a small percentage of goods is always calculated in advance as being liable to 'disappear' in transit, either by counting errors or pilfering. I don't condone it any more than you do. It's a fact of life.

"But after the war, people became used to doing everything on a larger scale. 'Big is beautiful' became a theme not only of the planner but of the petty thief. He began to steal items larger than he could easily carry—not, now, because they would be useful to himself or his family, but because he could sell them for untaxed cash.

"In time came a further change. The initiative to steal began to come not from the docker but from the man outside who was prepared to deal with the stolen goods. This was not new. The law has always recognised that the receiver—the 'handler' as we call him today—the 'fence' in criminal argot—was worse than the thief, because if the thief had no means of disposing of what he had stolen, he would steal no more than the things he needed. From a police point of view, the first problem was to identify all local receivers.

"But then in about the early 1960s came another development in dockland. Organised crime. This took the form of criminal gangs run from well outside the docks. They became almost like business firms—they had, for example, their own intelligence network made up of men who may never have been inside the docks in their lives but who knew all the dockland pubs, where they kept their eyes and ears open and often bought drinks for dockers, engaging them in conversation as a friendly, cheerful man can easily do, for the docker is by nature a warm-hearted, gregarious man. By such means, the gang would begin to get details of what goods were present in which shed—and what goods were going to arrive here, or pass through there, sometimes weeks in advance. For such plans must be made by the Port Authority well in advance. I mean, it's no good bringing say a lorry load of cigarettes to the Royal Albert Dock for loading on to a particular ship on a particular day unless there's going to be room in the right section of the right shed at the right time. Waiting cargo often has to be shifted around. And if you carefully question a few key men and fit pieces of information together like a jig-saw, you can get to know well in advance about all the major consignments coming through. The informants won't have been giving away any secrets—they wouldn't realise the significance of what they've mentioned in conversation. Indeed, it may not have any significance, until it is added to another item of information also insignificant in itself. But you will realise that the docks are not full of criminals at all. The big criminals of dockland are outside the docks altogether.

"Then the gang has to organise an efficient 'sales department'. This rests upon another fact of life. If you're a tobacconist, or a butcher, and life is not easy for you, and you're presented with an opportunity to purchase, say, a carton of twenty thousand cigarettes, or a side of beef—all brought to your door for about half the regular price, and all indistinguishable in appearance and taste from the legal ones—you're going to think twice about ringing the police. Anyway, you will have been selected in advance by the gang with some care, as a fairly honest, amenable type who's not having a very easy time just now. And if they have misjudged you—well, they also have a 'frightener' department, but that does not concern this case.

"Now, for these cheap goods you pay. In cash and in advance. That's part of the bargain. There is a guarantee that if the goods don't turn up you'll get every penny back. In such matters, the gangs are most scrupulous. Their reputation depends upon it.

"This brings me to the 'action teams'. It stands to reason that co-operation within the docks is to some extent necessary. There are a number of 'traitors' on the dock staff who get a regular retainer from the big gangs. Most of the time they pick this up for nothing. But some day a big load is going to have to be eased away from their shed when they and others will be reliably and reasonably engaged in looking the other way at a given moment. Pending such a moment, it is worth it to the gang to pay the 'traitor' a small salary.

"Now into the actual methods of theft I'm sure you will appreciate I do not intend to go. There are many ways of stealing from the docks. Most of them are known to the PLA Police. Some may have been thought out by the police that the gangs themselves haven't yet discovered, and we don't want to give them ideas, do we! Just let me ask you to remember this. In most cases of *bulk* theft, every item in that load has been bought and sold for cash before the theft itself ever takes place. So there is no 'fence' for the police to jump on. Within hours of the theft, the load has been taken to a distribution point, where it has been broken up and collected—or delivered.

"Well, that's the background, against which I will say this. We are dealing in this case with organised crime. The load which formed the target of the gang operating here was a huge sealed container of the type carried about by those huge juggernaut lorries hated by motorists and pedestrians alike. It contained seven hundred cases of an excellent Scotch whisky from the north of Scotland. Each case held a dozen bottles, each bottle indistinguishable from each other bottle. There was nothing anywhere to show the consumer that it was essentially export cargo. So if it was disposed of in small lots, it was virtually untraceable.

"And then one morning, acting on information received, the PLA Police directed that observation should be kept on a green Jaguar car which had been noticed in a street near the Royal Docks. Those watching it saw a man walk up to it. They saw that man being given some papers by the passenger from that Jaguar. Shortly afterwards, they lost all trace of the Jaguar for a time, although they did discover that the man who had been handed the papers was a long-distance lorry driver. A great many police officers were now alerted. You will appreciate that there was so far no evidence of a crime. There were merely grounds for thinking that one was about to be committed.

"And then two things happened. One was the reappearance of the Jaguar—on Silvertown Viaduct. One of the passengers got out and began to keep an apparently casual eye on the docks below. In that dock area, there appeared a lorry driven by the man who had been seen to take the papers that morning. It went, empty of all load, to a shed quite near the viaduct. There the driver produced papers to show that the whisky container I mentioned had to be transferred to another dock altogether. The papers were later found to be very skilfully forged. In fact they fooled the gate policeman when the lorry reached the gate. So up to now all was going well for the gang—until a foreman, back at the shed, put two and two together and set up a hue and cry. A series of dramatic events then followed in quick succession. For the moment it is enough for me to say that four men were arrested and, after police investigation, two more joined them in custody. I need now only sort them out for you as they sit before you in the dock.

"The gentleman furthest from you with the noticeable shortage of hair—which is of course no indication of criminality in itself (Oliver Rickler had a normal headful himself, but he knew that under his wig the judge was as bald as a button and would secretly enjoy the joke), his name is Harry Williams, one of the leading planners of this operation.

"Next to him sits Mr. Paul Burney, whose part in events is the exercise of a specialised skill. He is known as 'the wheels'. He drives vehicles with great skill. In his field, he is an artist.

"Third in line is Mr. Albert Delafield— in this operation the look-out up on the viaduct—a small cog in the engine but a cog, for all that.

"Next to him sits Mr. Rogers, who drove the lorry and who received from Mr. Williams the forged papers enabling him to secure the whisky container and to drive it to the gate heading elsewhere. When the alarm was raised, Mr. Rogers decided that the moment had come to abandon ship, as it were. Alas for him, he was within yards of a Welsh wing three-quarter, as you will shortly hear.

"That leaves the two gentlemen nearest the jury box. The fifth in line is a Mr. Willow—a man in a position of authority at the shed where the container lay, and who directed its loading on to Mr. Rogers' lorry, with the assistance of the sixth man in the line, a Mr. Lane. To be fair, Mr. Lane says he knew nothing about all this —he says he simply did what Mr. Willow told him. If you accept this, then you will be happy to acquit Mr. Lane. Mr. Willow denies all knowledge and all guilt, and whether that is the truth or whether he is exactly that kind of traitor of whom I was speaking generally, is a matter for you.

"One last point. Please do not concern yourself about various degrees of guilt. That is not a matter for you, nor for me. It is a burden which the law imposes upon His Lordship, who will reveal his conclusions in the course of his sentences, should you first find more than one of the defendants guilty. But a simple finding of guilt or innocence in respect of each of these six men is a burden that should be enough for you to bear.

"So much, then, for the background and the principal actors in our cast. Let me now turn to some of the particular items of evidence which the Crown's witnesses will reveal—assuming that you choose to accept the facts as they will give them on oath and after each has been fully tested in cross-examination by my learned friends."

20

THE back bar of the "Magpie and Stump" opposite the Central Criminal Court was packed, as usual, during the lunch adjournment, but by a stroke of luck a party of four got up and left just as they arrived. Quickly George Bryan and David Gunn sat down on two of the vacated chairs and held the other two manfully against all comers, while Evan secured a plate of sandwiches, and Stratton was soon elbowing his way through the crush with two pint glasses in each hand. Gunn looked up as he reached the table.

"My! That was quick!"

"Yes," said Stratton, sitting down. "It might have taken easily another ten minutes but the barman happened to look up just after I reached the bar and said, 'Let me see—yours is—?' and I said, 'Four pints of bitter' before anyone could get a word in. I hope it'll do."

George Bryan raised his tankard to his

lips. "Exactly right for me, thanks, Charles."

"Me too," said Gunn. "There's something about sitting in court that makes a pint of wallop much better than even a double Scotch—and I speak as a whisky man, myself."

"I think it must be the dust of ages which, for all Harry Wager's industrious hoovering, simply will not be shifted from the air," said Stratton.

"Yes," said Evan. "Besides—whenever anyone opens a volume of cases and smacks it to clear the dust from the edges, more is released. It's like Universities being great centres of culture because each freshman brings a little in with him and nobody takes any away when he goes down, so it sort of accumulates. But for the Old Bailey dust, beer is the only remedy, that's for sure!"

"Well," said Gunn, "how are we doing so far?"

"You've answered your own question, David. 'Well' is exactly how we are doing. Rickler played it very cool as you saw, taking all sensation, though not all interest, out of the opening. Even the villains have been presented as regrettable rather than evil, although Oliver can reverse that effect any time he wants. I'm sure he's right. The defence are going to whoop it up a bit—some of them anyway—and by that time it should have become a mixture of science and history—a quiet contest, with which any crash-bang-wallop stuff such as Miss Drew threatens will clash awkwardly. The formal stuff's over. The evidence will begin after lunch—plans and photos and such have all been put in and with any luck the jury are talking about it all over their first lunch together at this minute, getting some perspective into it."

"I'm a bit worried," said Evan. "Going too well." He swallowed a piece of sandwich reflectively. Bryan grinned at him.

"Oh come on, Evan! Professional pessimism isn't necessary in front of the guv'nor and me."

"It's not professional pessimism, George, it's my bloody toe!"

"Ah!" said Stratton. "A portion of Evan's anatomy that I have found more reliable than his brain, almost, over the years. What does it say?"

"That's the trouble—it's not saying anything. Just general apprehension. I smell trouble ahead, but too vaguely to make any definite forecast."

"Well, let's try and help it a bit," said Gunn. "We'll be leading off with the Matthew squad. They'll cover the spotting of the Jaguar, the handing over of the papers to Rogers and so on. Then there's a gap in the story, which is good, as the jury will imagine us collating that lot and directing a saturation of the area. Nothing to suggest that we had information straight from the horse's mouth."

"Speaking of horses—or one in particular," said Stratton, "I meant to ask you and forgot. What news of Jack Denny, David?"

"Well, as you know, he staged a very convincing stomach emergency, and we were able to fix him up in hospital with a *supposed* operation—ulcer or appendix or something—after which a period of convalescence was no more than reasonable. So if the Berry gang did have their suspicions when he went sick, I don't think they'll come to any firm conclusions yet. In the longer term, I'm more worried. For the moment, Jack is actually in London although reportedly somewhere in the Lake District I gather."

"Well, we've all got our fingers crossed for him," said Stratton. "Meanwhile—after the Matthew evidence, I presume we will have Bill Brewer next to show the lorry's arrival at 'F' Shed."

"Just so—and Bill can then carry on about its reappearance with the container aboard as it made for 6 Gate. After him I guess Rickler will ask for Pelham and then PC Abbott."

"Followed by J. P. R. Williams, sub nom Jenkins," added Evan.

"That's right—unless Rickler decides it might be better to have the two coppers *before* Pelham so that only then will there be any reason for cross-examination by Crane."

"Ah! I see!" said Bryan. "You mean that before Pelham there's no evidence involving Willow at all, so our evidence can be attacked only by Williams, Burney, Delafield and Rogers. By the way, I am a little surprised that we've had no Notices of Alibi from anyone."

"So am I," said Stratton, taking a swig

at his bitter. "No reaction from your pedal digit about that, Evan?"

"Not a tweak!"

"Right. Then once past Pelham, we go back to the good old cops and robbers bit —Peter Wilson with his leather waistcoat and 'Heigh Ho Silver!' and all that jazz."

"Exactly," said Gunn. "Followed by how Lucky Delafield got his."

"I can't help a sneaking affection for that poor sod," said Bryan with a smile. "He's so bloody hopeless it nearly makes you weep!"

"Well you buckle those tears back in your eyes, old son," said Stratton. "Because this is the point when you're going to need full 20/20 vision. You'll be on next after Wilson, and Willow's conviction may depend on the two slips he made in your interrogation."

"With Haines to back me, I know. But I'm the bull's-eye in Willow's target—I haven't forgotten."

"You don't need any tips, George," said Gunn. "You've handled this before. I'm more concerned about how young Haines will do."

"He'll be OK," said Bryan. "He's not

had all that much experience of the witness-box, of course, especially here at the Bailey. But I'm sure he'll keep his head."

"He won't get an easy ride, though," said Evan. "He has my sympathy."

"Mine too, but we've all got to go through it some time in this job," observed Gunn. "And if he starts falling abroad, much better that he gets his baptism of fire when his primary duty is simply to corroborate a very experienced senior."

"Anyway Haines will bring up the rear of our procession, I guess," said Stratton.

"And after the Lord Mayor's Show—," said Evan.

"I estimate our case will take until Friday tea-time," went on Stratton. "We certainly will if Oliver can work it. That will leave the defence to start nice and fresh on Monday next, the jury having had two full days to think over our case and let it all sink in. I confess to the ungallant hope that they'll be rotten days for Miss Drew."

"Now there's an odd thing," said Bryan. "It strikes me—I've had to be out in the hall for the whole of Rickler's opening, of course."

"Not only that," said Evan. "This is the last time we shall even be able to talk to you until you're out of the box, as you know."

"Yes of course. But it's occurred to me—I haven't seen a sign of the Drew girl all morning."

"Interesting," said Evan. "She hasn't graced the inside of the court with her busty little presence at all, so far. It's not compulsory, of course, though it's a mite unusual. Anyone else see her?"

"I haven't," said Stratton. "I know that when they came into court—the bar, I mean—after the session with the judge, Everett Crane was missing for several minutes, although all the others had been around, in and out of the court, as you'd expect. Probably the two of them were conferring together somewhere. The Bailey's got enough quiet corners for anyone who knows it well to disappear to for a while. And Crane duly turned up in court before the formalities began."

"No. I don't suppose it's important,"

said Bryan. "It just occurred to me in passing that I hadn't sighted her."

"Maybe that's why Evan's toe is playing up," smiled Gunn. "It had noticed the absence of our voluptuous villainess! First time I've come across an over-sexed toe, personally, but I suppose that, with Evan, all things are possible!"

"I like that!" said Evan in mock outrage.

"We all do," grinned George Bryan. "Only we don't all have a toe that twitches when there are prospects of it as yours apparently does!"

"Just for that you can get your own bloody second pint," laughed Evan as he picked up the tankards and moved towards the bar.

21

FOR Oliver Rickler the case had been, ever since the pre-trial conference, one of special interest, over and above its merits. His early curiosity about Everett Crane had been fed by most of the senior men to whom he had talked before the hearing. It seemed to be the universal view that Crane had been quite outstanding, and he was eager to see what a past master would do when picking up professional reins after years of absence. To some extent, of course, it would be like riding a bicycle—they say that one never forgets balance and co-ordination. He expected to see Crane employing little tricks here and there, especially at first, not least as a reminder of how they used to operate. Besides Crane would have a day and a half "assimilation period" before his first real hurdle came up—the confrontation with George Bryan in the box.

Stratton's forecast of the timing had turned out to be reasonably accurate. The early part of the Crown's case had gone as expected, without sensation and with no unexpected development. Rickler had watched the old master interestedly as he settled down in the saddle.

Crane's appearance had been the first surprise. Rickler had expected a basic scruffiness—the symptom of the alcoholic. He had visualised someone rather in the "Rumpole" line, and was unready for the neatness that was the dominating factor in Crane's appearance. He was of medium height and had kept his figure remarkably well. The limp was distinctive, but no more. The face was lined but the complexion was not blotchy—this was no ordinary boozer. Most striking of all was the voice. It had clearly been one of the old advocate's principal gifts and it was still rich, deep, clear and almost musical. Silent, Crane was quite ordinary. But when he began to speak, he acquired a kind of power, with which he could begin to weave magic. The voice, to Rickler's surprise, had lost no quality, as far as he could judge. He began to wonder whether the stories of an eight year binge had not been grossly exaggerated. Perhaps Crane had lost his nerve, more than his ability to remain sober.

In his younger days, Rickler had sat for hours in the back row, watching and listening to men who were artists at their work. But for a long time now there had been few real masters at the criminal bar. The cream of the old crop had naturally been elevated to the bench, but today's abundance of legal aid meant that counsel were appearing in court before they were hardly out of their pupillage. Some were good, but the potential master was something Oliver had not seen for ages. Appearing not only in the same case but in active contest with such a one as Crane was for him exceptional, providing a stimulation he had not known for too long —one he had forgotten how much he needed.

Out of court, Crane had kept pointedly to himself, exchanging no more than a formal nod in the robing room and disappearing as soon as the court rose, presumably into conference. Professional courtesy had precluded any of the other counsel concerned from trying to start a conversation. There was a tacit acknowledgement that this must be a trying experience for Crane, though the man himself showed no sign that he was aware of the gesture, much less that he needed it.

In court, throughout the early part of the trial Crane had sat alone behind all the others, in the third row. Rickler wondered whether this was a deliberate "up-staging" of them all, for it placed him not only on a higher level, physically, but if any of the other counsel wished even to see, much less to speak to, him, they had to turn round. It was a neat move, combining modesty with technical advantage. Rickler had smiled within himself and made a mental note.

Little of the early evidence had concerned Willow, and that which did was not damaging to him. The bitter, zealous Pelham had been the only one scheduled to do him any damage and, as Rickler had expected, Pelham had "failed to come up to proof". He had firmly refused to respond to any suggestion criticising Willow. So Crane had had little at all to do before George Bryan was called to the box.

But as soon as George took the oath, Crane was almost like an old war-horse sniffing cordite. Suddenly the back row was no longer the place of advantage. Rickler himself always occupied what was lightly referred to as "pole position"—the end of the front row nearest the bench—with Tom Alexander on his left. Beyond Tom there was room for two more advocates, though so far only Peter Dennis, for Williams, had sat there. But when the court reassembled on the day which would be climaxed by Bryan's evidence, Crane had taken the outside end of the front row on Dennis's left and immediately behind the bowed blonde head of Miss Drew, who sat at the outer end of the solicitors' table in the well of the court, sitting with her face to the jury and the witness-box, her back to counsel.

For a while, Rickler's inclination to watch Crane for his own instruction had kept him glancing to his left. But after a while, the presentation of the case as a whole had demanded all his conscious attention and the row might have been quite empty for all he knew or cared.

Bryan had been extremely strong.

Rickler had let him have his head almost completely, interjecting only the occasional question and standing silent for the most part as the Chief Inspector, with his long court experience, quietly recited the facts, referring only occasionally to his notebook. He had deliberately laid no emphasis on Willow, knowing that this would be the focus of Crane's questioning. He detailed the two vital slips—the revelation that Willow knew Burney as the getaway driver and the discovery of Williams' phone number in Willow's diary.

Bryan's evidence-in-chief finished at last, Rickler sat down and took his pencil to supplement for his own reference the detailed note that it was Tom's job to take. Dennis rose to have first crack, followed in turn by Smith, for Burney, and then Derek Morgan, the Welshman chosen by Nick Elkins to represent Delafield. Next would come the tall Scot Alec Glossop for Rogers the lorry driver and only when he had done would Crane's moment to rise be reached. So ran Rickler's mind—at which point he realised that Crane was not there.

He looked round to see if for some reason Crane had reverted to his former position above and behind. No—he had vanished. It was odd rather than serious. He would be unlikely to be reached for twenty minutes or so and he might well have wanted to slip off for a simple and obvious reason—everyone knows how tension can affect the bladder. Still, an instinctive concern remained in Rickler's mind as Smith ended his questioning, to be replaced by Morgan. In front, Miss Drew turned to say something to her counsel, realising only at that moment that he was absent.

Morgan finished and Glossop uncoiled himself for Rogers. Miss Drew was now glancing repeatedly over her shoulder and frowning. Rickler whispered to Alexander and took over the detailed noting as Tom slipped out of the pew and tiptoed away past the side of the dock. For a moment, as Glossop continued and there was no sign of movement on his left, time seemed to hover. Then Tom came creeping cautiously back. He slid into his place and whispered, "He's coming now."

Rickler turned directly to his left. Crane was limping past the end of the dock, as immaculate as before, his wig straight and with nothing about his appearance to give warning of trouble. Then as he stepped into the pew his foot seemed to catch and he pitched suddenly forward, throwing out a hand to prevent himself falling. Straightening at once, he made a quick, apologetic bow to the bench and another to Glossop for causing a distraction. Rickler remembered that he had tripped more than once over that very step, himself. It did not indicate alcoholic intake. And once in his place, Crane showed no sign at all of having boosted his courage. His papers had not even fallen from his arm, and he now laid them out neatly before him. Rickler felt reassured. Crane sat silent and motionless, gazing at the back of Miss Drew's blonde head.

Glossop thanked George Bryan and sat down. Crane's moment had come. He rose to his feet slowly, as if in deep thought. For a long moment he stared straight at the policeman in the box—a tactic often used by the experienced to meet the witness's eye, exert the personality and make some preliminary assessment of strength or weakness. When he spoke, it was without slur or hesitancy—the voice had all its vibrant quality. But the manner had changed from smooth ease to harsh aggression.

"Bryan—"

"Mr. Crane," came softly but clearly and immediately from the bench. Crane choked the next words back in his throat. For a moment there was anger in his glance up and sideways, but no more than that of anyone interrupted before getting out his first question.

"My Lord?"

"I am sorry to have to interrupt you at the first moment of your cross-examination, but one should start, I am sure you will agree, as one means to go on. The witness is not 'Bryan'. He is a Detective Chief Inspector, a rank that carries its own weight and the implication of a long police experience, to which he is entitled. I am sure the jury appreciate your position and your duty as an advocate. I am equally sure you would not wish them to remember you for your discourtesy, particularly for what was, I am sure, a mere slip of the tongue. Do continue."

Crane bowed with professional respect but let the gesture speak for itself, as if not trusting himself to speak. It was a difficult moment, and untypical. "Jimmy D", as Sir James Dover had been affectionately known throughout his career at the criminal bar, had been Treasury Counsel at the Old Bailey for some years before his elevation. He had always combined scrupulous courtesy with a strict obedience to the proprieties.

Crane had turned back to face Bryan, now. Rickler saw his throat move as he swallowed before he spoke—aggression still piercing the smoothness of his rich voice.

"Detective Chief Inspector Bryan—just how long an experience with this security force of yours does that rank imply?"

"I have served with the Port of London Authority Police for twenty three years, sir."

"I see. Probably done your time at the Gate for most of that?"

"In my earlier years, sir, certainly. There is much to be learned in our Force, sir—one might say especially at dock gates."

"How long have you held the rank you now enjoy?"

"Three years, sir. Before that I was a Detective Inspector for five and a Detective Sergeant for six. I had been a Detective Constable for several years before that again—I can work it out if you wish."

"Oh please do not trouble, Mr. Bryan. I will accept that you have had considerable experience, in years at least. Most organisations like yours do not boast the establishment of a CID, as you will know."

"No sir. That may be because we are a very ancient part of the police service and not a 'security force' as you seem to regard us."

"But you have no powers beyond the dock limits, have you?"

"We have, sir. With respect, our geographical jurisdiction extends for one mile beyond all the Authority's docks and works and anywhere in the country if we are in pursuit of a criminal."

"But you do not function as police beyond the docks, do you?"

"Only when circumstances demand, sir."

"And you have plainly no power to charge. These defendants all had to be taken by you to the Metropolitan Police Station at Newham to be charged, did they not?"

"All we lack, sir, is the provision of adequate cells for detention in the docks. So we have an arrangement of long standing with our colleagues in the Metropolitan Police at Newham."

"You regard them as colleagues, do you?"

"Mr. Crane," said the judge, "I regret having to interrupt you again. But while I have no objection to your receiving a most courteous education from the Chief Inspector on the subject of the PLA Police, I do not wish the jury to be under any misapprehension about that Force. It is a little known but greatly respected part of the British police service. Perhaps you will accept from me that their original foundation goes back to 1802, some 27 years before the Metropolitan Police. They are one of the oldest preventive police forces in the world. Within the docks they are the sole law enforcement agency. Their officers, whom I see quite often as witnesses, are all initially attested before magistrates, which as you well know is the sole hallmark of a constable in law. I really cannot have them reduced to the level of a private security force simply because you have not yet had occasion to become aware of those facts. I am sure you will treat Mr. Bryan and all his colleagues with the respect to which they are all fully entitled."

All quite unlike Jimmy D, thought Rickler. It was almost as if the judge was not quite within the iron control that every judge must impose upon his personal feelings at all times. Or could it be that he was putting Everett Crane calculatedly to some test? Crane's reaction was immediate and professional—the low bow and the use of the expression that can be said clearly to mean, "All right—it's your court and I can't hit back yet!"

"As your Lordship pleases."

And now, as if soothed by the silky quality of his own voice which had returned in full measure, Crane began to test George Bryan on every detail of his interrogation of Willow. Eventually he approached the moment when the knowledge of Burney's function had come up.

"Mr. Bryan, you will understand that

Mr. Willow's recollection of this part of the interrogation differs from your own?"

"Naturally, sir."

"He tells me—and will later swear—that when you mentioned Burney for the first time, in the course of running through all the defendants' names, you referred to 'Burney the wheels man'."

"He is quite wrong, sir. I deliberately refrained from saying that, in the faint hope that Mr. Willow might make the very slip that he did, a few moments later, when I pretended not to be able to recall the name of the getaway driver."

"Oh?" The loudness of the question and Crane's pause that followed it drew everyone's attention at once to the moment. "So you admit that you practised on Mr. Willow a deliberate deception, Mr. Bryan?"

"Certainly, sir. It is a move recognised —indeed, inherent—in all interrogation procedure, sir. It is quite unlike what I might call a wilful and improper deception, such as deliberately mis-stating known facts to a witness. There was nothing at all improper in what I said to him."

242

"That, Mr. Bryan, is a matter of opinion."

"Quite, sir. The opinion of the members of the jury."

Stratton, watching George Bryan intensely from below, spotted the constriction of the throat as he swallowed—the scarcely noticeable pressure of upper teeth against lower lip. It had been less smooth than George had made it look. It had shown him the acuity of the old master—the danger even to an honest witness. The suggestion that Bryan had been a deceiver was neither inspiration nor luck—it was a shot, planned, aimed and fired with the precision of the natural advocate. It also showed Crane to have been quite unaffected by the earlier judicial reprimand.

Crane now turned to the issue of the diary. He suggested that the first time it was seen or mentioned was when it was listed with Willow's pocket contents at East Ham. Bryan was quietly adamant that it had been discussed and looked through at the interrogation.

"So you insist, Mr. Bryan, that the diary was not only there but that Mr. Willow produced it before you went downstairs for the formalities and later to East Ham for him to be formally charged?"

"Exactly, sir. I do so insist."

"Very well. Then let us suppose that he produced the diary. Will you not agree that there was ample opportunity for you to add to its contents to the extent of the name 'Harry' and the phone number?"

"There was ample time, sir, and, had I wished to do anything so wickedly criminal, right under your client's nose moreover, there was what you might call opportunity. But the suggestion is totally wrong."

"I put it to you, however, that that is exactly what you did."

"I deny it categorically."

The judge looked up from his book.

"Mr. Crane—forgive me—I may have misunderstood. You have just put to the witness two courses of action."

"That is so, my Lord."

"But are those two courses not mutually exclusive?"

"My Lord?"

"You put it in terms that your client never produced a diary at all—that the diary itself was 'planted', if I may use the word, complete with every entry we see in it today—that it was secretly added to the list of pocket-contents which Mr. Willow had signed."

"That is so, my Lord."

"And you have now put to the same witness that Mr. Willow *did* produce a diary during the interrogation—this, his own diary—but that in it the witness falsely inserted this single incriminating entry."

"Your Lordship is quite right. I put the first suggestion to the witness. He denied it. I then put to him an alternative proposition based, this time, upon the witness's own denial."

"Mr. Crane—we do not seem to be quite 'ad idem'. You know the old basic rule of cross-examination which runs 'You must not prove what you have not put and you must not put what you cannot prove.' In the context of this situation you know exactly what Mr. Willow will say on oath in the box in due course, and therefore you know which of those two allegations he makes against Mr. Bryan. That one you are thus able later to prove—the term here meaning 'adduce in evidence', of course—so it follows that you have just put to Mr. Bryan an allegation—the other one—which you know that you will later be unable to prove."

"My Lord?"

"Are you then not necessarily breaking that rule, Mr. Crane?"

"My Lord, I am surely entitled as defence counsel to every latitude to examine every possibility which may lie behind what I am instructed is false evidence?"

"Such latitude, Mr. Crane, can never be extended to flagrant breaches of established rules."

"If your Lordship pleases."

"But I do *not* please, Mr. Crane. And I must insist that you now withdraw one allegation or the other. As to which, only you know which is in your client's proof of evidence. Will you now please tell the court which proposition you propose to withdraw—the first or the second?"

Crane's answer sounded as calm and formal as if this sort of thing was an everyday occurrence and without any great significance.

"The first, my Lord."

"I am obliged, Mr. Crane. Now let it be plainly noted. You no longer suggest that Mr. Willow never had a diary. You are saying that he will in due course swear that he did produce a diary but that it did not contain the entry in question. You have put that to Mr. Bryan. He has categorically denied it. Is that clear and correct, Mr. Crane?"

"My Lord, it is."

"Then may we now proceed?"

Oliver Rickler was staggered. The judge was technically correct but such cross-examinations took place every day by defence counsel and were always ignored —never picked up by the judge. It was commonly treated as a defence latitude. It was totally unlike Jimmy Dover of all people to call Crane to a halt and haul him publicly over the coals like this. As for Crane—he was conducting his case with a certain panache but in a way that showed a quite amazing lack of professional discretion. His mind was alert—his speech unslurred—could he have taken some stimulant? And now he was going off on to a course quite as perilous as that on which he had just been judicially wrecked.

"These suggestions are not new to you, Mr. Bryan?"

"I don't understand you, sir. Are you suggesting that I have forged evidence in other cases?"

"Oh no, not at all. I meant only that today is not the first time that you have heard these suggestions."

George was out of his depth. After a pause for furious thought, he raised his shoulders and slowly shook his head. The judge looked at him with a smile.

"What is the cause of your obvious concern, Mr. Bryan?"

"My Lord—my answer will involve matters which, with the greatest respect, must raise questions of admissibility."

"Oh, well I can relieve you there. You go ahead and answer all the questions you are asked. If Mr. Rickler or I see anything wrong in the question, we shall intervene before you answer."

"Thank you, my Lord. The answer to Mr. Crane's question is 'Yes.' I have had occasion to discuss these matters before today."

Crane nodded gravely. "You know a Mr. Dickenson of South Woodford, I think?"

"Slightly, sir, yes."

"Well enough, I think, to discuss with him the merits of this case in the knowledge that he had already been professionally instructed for the defence?"

"He telephoned me, sir. He reminded me where we had met before. When he was in the police. Then he told me something about this case."

"To which you were only too eager to listen?"

"There was nothing eager about it, sir. I listened."

"And what did Dickenson tell you?"

Oliver Rickler was on his feet so quickly that he seemed almost to have been standing before the question was asked.

"My Lord, the answer to that question . . ."

"Must be inadmissible? I take your point, Mr. Rickler. But it is surely so only if Mr. Crane does not later call Mr. Dickenson."

"Naturally, my Lord. However, I am aware that since the conversation about which my learned friend was asking, the defence have withdrawn instructions from Mr. Dickenson."

Crane, who had sat down the moment Rickler had risen, now rose with a smile as bland as if this was the point he had trapped Rickler into making.

"My Lord, it is true that Mr. Dickenson and the defence have, so to speak, parted company. But that does not prevent my calling him. And though he is not here at this moment, he will soon be so. I have issued a subpoena with which he has been served, compelling his attendance. He pleaded essential business this morning and I directed that he should attend from this afternoon."

"I note what my learned friend says," said Rickler. "However, the presence of Mr. Dickenson in the building is hardly sufficient to make the question admissible. Only an undertaking in open court would do that."

He looked at Crane as he spoke and was conscious of a regard that combined amusement with professional respect. A movement below him made him aware that Miss Drew had turned anxiously as if to ask Crane what he intended to do. Crane either did not see it or ignored it.

"My Lord, I give such undertaking," he smiled.

"I accept it at once, of course, my Lord," said Rickler. "My learned friend is free to ask his question as far as I am concerned."

The judge nodded, made a note in his book, and turned to the box. "Mr. Bryan, you were asked what Mr. Dickenson told you when he phoned."

"My Lord, he told me that he had been requested by Mr. Willow's solicitors to carry out certain investigations in this case. He said that he was troubled because the suggestions made to him were—if I may use your Lordship's words—'mutually exclusive'. Then he asked me exactly what had occurred during Mr. Willow's interrogation."

"But you told him more than he asked, didn't you Mr. Bryan? You urged him to write to my instructing solicitor declining the instructions, didn't you?"

"Not in so many words, sir, although this is what I know he did do. It was rather what Mr. Dickenson told me he was going to do."

"As a result of your advising him?"

"No, sir. Following what I told him, he made his own decision and then asked me if I agreed with him. I replied that I did. With great respect, sir, I still do."

"Yes—well, we won't go into the merits of the decision until we hear from Mr. Dickenson in the box. I want now to turn to a completely fresh aspect of the case." He paused and looked up to the bench. "Unless, of course, your Lordship was proposing in any event to adjourn at this point? It would be a convenient moment, if so."

Mr. Justice Dover looked at the clock high on the wall below the public gallery on his left. It was eight minutes to one.

"Thank you, Mr. Crane—yes, if you are proposing to turn to a fresh aspect of the case, it would perhaps be suitable if we did not interrupt you in the middle of that. The court is adjourned until a quarter past two."

He closed his large judicial ledger as he spoke, and rose. He bowed to the jury on his right, to counsel on his left and a third time more briefly to the centre. Then he turned to his left and strode to the door of his room at the far end of the bench, which an usher had already opened for him to pass through.

It closed behind him.

22

FIVE minutes later, Rickler, Alexander, Stratton, Baunton and Gunn filed into a small room occasionally available to senior counsel at the top of two flights of back stairs. George Bryan being still in the course of his evidence, he was untouchable in any event, and when he came out of the box he would be as confined within the court for the rest of the Crown's case as he had been excluded from it before being called.

Oliver took off his wig, lobbed it gently on the table and lit a cigarette. Hungrily he took the first long pull on it, inhaled deeply and exhaled with a sigh of satisfaction.

"Better than we'd hoped," said Stratton tentatively.

"A little too well, perhaps," said Rickler.

"Well, we shall be cross-examining our own witness in Dickenson," said Tom

Alexander,—"and that doesn't often happen."

Rickler lifted an eyebrow. "There was a poem in Latin which I had to learn and translate at school which began with a line like 'Timeo Danaos cum dona ferentes', which meant, as I recall, 'I am wary of the Greeks when they bring gifts'."

"A reference to the Trojan Horse," said Stratton.

"Yes. I rate it higher as a principle than the old adage about not looking a gift horse in the mouth. In the context of a criminal trial the Latin tag is the more reliable, particularly when the horse is presented by someone of the calibre and experience of Everett Crane. What do you think, Tom?"

"I'm probably wrong, Oliver, but I felt it was simply that Crane has lost his touch. Out of practice in both senses. I think he failed to see the case in perspective. He needed to ask George Bryan about Dickenson—he found he couldn't do that without giving the undertaking—so he gave it—just like that!"

"I'm not so sure," said Evan, thoughtfully. "Granted it looks just like that, but

I wonder if perhaps it wasn't meant to. You see, Crane had already decided to subpoena Dickenson, so he must have anticipated your challenge and he had his answer ready. Sorry to disagree, Tom, but I've a feeling that Crane is playing it this way intentionally—that he's made a few deliberate slips to make us think he's a has-been, and that this is only another one—whereas in truth it's deliberate. He may have decided as a matter of cool tactics that it's more important to go for George Bryan now than to let you cross-examine Dickenson later. And I can't see why."

It was David Gunn who broke the silence that followed Evan's remark. "Look—I'm the only layman in a bunch of lawyers, and tear me to bits if I'm wrong—but from a copper's point of view, I think Evan's partly right but not entirely. I've got a feeling that this whole Dickenson business is a carefully planned diversion, and Willow's defence, when it comes, is going to centre on a different point altogether."

"David," said Stratton "—you are a crafty old bastard!"

"A crafty old bastard who just may be

bang on target here," smiled Rickler. "I am most grateful to you all for the ideas. I think we'll play it by ear for the moment, and I intend to remember what you said, Mr. Gunn."

"Thanks, but my idea was only a follow-up to Evan's."

"The putt that falls short will never win the hole," said Evan modestly. "No—what I can't understand is what the hell Crane's doing getting Jimmy D's back up like that. I know there are judges who are so bloody-minded that counsel can win the sympathy of the jury just by refusing to be bullied by the bench. But Dover's a gentleman and that's not on. That's where I thought Crane had lost his touch."

"I'm not sure, Evan," said Stratton. "Oliver—haven't you met lots of cases where defence counsel has simply thrashed about, putting everybody's backs up, *and* lost the case in the process, only to have the convicted defendant praise him to the skies as someone who gave him his full money's worth?"

"Oh yes—there are a few old advocates who do that often and never lack clients. The defendant seems to think it's a question of loyalties. The thrasher is loyal to him personally, whatever the consequences, whereas they regard the quiet, skilful defender as loyal to the ethics of his profession first and to his client second. It's interesting, Charles, because I really don't think Crane was thrashing about, this morning. There was a tangible aggression about him, as if it was involuntary. Tom—you were right alongside him."

"I know what you're thinking but no—not a trace of a smell on his breath."

"Vodka?" suggested Evan.

"No," said Rickler. "I don't think it was drink, for all the stories. It could have been one of the amphetamines. But I think it was deeper. This was the first direct confrontation that Crane has had in court for eight years. I think it may have been like the burning-off of a rust of antagonism that's been there ever since his wife killed herself. It was a kind of compulsive hatred of the police."

"Oh surely not, Oliver," said Stratton. "I mean—if the copper was from the same lot, I could see it. But Crane's never come up against our Force in his life. Whatever the reason behind his aggression, I can't think it was that."

"Well," said Evan, as cheerful as ever—"I must say I don't find myself very impressed by the famous Crane, whatever his motives. And if I was a criminal, innocent or guilty, I wouldn't touch him with a ten foot pole—not if my liberty was at stake. I think the real blob is old Drew selecting him as counsel. I mean—good or bad, it was one hell of a risk, surely, from her angle!"

"Anyway, our case is going exceedingly well, so far," said Rickler. "And in a six-handed job like this, one can normally expect *something* to go seriously cock-eyed through nobody's fault. Even a case of yours, Charles! But here not only has nothing gone wrong—we've landed a bonus or two. Takes the edge off my enjoyment, that does."

Stratton winked at Baunton. "Some people are never happy unless they've got something to be unhappy about!"

"I know the type," grinned Evan. "If there's nothing to worry about, they worry because they're not worried!"

"Well, if that's your kind of worry, Mr.

Rickler—just you go on suffering from it," said David Gunn. "Me—I'm just a superstitious old copper and I shall continue to keep all my fingers and toes crossed, if nobody minds!"

23

IT was as if someone had read Everett Crane a kind of individual Riot Act during the adjournment. When the case resumed after lunch, he was like a different person. Polite, respectful, smooth, confident—he went out of his way to erase the impression that his earlier cross-examination had left behind. And, so elegant was his style, so great his command of the art of advocacy, that it took only a short time to achieve the effect he wanted, on everyone from the judge down to the court usher. None watched it more appreciatively but more warily than Oliver Rickler.

Once the case was well under way again, with George Bryan riding all the blows thrown at him with relative ease, Evan Baunton slipped quietly out of his chair at the solicitors' table in the well of the court and, with a light bow to the bench, moved softly round the side of the dock to the swing doors on the far side which gave first to the little dark lobby and then to the main hall. Quietly he moved out into the marble expanse of this, and his keen eye spotted at once the tall, slim figure sitting on the central bench. He was about to slide back into court when there was a soft but warm voice from behind him.

"Evan! How's things, you old scamp?"

He turned to see the tall figure of Michael Black who, until a year before, had been a detective sergeant in the London Dock division and who had recently joined the staff of Harry Wager, the bearded, ebullient Keeper of the Central Criminal Court.

"Mike! Great to see you! You look as if your new life suits you! It's years since you've looked so well."

"I'm fine. I hoped I might see one of you—I noticed from the lists that the old mob was in Court One. Six-hander, eh?"

"Aye. The Berry gang, no less. The complication is really only in one corner. Foreman of ours who was one of their inside men. Bit of discretion called for. Look—see that tall young fellow at the far end of the seat there? He's an ex-Met man. Name of Dickenson. A lot is going to centre on him. I can't talk to him myself, because he's being called by the other side, technically. But if you're passing this way, I'd appreciate it if you and your pals will keep a fatherly eye on him. I don't want him to get decoyed away or generally lost. Early part of next week will be the key time. Don't talk to him—or if you do, don't mention you're an ex-PLA copper. He's a private eye now, by the way."

"Message received and understood. I'll have a word with one or two of the lads and an eye will be kept on Dickenson until he's actually called."

"Great—thanks! I'll pop back now. Just slipped out to see if he'd arrived. Nice to see you, Mike. One of these days when we're not both too rushed, we'll have a jar together, eh?"

They exchanged farewells and Evan tiptoed back into the lobby. He took a notepad from his pocket and wrote neatly on it. Then he had a brief whispered word with the B Division City policeman inside, and crept back the way he had come. Regaining his seat, he passed the note he had written to Stratton, who glanced at it and indicated for him to hand it up over his shoulder to Tom Alexander.

Tom saw the hand and took the note. He read: "DICKENSON THERE—SITTING ALONE IN MAIN HALL" He nodded and put it where Rickler could see it.

"Mr. Haines—you and Mr. Bryan have no doubt discussed the details of this series of investigations and arrests on many occasions before today, haven't you?"

"On a number of occasions, sir—yes."

"And no doubt your note-books were made up in collaboration soon after each defendant had been questioned?"

"Yes, sir. The procedure is perfectly permissible."

"I am aware of that, Mr. Haines. I was not criticising it, nor you. I meant only that it was probably you who did most of the writing while the defendants were questioned, leaving Mr. Bryan as the senior officer free to ask the questions, probably glancing at you occasionally to make sure he wasn't going too fast for you—probably pausing every now and then for you to catch up."

The voice was soft, conveying appreciation, understanding, even familiarity. Crane had obviously been present at interrogations. The effect was calming, reassuring, unmenacing.

"That's right, sir."

"Indeed, that is what was happening during the whole time that Mr. Willow was being questioned?"

"Yes, sir."

"*Every* moment, Mr. Haines? Think again—carefully."

"As far as I can recall, sir." He glanced quickly over his notebook. "Yes, sir."

Crane smiled disarmingly. "And isn't it the custom in your excellent Force, Mr. Haines, to offer men in custody for some time so much as a cup of tea?"

"Oh—you're right, sir. I remember now. Yes, we did ask Mr. Willow if he would like some tea."

"Thank you, Mr. Haines. And up to that moment, there had been the three of you in that office and no other—Mr. Bryan, Mr. Willow and you?"

"That is so, sir."

"And Mr. Willow said he'd like a cup of tea, I think."

"I didn't make a note of it, sir, but now you remind me, yes I believe he did."

Stratton heard George Bryan on his left at the table breathe softly, "No he bloody well didn't!" He looked round with raised eyebrows. Bryan had closed his eyes as if in pain, waiting for the next question and answer.

"And so, Mr. Haines—it being your part in the routine—you probably went and got the tea for the three of you."

"That's right, sir."

"Jesus!" breathed Bryan. "That was during the session with Teddy Lane! Willow said he wouldn't touch our beastly tea—he suggested we'd probably poison it first!"

"And of course, Mr. Haines," went on Crane's mellifluous voice—"getting that tea took you down one floor to the canteen, I imagine—and back up when you'd been served?"

"Yes, sir."

"Taking what—five or ten minutes, perhaps?"

"About that, yes, sir."

"During which time, Mr. Bryan and

Mr. Willow were alone together upstairs, as far as you can say that is?"

"As far as I can say, sir."

"They were certainly alone together when you returned with the tea?"

"They were, sir—yes."

Stratton reached for paper and scribbled: "IT WAS LANE WHO HAD TEA, NOT WILLOW, WHO REFUSED IT. HAINES NOT ABSENT DURING WILLOW SESSION" He folded it in half and held it over his shoulder without looking round. Out of the corner of his left eye, he saw Alexander's hand. The note was taken. Stratton felt, rather than heard, Tom nudge Rickler. He was concentrating so much on what was going on behind him that he missed Crane's next questions to young Haines. Doubtless the breach so skilfully made in the Crown's wall was being gently, tactfully, widened. Then he heard a long, quiet sigh of intense relief escape Rickler's lips. Stratton lowered his head and smiled. Rickler was happy at last. Something had finally gone wrong. No longer was he waiting for the moment —dreading it—magnifying it in his mind. It was out, now. And damaging, but hardly fatal. And re-examination was still to come. Contentedly, Stratton reflected, knowing his friend and colleague very closely from a forensic point of view, that Oliver would betray nothing in his voice as he rose in due course—"just to clear up a little point or two"—and ask Haines something like "Mr. Haines—about this little expedition to fetch the tea—at what stage in the interview with Mr. Willow did this take place? At the beginning? Or perhaps at the end, after the diary had been produced? Or somewhere between? Think carefully, will you?" It would be enough to make Haines realise suddenly the mistake he had made. A nasty moment for him. No doubt in years to come he would warn many a novice against the situation and cite this as an example. To Oliver Rickler, it would be a mere passing forensic challenge. Charles Stratton smiled quietly to himself.

24

MONDAY had dawned bright and clear—usual in what had now become a memorable summer. About Oliver Rickler in particular there was a marked air of confidence, which appeared at the precise moment on the previous Friday afternoon when the unfortunate Colin Haines had made his error. Rickler had been little short of jubilant during the brief chat in the lobby at the end of the day's hearing. When Stratton arrived at court on Monday morning, half an hour early as usual, he was amazed to find his leader already robed and gowned and in his seat, working on his notes and full of breezy comments about how well it was all going.

The Crown's case was now virtually finished, and only a formal witness or two remained to be called. Rickler spent Monday morning rounding off his case with the forensic elegance which was his *forte*. The court adjourned for lunch, after which the defendants at last began their procession through the witness box to give their stories and to submit themselves to cross-examination—unless any of them decided to make an unsworn statement from the dock, which was a course in which few indulged. The law forbade any comment on the tactic, however pertinent, from the prosecution, but the move seldom indicated anything except an admission that its maker would not face questioning. There were occasionally circumstances which could render the move justified, but hardly in a case such as this.

Harry Williams, first of the six to be heard, could never be said to lack gall. He met his ordeal with the same full-frontal insouciance which had marked his conduct since the start of the trial. He knew very well that the guilty man in the witness box, unable to let the truth emerge, could not afford the lie direct, as the cross-examiner's joy is the lying witness, of whom a veritable banquet can be made. The professional criminal learns that the only thing to do is to create a version consistent with the provable facts and his own innocence, and then to convince himself that this is what actually happened. Once this had been achieved, he could take the oath and recount this "new truth" with a clear conscience. The method, if it is done efficiently, is by no means easy to dent and very difficult to crack wide open. It was the method by which Harry Williams, who was a very professional criminal, had several times escaped conviction. It helped that he had a face as inscrutable as a block of granite, over which he could glue the veneer of a polite, tolerant smile.

Oliver Rickler and Harry Williams had had more than one major confrontation across the well of a criminal court. Now there came out exactly the story that Rickler had calculated would emerge. Williams denied being anywhere near Prince Regent Lane on the day of the crime. He pointed out that green Jaguar cars, if not all that common, were surely not all that rare, and mistakes in reading number-plates could be made easily and honestly. He challenged the accuracy of the police but not their integrity. He had not, he said, advanced an alibi for the period in question because he had spent the morning alone at home and could not call any witness to support it. As to the drama of the early afternoon, all he could say was that by coincidence he was out for a drive in his car, being driven by his friend Mr. Burney out of kindness since he, Williams, had a serious back complaint —which was why he had to have a specially constructed low bucket-seat in the back on medical advice. They had happened purely by chance, he said, to be moving south along Silvertown Way when of a sudden they had become aware of being trailed by a nasty thug—a motorised mugger, he looked. Understandably, but in the event unwisely, he had told Burney to accelerate in order to escape this unwanted attention, which had given rise to the pursuit which PC Wilson had accurately described. Had he known—had he even dreamed—that the pursuing thug in thug's uniform was in fact a PLA policeman in fancy dress, he would have stopped at once before trying to escape at all. He gently reproached a CID for allowing its men to dress in such a way as to frighten honest citizens passing by upon their lawful occasions.

This note of gentle reproach was one in which Harry Williams was very experienced. Rickler, who was familiar with it, countered with smiling courtesy, conveying to the jury that this encounter was a regular formal comedy which they might choose to admire but to the contents of which they should pay little serious attention. In the end, honours came out fairly even, as usual. But Rickler was confident that this battle was one which Williams was going to lose. The evidence of the police about the morning "meet" when the forged papers were handed over to Rogers had been quite unshaken and would be remembered.

When Rickler had finished, there was little cross-examination on behalf of Williams' co-defendants. James Smith, for Burney, and Derek Morgan for Delafield had each asked Williams if he had seen or heard any sign of their client that morning near Gresham Road. Each had received the assurance they sought. Harry Williams, as calm and unruffled as when he started, returned to his corner of the dock, calling no witnesses. Peter Dennis, his counsel, was replaced by James Smith, as Burney was escorted from dock to witness box. The young man with the high voice and nervous manner, whose wig seemed too large for him and was always slipping towards his nose, being repeatedly and distractingly pushed back again, led a nervous and quiet Burney through a tale supporting that of Williams. It revealed what an artist Burney was not. Asked about the "meet" at noon, Burney claimed to have been drinking in a pub where he had seen no-one he knew and could therefore call no-one to give him an alibi. He had picked up Harry Williams at 1.45, he said, and they had gone for the peaceful drive which had turned out so eventful.

Cross-examining him, Rickler was gentleness itself, encouraging Burney to describe the inside of the pub where he claimed to have been and slipping in occasional references to re-filling his glass, all so casually that when he finally asked, "Did you have one more for the road?" and Burney said no, he hadn't, Rickler was able to comment that it was as well: "You have just retailed a consumption that would have left your blood/alcohol about double the legal limit!" Maybe, he suggested, it was lucky for Burney that PC Wilson had produced a radio and not a breathalyser when he had finally caught up with the Jaguar. Burney did not answer. Over a long pause, which seemed to him even longer than it was, he stood licking his dry lips in silence. Rickler smiled broadly and finally resumed his seat, leaving the silence to comment on itself.

With Burney back in the dock, his ordeal over at last, it was the woebegone figure of Delafield that crossed the well of the court beside the warder and mounted the steps to the witness box, while Smith was replaced by Derek Morgan, the Welsh boy whose forensic delicacy contrasted with his florid Celtic appearance. Tom Alexander exchanged a smile with Rickler.

The hapless Delafield began by making a memorable hash of the oath, which finally brought a kindly smile from the bench. "No, don't worry, Mr. Delafield—lots of people find themselves a bit flustered by the wording. It's so often misquoted that it's easy to go wrong. Now, take a deep breath and start again quite calmly. Nobody's going to jump on you, you know!"

Somehow Lucky managed it at last, handed back the testament and the card to the usher, flashed a nervous smile of gratitude to the judge, swallowed hard and faced Morgan, who beamed encouragingly. Slowly he got his story out, sentence by sentence—the story that Harry Williams had given him a week ago and which he had committed so laboriously to memory. It didn't sound convincing even to him. The whole idea of his taking a walk with no particular motive in the middle of his normal lunchtime, and then just happening to stop and lean on the parapet of Silvertown Way to take a little rest—it wasn't impossible but it was so unreal! Then to have "noticed" a lorry approaching the gate from inside and yet to have taken no interest in it but to have turned to resume his stroll when he had become aware of a passing green car accelerating sharply, hotly pursued by a man on a motor-bike in jeans and a leather waistcoat—it was like a cheap novel, but doggedly on he went. Then a taxi which seemed to come from nowhere had stopped beside him and a man in a grey suit had jumped out of the back and had grabbed him saying, "All right, Lucky—you're nicked!"—it was all bewildering. He reflected that the last bit was true, anyway.

He swallowed once more as Morgan sat down and Rickler got up. Oliver's manner was deceptively gentle, sympathetic, as if to persuade him to forget the menace he had been ready to face.

"My! You *do* seem to have been dogged by misfortune, don't you, Mr. Delafield!"

"Er—yes."

"Not only in this case but in every way."

"How d'you mean?"

"Well that nickname of yours that you just said the stranger called you—'Lucky'. You're called that because you're accident-prone, aren't you?"

"I dunno. I am a bit, though."

"Yes, exactly. And whether it was typical or not, that docks business was a bit of a disaster all round, wasn't it!"

"Yes."

"I mean—there you were, right at the scene of a major crime, stranded by all your mates on a lonely pavement and arrested by a stranger who leaps out of a passing cab and shouts 'You're nicked!' And bless me, you were too, weren't you!"

"Yes."

"But it had already been one of those days, hadn't it?"

"I don't remember."

"No?"

"No. I was out for this walk."

"Honestly? Well, when did it start, Mr. Delafield?"

"I can't remember. Middle of the day, some time."

"All right—where were you about noon?"

"About noon?" He was completely stumped, now. The script they'd given him started with the walk. That must be well after noon. Where was he supposed to have been at noon? Harry hadn't said. His head swam. The voice quietly persisted:

"Yes—about noon. Where were you, Mr. Delafield?"

"Let me think, then."

"Of course, Mr. Delafield—don't let me rush you! Have a jolly good think. Take all the time you want, within reason. All we want to know is where you were that day about noon."

Lucky nodded, thinking furiously now. Where was he? Oh Christ! At noon he'd been sitting in Harry's Jag, waiting for Rogers to collect the forged notes—he mustn't tell them that! Anything but that! Where could he say he'd been before that silly walk business? Where might he have been if he hadn't been scooped into this daft caper? Betting shop, he supposed. Yeah—that was safe enough.

"Betting shop," he said.

"Ah—really?" said Rickler.

"Yes—really!" said Lucky.

"Which betting shop?"

The voice was still polite, but there was an edge behind it now, though not obviously. Which betting shop would he have been in? Sweet Jesus help me! What was the name of that big one up by the roundabout?

"By the big roundabout. Can't remember the name."

"Can't you? Pity—still—I expect we can find it. On the main road, that would be—to the east? Yes, I think there is one there. That's most helpful, Mr. Delafield. Now—*when* would this be?"

"Not sure. From noon till maybe 1.30?"

"Fine! That's near enough. Anyway, you couldn't have been a passenger in a green Jaguar in Gresham Road at noon, then?"

"No, sir. I couldn't. No."

"Mr. Rickler," interrupted the judge, "I don't want to stop you but perhaps, for the record—the Crown have not, I imagine, received any formal Notice of Alibi for this defendant?"

Rickler noticed that below him Evan was scribbling furiously and whispering to Stratton. He smiled up at the bench.

"My Lord—none that I know of—none before this morning, anyway. But if your Lordship would grant me just a moment —I apprehend that I am about to receive some relevant instructions."

"Certainly," said the judge, and turned to the witness box. "I'm sorry about this, Mr. Delafield. A small technical point has arisen. We'll be back to you in a minute. You relax!"

Bemused, Lucky returned the open smile and waited patiently, his mind in the blank that nature seemed to have prescribed for it. Meanwhile, Rickler and Alexander were reading the note that Stratton had passed them. It read: "GET MORE DETAILS. THEN WAIVE NOTICE ON TERMS THAT WE CALL REBUTTAL EVIDENCE LATER. WE THINK WE'VE GOT HIM!"

"My Lord—I think a few questions will enable me to help the court about the Notice."

"As you wish, Mr. Rickler."

"Mr. Delafield," beamed Oliver, apologetically, "I'm so sorry—you took us a little by surprise there with your mention of the betting shop. Let me just check. We know now roughly where it is and that you were there from about noon till about 1.30 p.m. Can you remember which horses you were concerned to back? Or which races? Even which meeting?"

Again Lucky thought furiously. "I can't remember the meetings, nor the horses. But the race would have been probably the 1 o'clock, then probably a 1.15 somewhere —maybe a 1.30. I could check—"

"Oh no, please don't bother—we can do all the checking and bring it up, later, don't worry about that. As long as you're sure that on the day you were arrested on the Viaduct you had been in the betting shop on the big roundabout from noon till 1.30, placing bets on horses running probably in the 1 o'clock, the 1.15 and the 1.30. Right?"

"Right."

"Er—they lost, I presume?"

"I expect so. Mine usually do."

"Ah. Something we have in common, Mr. Delafield," said Rickler, never having placed a bet on a horse in his life. "But I'm sure you realise that several witnesses have said you were in Gresham Road in the green Jaguar on that day and not in a betting shop at all. So I have to put it to you formally that you're quite wrong, whether deliberately or accidentally, and that you weren't betting on horses that day. Understand?"

"Yes. It's up to the jury, then."

"In the last resort—of course."

"Can I go now, then?"

"As far as I'm concerned, certainly—but only if Mr. Morgan has finished with you and if his Lordship doesn't want to ask you anything."

The judge, who had noticed Derek Morgan's silence and did not want to embarrass him, released the unhappy witness, who was escorted back to the dock, which felt to him like a sanctuary all of a sudden. Then Rickler rose again.

"My Lord, I am instructed that provided I may call rebuttal evidence in due course, the lack of any Notice of Alibi will be waived by the Crown. These things happen. I have nothing but sympathy for Mr. Delafield's advisers."

"My Lord," said Derek Morgan, rising—"I am much obliged. I shall of course not object to my friend's calling evidence later, and I am most grateful to him for his professional compassion."

He bowed, and sat. The judge looked at the clock on the wall. Then he smiled towards counsel.

"Gentlemen—although it is only ten minutes to four, I feel it might be more appropriate to the defence and also to the jury, if we start a fresh defendant on a fresh day. Therefore, unless there are any objections, I propose to adjourn now, until half past ten tomorrow, Tuesday, morning."

Everyone bowed assent. The judge rose and made his triple acknowledgment, then swept off. Everyone relaxed at once, and there was a buzz of conversation. The six defendants were wheeled away down the stairs from inside the dock to the cells below. Charles Stratton turned round to Oliver Rickler.

"I'm not sure exactly what it is that Evan is planning to spring on us in the shape of rebuttal, but I gather it could be fairly spectacular, eh?"

"You could say that," grinned the little man. "But I'd rather not say exactly what it is until I'm sure I've got it, if you don't mind."

"My dear Evan," said Rickler—"be as discreet as you like. Provided I know the surprise is going to be pleasant rather than unpleasant, I never mind being surprised. By the way, Charles—I've asked Tom to cross-examine Rogers. Gives the jury a fresh face to look at, you know."

"Fine. Fine. Enjoy it, Tom!"

"By the way, Charles—no sign of our lady solicitor today?"

"No, Oliver—neither here nor outside. I expect she's arranging to be here all day tomorrow. Willow's bound to be in the box by lunchtime, at latest."

"Bound to be. You know, I wish it was Miss Drew herself who was going to be in the box. Not that I mind cross-examining Dickenson, who is virtually our own witness. But I enjoy a real contest more!"

"So I've noticed!" laughed Stratton. "Still, we solicitors as a breed are a fairly canny lot. We rarely leave the well of the court for the open spaces of the witness box!"

"So I in my turn have noticed, if I may return the compliment, Charles! And now, if you'll excuse me, I'm gasping for a cigarette, as usual."

25

ERICA DREW was at the solicitors' table in the well of the court in good time on Tuesday, smart as ever in a dark red costume. It was to be anticipated that the first half hour or so would be occupied by Rogers and his cross-examination. Indeed, Miss Drew might logically have thought that she would scarcely be needed before, say, 11.15 at the earliest. But in the event, no sooner had the judge taken his seat, opened his huge book and looked up with his usual courteous smile, than the lanky Alec Glossop uncoiled himself and announced that his client had issued instructions that morning to the effect that he declined to give evidence from the witness box, but would make an unsworn statement from the dock.

Tom Alexander groaned almost audibly. Keen to make the most of his one chance in the entire case to take and hold the floor, he had been up until the small hours alone at his desk, poring over his papers, studying every aspect of Rogers' possible defence, anticipating every move and constructing a counter-move to it. After a short and restless night, he had slowly keyed himself up to that exact pitch of nervous tension which falls just short of flutter—he was as taut as a sprinter on his blocks—only to hear the starting gun go off twice in quick succession. Indeed, for Tom Alexander it was worse than a false start—it was no start at all! Under his breath he swore so profanely that he surprised even himself.

Rickler made a sympathetic grimace, knowing from his own early experience just how the younger man would be feeling. Tom gave him a rueful grin back. Meanwhile, Rogers was standing in his place in the dock, a grubby sheet of paper in front of him, from which he now began to read.

"My Lord—members of the jury. I have decided not to go into the witness box because I can't explain even to myself why I panicked for no reason when that chap came up behind my lorry shouting about theft. I've been concerned in crime twice before, you see, and you get to feel that as soon as the police know you've got a record, they jump on you and you'll never be believed. All I can say is that I didn't know those delivery notes I had weren't perfectly genuine. I had no reason to think they was forged. I gave them to the copper at the gate and he seemed satisfied. But when I heard that yell, I went barmy—I just panicked—I jumped down and ran. I wasn't going nowhere—just out of it. And then I was crash-tackled from behind. I couldn't say any more than that even if I went over there to the witness-box and opened myself up to all sorts of attack from the barrister. I just don't want to be attacked any more. I can't help it—I panicked. I wish I hadn't. I'm sorry I did. Look where it's landed me! I didn't know about theft or conspiracy or nothing. I'm not guilty and that's all I can say. Thank you."

He finished reading and stood, silent and confused. It was a good performance, conveniently ignoring all the evidence about the Gresham Road rendezvous. For a moment, a wave of sympathy for him passed over the jury box, visible only to the most experienced watchers. The judge completed his note and looked up.

"Thank you, Mr. Rogers. The jury have heard you and I am sure they will remember what you have said. You may sit down."

Rogers nodded and resumed his seat. So also in his pew did the string-bean Glossop. At the solicitors' table, Victor Everett closed his notebook with a sigh and smiled sadly across at Charles Stratton, who looked sympathetic. They both knew that nobody could get off in a case such as this by refusing to fight. Rogers had thrown his hand in. But at least he hadn't let any of the others down. The gang would remember that.

Thus it was little more than quarter to eleven when Everett Crane rose to present the case for the fifth defendant—from Stratton's point of view, the most serious, the most important, the most guilty and the one most likely to cause trouble. Oliver Rickler took a deep breath. He was half way through the exhalation when Crane's voice cut across the court.

"My Lord—I call my client, Ian

Willow!" he said, with an imperious gesture towards the dock.

As Willow pushed back his chair and was ushered through the little gate in the side of the dock, down the steps and across to the witness box, Rickler's attention was on Crane, with grave concern in his eyes. For unless he was mistaken, the older man's speech was not quite normal. There was something in it which suggested that Crane had—might have—taken steps to ease the tension that must be gripping him. Rickler's stomach turned over.

Willow was entering the box, his height and bulk more noticeable than in the dock. He stood there like an ungainly heavyweight wrestler, fumbling with the testament and the printed card, straining to follow the usher's instructions.

To Rickler's intense relief, Crane's handling of his client's evidence in chief was immaculate. The style was not as elegant as it had been earlier. Aggression seemed to hover near all the time. But Crane was exercising rigid control over himself, even though only one as close to him as Rickler could see it. Indeed, it was so effective that

Rickler began to wonder whether the minimal slur might not have been a deliberate red herring on Crane's part to divert attention from what was coming out of Willow's mouth.

Slowly, patiently and very clearly Willow's evidence emerged. Rickler divided his attention—something that long practice as an advocate enabled him to do—half his mind engaged in pre-planning the cross-examination to come, giving it not only clarity but positive shape—a series of points arising from a base like peaks from a plain—while the other half was monitoring what Willow was saying and noting it briefly so that if anything emerged which was either unexpected or significant, the whole attention could be switched instantly to it.

When Willow came to the events of the charging procedure, Crane began gracefully to round the story off. Rickler was now concentrating almost wholly on choosing his opening questions—so often an incalculable amount depends on this—they were like the tentative blows exchanged by boxers during the first minute of a fight. Occasionally an immediate attack was called for. Similarly, advantage might be gained over a witness who is expecting such an attack by asking a series of harmless formal questions on a level of importance so low as to induce the witness to lower his guard just long enough for the advocate to deliver a telling punch. Rickler would not make the final decision until he rose and held Willow's eye for a moment. It was a moment that could not be long delayed now.

Half an hour later, he could review the situation as he moved toward the key points of his offensive. It had gone well. He had made a very unhurried approach which had so stretched Willow's nerves, taut in their expectation of an immediate frontal attack, that once or twice they had snapped, so that he answered a mild question with a savagery that made the answer stand out as not merely singular but sinister. At once Rickler had paused with half-open mouth as if completely taken aback by this unnecessary and unjustified wrath on the witness's part.

Patiently, slowly, he had covered the ground of the events at "F" Shed—the arrival of the lorry, the conversation with Rogers, the identification of the container to be reloaded in accordance with the papers, which seemed perfectly genuine, and which Willow said had totally deceived him.

"Those papers were really good," he said. "They'd fooled Rogers and all!"—throwing this gratuitous assistance to the sulking Rogers in the dock as if it were a 16 pound shot and he Geoff Capes.

"And then you selected Mr. Lane to arrange the slinging?"

"Lane happened to be there at the time."

"You say that almost as if you would have been glad if it had been someone else, Mr. Willow. Have you not much respect for Mr. Lane as a dock-worker?"

"I've got no respect for Lane at all. I'd have preferred anyone else. He happened to be there, as you say. My bad luck. He's useless and he knows I think that."

"Oh I'm sure he does. Not a particular friend, obviously."

"You can say that again."

"I could but I won't. You have nothing to do with Mr. Lane socially—outside work, I mean? I notice you live not far apart. But there's nothing relevant that decided you to pick him for this job?"

"I don't know what you're getting at. I've got no use at all for Lane. Except at work, when I've got to see him, I don't want to know him."

"Right. Then let me turn to the more significant matter of your acquaintance—or lack of it—with Mr. Harry Williams."

"I've told you—until this case blew up, I'd never met Harry Williams. I met him first in the van going from the docks to East Ham nick. Didn't know him from Adam till then. Name meant nothing to me."

"And yet here it is—name and number—in your diary."

"That evidence was fake. Bryan forged that!"

"There could hardly be a more serious allegation against a serving police officer, Mr. Willow."

"Oh I agree with you—there couldn't!"

"And yet you make it. On your oath?"

"Oh yes I do."

"Very well. Then may the witness please be handed Exhibit 14?"

The usher took it from the collection on the Clerk's desk, checked briefly with Rickler that it was the one required, then went across and handed the little diary to Willow, who reached down over the ledge to take it. He did not attempt to open it —just stood blank-faced, holding it.

"Right, Mr. Willow. Now, as we all know from earlier evidence, what you have in your hand is indeed your personal pocket diary owned and used by you for several months before this case arose—by you and no-one else, indeed. Check it, will you?"

Willow did so. "Yes, it's mine."

"You have completely withdrawn your earlier allegation that it never was your diary—that you never had such a diary— that the police wrote every entry in it and planted it among your belongings—that's all quite withdrawn now, is it?"

"My lawyer said that. I didn't."

"Ah—but we won't go into that. I merely wanted your personal confirmation that no such allegations remain."

"I never made them. I make others."

"I know. Now—will you turn to the

memorandum pages which follow the dated section of that diary?"

"Yes."

"Will you please read aloud the entry that all the fuss is about?"

"Yes. 'HARRY—246 8071'. It's here."

"That's the note that you say Mr. Bryan made in your diary?"

"He did. He must have."

"When?"

"When his side-kick went to get the tea."

"I put it to you that Mr. Haines never left the room."

"He said himself he did!"

The judge smiled. "The witness has a point there, Mr. Rickler. Mr. Haines undoubtedly did say so in cross-examination."

"My Lord, I concede he did. But since I am instructed that Haines was simply confusing the interrogation of Mr. Willow with that of Mr. Lane, I had to see if the witness had the same recollection."

"Of course. Do proceed."

"Thank you, my Lord. So—you say, Mr. Willow, that Mr. Haines left you and Mr. Bryan alone and that then and there, in that room, Mr. Bryan took that diary and made that entry?"

"He didn't take it because I'd given it to him. Otherwise, yes."

"Mr. Willow—I put it to you that that is a direct and deliberate lie which, since you are on oath, amounts to perjury."

"Well you've got to, haven't you?"

"I haven't *got* to do anything except test the accuracy of your evidence with admissible questions. But I do put it, yes."

"Well I do so deny it, then!"

"I hear you. It will be for the jury to decide. Meanwhile, let us consider the diary entry further. You know that *is* Harry Williams' phone number, don't you?"

"Yes."

As the word left his lips, Crane was on his feet on Rickler's left, just beyond Alexander. Rickler sat down at once.

"My Lord—"

"Yes, Mr. Crane?"

Whatever words had brought Crane to his feet died in his throat. It had been instinct, and it had played him false. Rickler could remember occasions when the same thing had happened to him. He smiled, understandingly. Crane could not formulate an objection.

The judge smiled patiently. He too knew just what had happened.

"I hear you, Mr. Crane, but I cannot see that there is any valid objection that I could sustain. Mr. Rickler's question was perfectly proper. Your client's answer was perfectly admissible. It was not at all incriminating."

"My Lord, I know. I do not object."

"I am glad, Mr. Crane. We all know how sometimes a word can bring counsel to his feet instinctively. Mr. Rickler?"

As Crane subsided, Oliver Rickler rose, curbing a natural urge to smile openly. It was only when he went to put his next question to Willow that he became aware of the appalling effect, whether intended or not, that a sudden interruption can have on an advocate in full flow. The thread of questioning—the whole logical long process of thought—which the interruption had snapped, should have been there to pick up again. It had vanished. His mind, progressing so smoothly before Crane rose, was now a whirling blank. He put his hand to his forehead, wondering whether Crane had done it as a deliberate forensic trick. Where had he got to? He had asked Willow about the phone number. He had suggested that the number was indeed that of Harry Williams. But now he could not for the life of him remember just where he had intended to go from there. It is, he realised, one of the most disconcerting things that can happen to an advocate, and no-one is immune from it.

"My Lord—I'm so sorry. For a moment—"

"Take your time, Mr. Rickler. I'm sure we all know how easy and how upsetting it can be to find one's train of thought unexpectedly de-railed, so to speak. These things happen. We await your convenience."

Bowing his thanks and staring blankly at his notes, Rickler realised that the one thing that might put his memory back on the rails was a question—any question. The sound of his own voice was the factor that could do it. What could he ask Willow, who was now standing in the box openly grinning at his adversary's discomfiture? Something formed itself desperately in his puzzled mind—only vaguely—a trigger to set the train of thought in motion again—for no other reason.

"Assuming that that number is Harry Williams' number and that 'Harry' in the diary refers to him—will you please now specify in terms exactly what impropriety you allege against Det. Chief Inspector Bryan?"

It meant almost nothing. Willow had alleged forgery. The question had not even brought back whatever had been in his mind before. And yet, as he asked it, he saw with astonishment that the question had had a marked effect upon Willow. His grin faded with his concentration. Now it seemed as if Willow in his turn was about to suffer a mental blank. What on earth, he seemed to be asking himself, was Rickler after? He had been understanding and following and countering, depending without realising almost as much on the barrister's logical process of thought as Rickler himself had been. Now he was thrown, and in the same way. Did Rickler want the forgery allegation repeated? Why? What was the significance of the question? He could not see behind it. His incomprehension turned to fear. And, as quickly, to anger. That damned Drew girl had worked out all the possibilities in advance, she said—hours of rehearsal, she'd given him. Smart kid, he'd thought. And now look what a spot it had landed him in. Defensively, he thought, "Right! She's got me into this! Then let her bloody get me out of it!"

"That's a matter for my solicitor!" he snapped.

"I am not concerned with your solicitor, Mr. Willow. I asked you a simple question. Exactly what allegation are you *now* making against Mr. Bryan in the light of your last answer?"

Rickler was blindly following his own instinct. Accidentally, and without knowing how, he had suddenly got his quarry on the run. Never mind how or why—the necessity was to press further. Wherever it might lead, he must press on. Willow licked his lips.

"It's privileged."

"Privileged? Privileged? Mr. Willow, I think you have got hold of the wrong end of some stick. No doubt you have heard that some communications between a solicitor and his client are protected from disclosure in court. But—subject to his Lordship correcting me—that is a protection from disclosure *by* the solicitor. It is the client's privilege to insist that the solicitor remains silent under questioning about certain limited matters."

"Right. I exercise that privilege."

"Mr. Willow—there is no privilege exercisable by you in this context. You cannot render my question improper, nor your answer avoidable. Or are you possibly trying to convey that you decline to answer my question altogether, leaving it to your solicitor to face the question of privilege later, if she should be called?"

Willow was right out of his depth, now. He did not know what to answer. He could hardly say no—that would lead to worse trouble!

"Yes," he snapped.

"Oh! Well then, let us look ahead, a moment. If in due course your solicitor is called to give evidence, and if I should ask her about these allegations you now make against Mr. Bryan—she could refuse to answer some questions on the grounds that she would be offending against that privilege which is yours and not hers. Are you with me so far?"

"Yes." It was a lie. He was not.

"Then let me tell you now that you have a right to waive that privilege if you choose. I ask you—will you do so?"

Willow's mind boggled. That bloody girl had got him into this with her scheming. What should he do? What *could* he do? He glared at her as she sat at the table below him and below Crane, looking steadily down at papers in front of her. At last she raised her head and looked up at him. Her face was a blank. In the continuing silence, Rickler's soft voice repeated the question.

"Will you waive that privilege?"

Vehemently but within a very small compass of movement, she shook her head. It was enough.

"No I won't!"

The judge put down his pen and slowly moved his head from side to side in puzzlement and concern.

"Mr. Rickler—I am indeed sorry to interrupt you again, but I feel that somehow we have strayed from a normal path. We seem to be engaged in an aspect of professional privilege in which Mr. Willow's solicitor—whom I take to be the young lady sitting at the table there—is directly involved. If that is so, I have to record with the most serious displeasure that I have just now observed a solicitor telling her client in the box how to answer a question. She made a small but distinct movement of the head, to which he immediately responded. I presume she has a professional right to stay in court even if she may later be called—I suppose it is relevant whether or not Mr. Crane intends to call her. Can I seek your assistance, Mr. Crane?"

Crane rose. Rickler decided that he himself was sufficiently part of the development to remain standing.

"My Lord," said Crane, "I *am* intending to call my instructing solicitor Miss Drew to give evidence on behalf of Mr. Willow."

Oliver Rickler felt his mouth open in surprise and shut it with a snap. How this had all happened mattered no longer. His function was now to exploit the situation in the interests of justice.

"My Lord—"

"Yes, Mr. Rickler?"

"I cannot of course ask my learned friend a direct question. But I cannot hide the fact that I need to know whether he intends to call Miss Drew before or after he calls Mr. Dickenson, who to my knowledge has been within the precincts of this court ever since last Friday."

"My Lord," said Crane, "I can clear up the point easily. I shall not now be calling Mr. Dickenson."

There was a long silence. Out of it, eventually, came the soft, shocked voice of Mr. Justice Dover.

"I do not think I can have heard what I thought I did. Unless you made a slip of the tongue, Mr. Crane, you seemed to say that you were not now intending to call Mr. Dickenson."

"That is what I said, my Lord."

"But Mr. Crane, that cannot be so. Last Friday morning in open court you gave a professional undertaking that you would call Mr. Dickenson as a witness for Mr. Willow. In direct consequence of that undertaking, you were permitted to take up a line of cross-examination of Mr.

Bryan that would have been grossly improper save with your undertaking that you were calling Mr. Dickenson. You cannot now withdraw an undertaking having first gained an appreciable unfair advantage by means of it."

"I do, my Lord. I withdraw my undertaking."

"Mr. Crane, you cannot mean what you are saying. Counsel cannot treat a court in such a manner. It is beyond my comprehension. How do you *dare* go back on your solemn professional word?"

Rickler's impression had been that Crane had gone red, but now as he looked at him he saw that Crane had turned pale, almost white. He looked ten years older than before and his voice was uncertain, wavering.

"My Lord—circumstances have greatly changed from those in which I gave my undertaking."

"Mr. Crane—you know well the adage that 'Justice must be done though the Heavens fall'. I tell you now that it would be wrong to permit you to go back on the undertaking you gave although the Heavens fell, much less on the grounds that circumstances had changed, however radically."

"My Lord, believe me I deeply regret the necessity of taking this course. But I understand there is nothing that can be done to compel my calling Mr. Dickenson. I apologise to your Lordship and to my learned friends for having to withdraw my undertaking. I can only say that circumstances alter cases."

"They may alter cases, Mr. Crane. They cannot alter professional obligations. If you intend to convey that there is no way in which I can *make* you call Mr. Dickenson, you are perfectly correct. A judge cannot call a witness nor can he force an advocate to do so. I can, however—and I do so now with deep regret—censure you publicly from the bench in open court—a court as open, I would remind you, as that in which you gave me your solemn professional undertaking last Friday morning. And when this case is over, irrespective of the result, I propose to send the papers with a personal report to the General Council of the Bar which, I would remind you sir, is my profession as well as yours. They will consider the matter."

For a moment Crane's head bowed. His speech when he lifted it was definitely slurred, but clearly through emotion, not alcohol.

"My Lord—your words leave me in what I can only describe as acute distress. I find it impossible to proceed further without immediate instructions. I must consult urgently with my instructing solicitor. Under the circumstances, I beg your Lordship to grant me leave to see what can be done to put matters right— or at least less wrong. Would your Lordship allow me to request that the case against Mr. Willow might be put back for the moment—say until after the luncheon adjournment? It is, I notice, already half past twelve. Then, if your Lordship permits me, I will on the resumption at once call Miss Drew."

"Mr. Crane, your proposal directly affects Mr. Rickler and those associated with him. We must hear from them before any decision can fairly be made. Mr. Rickler, I am minded to say that I will adjourn now until after lunch, not least because what has occurred has left me gravely upset. I, too, can do with time to let these unprecedented events assume some degree of perspective. I imagine that an adjournment now would not seriously concern you. As to what should happen on the resumption—can you give us your reaction to Mr. Crane's proposal?"

Rickler's mind had been racing. He was in favour of an immediate adjournment. True, it would deprive him of carrying on the chase of Willow who was in full flight —but with any luck he could put him to flight again. The Drew girl and Crane would be allowed no contact with him until he was back in the box and finished with, and if he really had "lost his bottle", then time would be likely to make him weaker rather than stronger. But he had now realised what Crane was really after —drawing attention away from Miss Drew so that he would be unprepared to attack her in the witness box. And that implied that there were facts about her which Crane had deemed it worth risking his professional career to conceal. He must secure time enough to investigate her before she gave evidence.

With a quick look of request towards the judge, which gained him an immediate nod, Rickler bent down over Stratton's shoulder. Very quietly into his ear, he said, "Charles, I think I've spotted their game. We must have time to follow up a few lines before we put that girl through it in the box. Can I go ahead on that basis?"

"Of course, Oliver—you have my full agreement in advance to whatever course of action best suits you. All yours!"

Rickler straightened with a smile.

"Yes, Mr. Rickler?"

"My Lord—as regards the immediate adjournment, I am entirely agreeable. But I fear I cannot agree to my learned friend's other proposal. I regard it as important that Mr. Willow should continue in cross-examination until his evidence is finished. Thereafter, while it is a matter for your Lordship, I would respectfully oppose having to question Miss Drew without an opportunity of considering the position in detail with those instructing me. Indeed, I would go so far as to suggest that Mr. Osborne might be asked if he and Mr. Tomlinson his instructing solicitor would be prepared to have the case against Mr. Lane dealt with on the retirement of

Mr. Willow from the box at the end of his present questioning."

The judge turned to Charles Osborne.

"Mr. Osborne, I am sure Mr. Rickler would not wish to prejudice your client in any way but, subject to that, I feel I should like to assist him as far as possible, for he has been stopped in the middle of a key passage of arms with Mr. Willow."

As the judge was speaking, the chubby Neil Tomlinson on the far side of the solicitors' table was grinning cheerfully through his beard. Nodding reassurance to the bemused Teddy Lane in the dock, he gave Charles Osborne a clear and open "thumbs up". Osborne rose.

"As your Lordship will no doubt have seen, I am instructed that such a course will give us no trouble. We have been ready for some time to do our duty by Mr. Lane at the drop of the proverbial hat. If the hat drops during this afternoon, that will suit us as well as we hope it may suit your Lordship."

"Thank you, Mr. Osborne, and through you I thank Mr. Lane and those immediately instructing you. Very well—I will adjourn now until a quarter past two."

He rose—so anxious to be back in his room that he even omitted the customary triple bow. Shutting his book, he picked up his pen and walked quickly, with head down, along the bench to the door of his room, into which he disappeared.

26

MINUTES later, in the main hall outside the court, Charles Stratton with Evan Baunton and David Gunn was approaching Joe Dickenson. Stratton, after identifying himself, looked slightly quizzical.

"Forgive me but haven't we met somewhere before?"

"We have, Mr. Stratton, yes—though I didn't remember myself, till this moment. It was 1966, actually—I was in one of the squads engaged in the special search for Harry Roberts, the Shepherds Bush cop-killer. We were offered an office in your Headquarters and honorary membership of the Police Club while the search was on —really memorable co-operation. You and I met in the bar a few times and at lunch. I wouldn't have thought you'd remember me."

"It was really just a sense of familiarity, I confess. I'd never have pinpointed it if you hadn't reminded me. Let me introduce Evan Baunton, my Assistant. David Gunn you'll remember, of course—he's the head of our CID now."

"Curiously enough, we haven't met," said Gunn, shaking hands. "I was CID Royals, at the time, visiting HQ only rarely, more's the pity. I know you were linked with George Bryan, but he went from HQ to take over my job when I came up to handle my present one. He's spoken very highly of you and I'm glad to meet you."

"Thanks. By the way, I gather that I'm openly on the side of the angels in this case now, then?"

"That's right," said Stratton. "Mr. Crane's withdrawal of his undertaking has entailed the cancellation of his subpoena. Technically there's no property in any witness, of course, but to speak to you before would only have caused trouble and embarrassment all round. But now we can speak freely—and frankly I think you may be able to help us quite a bit."

"More than you think, perhaps. One thing—has Lane been in the box yet?"

"No. Straight after lunch, in fact," said Evan.

"His case has been interposed in the middle of Willow's," explained Stratton. "Mr. Crane seemed anxious to call Miss Drew straight away, but Oliver Rickler, who's leading for us, insisted this would put us at some disadvantage for some reason he hasn't yet told me. So she will be called tomorrow morning."

"Mr. Rickler's instincts are infallible— that will be ideal. I can give you some relevant facts about Teddy Lane first, though, which will help you considerably this afternoon when you cross-examine. I may say that I don't think Lane's guilty— I think he was used as a tool by Willow— but you may know differently, of course."

"No," said Gunn. "That's been our view for some time. We hope and expect he'll get off. But what can we bring out through Lane that will strengthen the case against Willow?"

"Some facts and a photograph."

"Right," said Stratton. "There's a little conference room up the back stairs where Oliver Rickler has arranged to meet us in a few minutes. There are technical rules about counsel seeing witnesses, but they can be waived now and then, and he's no more worried on that score than I am. So let's go up there and have a chat. I don't anticipate that we'll be actually calling you to give evidence, by the way, but we can do with whatever information you can give us. Come along—this way."

Up in the little conference room, Dickenson was introduced to the two barristers and then began telling the group what he had been able to find out. It seemed that he had made it his business to visit several dockland pubs over the last week, with no specific motive other than finding out how and what the average docker thinks—background information which would help him, if not in this case, then in other possible cases in the future. And in one of them, he had got into conversation with a very expansive docker, who loved showing how much he knew about the events *behind* the current dockland topics. The conversation had led to others, in other places, and Dickenson had wound up looking through back numbers of a small East London local weekly newspaper. The faces of his listeners began to take on smiles of high amusement—smiles which broadened still further when the young investigator took from his brief-case half a dozen copies of a photograph which he had quietly obtained.

When this, and all its potential advantages, had been fully discussed, Rickler paused and smiled across the table.

"And now, Mr. Dickenson, I want you to be good enough to tell me exactly what was in the letter you had from Miss Drew which caused you to phone George Bryan at the docks. I need to know because her counsel has said in terms that he intends to call her tomorrow morning and we need to know all we can find out about her before then."

"Well, on that topic, Mr. Rickler, I think I can provide you with a pleasant surprise. I can also save your team a great deal of trouble. Because after I had declined her instructions, I was naturally curious about what sort of solicitor would do anything that was frankly so bloody silly! So I did quite a lot of detailed research into Miss Erica Drew. I thought I might need it for my own defence. And as I don't appear to need it for that, and it will materially assist you, I will gladly tell you all that I managed to dig out about her. It's an interesting and unusual story. It will explain a number of things that might have puzzled you in this case, too. But as you rightly asked—let's deal first with that stupid letter which set the whole business off. I have it here."

He reached again into his brief-case.

"Mr. Lane," said Rickler, stressing again the warmth in his voice, "I want now to turn to another aspect of this matter. You have already made it clear that you acted that day at 'F' Shed solely on the direct orders of Mr. Willow who, before he gave you those orders, had prepared for the coming of the lorry by making an arrangement with a man who could drive cranes but who was *not* the regular driver of the crane that was used. We know that the regular crane driver was sent off for an early lunch-break. You have also told us how, when the lorry did arrive, the driver showed Willow the papers he had—quite a pantomime was gone through about them, indeed, presumably necessary so that Willow could cover himself. And then it was after that, I think, that you were given direct orders by Willow. Is that right?"

"That's right, yes."

"Were there any others about at that time, on the pitch, Mr. Lane?"

"No. Willow, the lorry driver, the crane man—that was all on the pitch. Except me. Willow had told me to stay."

"I see. Mr. Lane—may I put it this way? It would seem as though Mr. Willow was exercising some pressure of some kind over you. Would that be a fair assumption?"

"I'd rather not answer that."

"Very well, Mr. Lane. I understand. I think I can get what I want another way. Would it be fair to suggest that Mr. Willow always picks on you if there is something awkward to be done?"

"Yes."

"Right. That of course means little in itself. We all have our own '*bêtes noirs*'. But he did say on oath in that box that outside of work he didn't even know you. That you were barely a name to him, once you were both off the docks."

"I heard him."

"That's not true, Mr. Lane, is it?"

"No."

Rickler picked up the photograph from the desk before him. Then he nodded towards the usher, who came across and took it.

"Mr. Lane, the photograph which the usher is now bringing over to you is an enlargement of a press photograph taken during the summer of 1966. Will you look at it first without comment?"

"Yes."

"My Lord—I have shown my learned friend Mr. Osborne a copy of this photograph and he has discussed it with those instructing him. I propose to ask Mr. Lane first if he remembers it being taken. If there should be any need to prove it formally, I can arrange for the photographer to attend here. Mr. Osborne kindly indicates he does not think there will be any such need. Mr. Lane—do you remember the occasion?"

"Yes. I remember it being taken and appearing in the local weekly, afterwards."

"Thank you Mr. Lane. My Lord—here is a copy for you, and I have copies for the jury, if my learned friend has no objection."

Osborne rose. "None, my Lord. Procedurally, if it will make it easier, I will admit the photograph under s. 10."

The usher handed a copy to the Clerk who, after a glance, handed it up at once to the bench. Meanwhile the usher was distributing four more copies among the jury.

"Now, Mr. Lane—what we see here is a wedding group."

"Yes."

"Who is the bridegroom?"

"My brother Jimmy."

"Is that you yourself on his right—best man, perhaps?"

"That's right."

"I believe the bride's parents were both dead, and the bride was given away by her brother."

"Yes."

"That's her brother standing on her left, isn't it?"

"Yes."

"What was your brother's bride's maiden name, Mr. Lane?"

"Margaret Willow."

"And in case the jury have not yet

recognised him—the name of her brother there in the picture beside her?"

"Ian Willow."

"Your co-defendant?"

"Yes."

"Related to you thus by marriage?"

"Yes."

"Thank you, Mr. Lane," said Rickler and sat down without comment.

Osborne rose. "Subject to any questions your Lordship may wish to ask Mr. Lane . . .?" The judge shook his head. "Then, Mr. Lane, will you return to your place in the dock?"

Prisoner and escort moved slowly down to and across the well of the court, up the steps and in through the little gate into the dock. Lane sat down nearest the jury as before, looking rigidly to the front—no trace of a glance to his right where the big man sat next to him. Willow closed his eyes.

"My Lord," said Charles Osborne. "That is my case."

"Thank you, Mr. Osborne," said the judge, making an entry in his huge ledger and drawing an obvious line across it under his notes. Then he turned to Oliver Rickler.

"Mr. Rickler, though it is only quarter past three, I think we now have no alternative but to adjourn until tomorrow morning."

Rickler's attention was caught by a movement below him. "If your Lordship will grant me one moment—" he said, and looked to where Evan Baunton had appeared at the side of the dock, nodding energetically to Charles Stratton at the table. It was all he needed.

"My Lord—the witness whom I am anxious to call in rebuttal in the case against Mr. Delafield has just arrived. It occurs to me that if it is not inconvenient to Mr. Morgan and his instructing solicitor and if it suits your Lordship, we might hear from him now."

"It suits us, my Lord," said Morgan, half rising.

"Then let him be called with pleasure," smiled the judge, turning back several pages in his book. "Let me just remind the jury. You will recall, members of the jury, that the statement made on oath by Mr. Delafield was to the effect that he could not have been at the rendezvous in Gresham Road as alleged against him, because he was at that time in a betting shop near the Canning Town roundabout, where he was placing bets on a horse or horses running in either the 1.15 or 1.30 or maybe both. He had not delivered a Notice of Alibi as the law requires, but this was waived by the Crown provided a witness could be called by them 'in rebuttal' as it is called—one who can prove that the alibi was false. That witness has now arrived and we will hear him directly. Let him be sworn."

Evan Baunton signalled. The swing door opened and a man walked into court, past Evan, down into the well and up the steps to the witness box. There was a stunned silence as he took the oath.

"Thank you, sir," said Rickler as the witness gave the testament and card back to the usher. "Your names?"

"Robert Cerney, my Lord. I am the licensed proprietor of a betting shop on the south side of Barking Road some fifty yards east of the main Canning Town roundabout at the top of Silvertown Way."

"Mr. Cerney—I ought perhaps to say

that if the quality of your reception puzzled you, it did not indicate discourtesy. On the contrary—"

"You mean I look exactly like the traditional bookie is supposed to look? Sir—I know I do. I go out of my way to keep it so. It's my little personal gimmick, if you like. I'm known everywhere as the bookie who looks like a bookie's supposed to look. Fat, red face, bald head, loud tie, check suit—the lot. Helps business, you know!"

A wide grin at once endeared him to everyone from the judge to the public gallery in which one appreciative guffaw was at once shushed by an occupationally scandalised usher.

"Well, then, Mr. Cerney," smiled Rickler, who was working without any note—"do you know a Mr. Albert Delafield, one of the six men over there in the dock?"

"No, sir. Never seen any of that lot in my life, that I can recall. Nor does the name mean anything to me."

"Oh. Then—do you remember Thursday June 10th last?"

"No sir, not particularly."

Rickler paused. For a moment, the joke seemed to be on him. He caught a smothered giggle from Derek Morgan behind him. The judge and several jurymen were smiling amusedly. Stratton turned and mouthed some word Rickler couldn't catch. He looked cheerful enough, though. And then the situation seemed to penetrate to the witness.

"Ah! I think I can help you, sir," he said, bending down and lifting up to the ledge of the box a neat black executive briefcase. Opening this, he took out a large foolscap desk diary—a week at an opening, in common form. Rickler realised that it was the word "DIARY" that Stratton had mouthed at him.

"This, my Lord," said Cerney, "is my office desk diary. I keep it made up every day with the meetings and my gross profit for each—just a rough note for my own information, sir—we keep proper accounts, naturally. Got a staff for that."

"I see, Mr. Cerney. Perhaps you'll turn to Thursday 10th June of this year and tell us first what horse-race meetings were held on that day?"

The big man flipped over the pages until

he found the right week. Then he looked up and beamed at Rickler.

"Thursday June 10th, you said, sir? Ah! Well, that's an easy one to answer. Horses, you said, sir? The answer is none."

"None at all, Mr. Cerney? Isn't that rather unusual?"

"Normally, sir, yes very. At the beginning of last June—not at all."

"You do surprise me. I happen to remember that the day was a particularly fine, sunny one—in London at least."

"Right across the country, sir. But you may also recall that it was the first fine day for three weeks. We'd had nothing but belting rain for 22 days all over the land. It stopped during the afternoon of June 9th, actually, but there wasn't a racecourse in the country that wasn't waterlogged, and the stewards at every meeting had pronounced them abandoned. In fact there were three stadiums that did manage a bit of dog racing that evening—greyhounds, you know. But they were all wealthy ones that had tarpaulins covering the track throughout the wet—well, it's not impossible—it's only about 400 yards a lap, see. But horse racing on June 10th last? No, sir—not a single meeting. Indeed, we didn't open the shop until about half past five, just for those dog races. Makes a bit of a change for us."

All this was reeled off at high speed in ebullient full-bodied Cockney dialect. Long before it ended, Rickler was choking back his laughter. He did not dare glance at the dock—but if ever "Lucky" had deserved his sarcastic nickname, it was now. He forced a straight face.

"We really are most obliged to you, Mr. Cerney. I hope you have not been inconvenienced by coming. You have greatly assisted the court. I have no further questions. I imagine there will be little, if any, cross-examination."

Out of the corner of his eye, Rickler could see the headshake of the crestfallen Derek Morgan. The rich Welsh voice intoned sadly—"There will be none, thank you my Lord."

27

"YES, Mr. Crane?" said the judge. The icy formality with which he was treating counsel was the only indication of the judge's continuing concern.

"My Lord, I have now been able to take further instructions in this case, thanks to your Lordship's kindness in putting it back yesterday. I am glad to say that the position is by no means as serious as your Lordship quite justifiably thought it was yesterday."

"I am very glad to hear it, Mr. Crane."

"Quite, my Lord. The position is now that although I shall not be calling Mr. Dickenson as I originally intimated—"

"As you originally undertook in open court, Mr. Crane."

"Quite, my Lord. I shall instead be calling my instructing solicitor who, by the way, I have directed to remain outside until she is called. The important point I wish to make first, my Lord, is that if the undertaking that I gave had been the same but had specified Miss Drew's name instead of Mr. Dickenson's, then the cross-examination that your Lordship permitted me to conduct would have been exactly the same. In other words, although the witness's identity will be different, the same points will come out in evidence and I shall have gained no earlier advantage."

"I take your point, Mr. Crane. If it proves correct, then I shall be glad to know that you will not have gained that grossly unfair advantage from your cross-examination of Mr. Bryan. But while that may be so, it does not lessen at all the seriousness of giving an undertaking in open court and later withdrawing it, despite the availability of the subject of it. That, however, is a matter which will be considered at another time and in another place. Do not imagine that it will not, Mr. Crane. I shall still, though reluctantly, draw the attention of the Bar Council to the case."

"I understand, my Lord. Er—there is one further point I should perhaps raise. Pending her evidence, Miss Drew remains outside. Technically Mr. Willow is in mid-cross-examination, during which I must have my instructing solicitor in court with me. I therefore seek not to recall Mr. Willow until Miss Drew has completed her evidence."

"I see. What do you say to that, Mr. Rickler?"

"I have not heard of it before this moment, my Lord. However, I do not wish to obstruct Mr. Crane further. I will raise no objection."

"Thank you, Mr. Rickler. Very well, Mr. Crane."

"I call Erica Drew."

There was a pause. The name was called again in the hall beyond the lobby. Then the door swung and in she came. The suit was black—either very fine corduroy or velvet—cut on classical lines, with a single row of black buttons down the centre, set off by the collar of a white blouse or shirt which emerged from the square cut lapels and fitted neatly—demurely was the word which came to Stratton's mind—over the velvet collar. As she crossed the well of the court and mounted the steps to the witness-box with a small handbag tucked into her side from a strap over her left shoulder, it was possible to see the pencil-line skirt, impeccably cut, smart stockings and markedly high heeled shoes. Altogether a picture of quiet, professional elegance. How exceptional a picture it was, Stratton had no idea. But it was impossible to fault her on it.

She emerged into the canopied witness-box at the top of the steps, slipped the bag strap from her shoulder and put the bag on the ledge to her left. Her hair was short and neat—fair, with blonde highlights—and her make-up so right as not to be noticeable. What surprised him more than anything was how effectively the cut of her jacket had eliminated her former bustiness—or was it perhaps that her earlier clothes had emphasised this? Certainly there was no pouter-pigeon effect now as she stood very straight in the box, a half-smile flickering on her lips. Yes, thought Stratton—full marks for appearance.

The usher made no move. As a legally qualified witness, she was to be credited with experience of courts and oath-taking. With her right hand she took the testament, in her left the card. In a low tone but with perfect clarity she recited the formula. Then she replaced testament and card, turned to the judge with a hint of a bow to indicate that she was at the service of the court, and spoke, unprompted.

"Erica Drew," she began, giving not a private address but that of her Loughton office—a privilege automatically accorded a professional witness. "I am employed by Edwin Poulter and Co., solicitors at that address. I am the person having charge and conduct of the case against Mr. Ian Willow."

"Thank you," said Crane. "And, having taken details of the facts from your client, what initial steps did you take?"

"I found myself particularly concerned about a pocket diary in which it was alleged there was an entry linking my client to his co-accused Mr. Williams, though my client insisted he did not know Williams at all. Being at that time unfamilar with the docks, I decided to make use of an Enquiry Agent. I had heard of an ex-policeman who had recently set up practice in his field at South Woodford, and, having located him, I telephoned him. His name is Dickenson. As a result of what he told me, I wrote to him, setting out the several lines of enquiry I wished him to undertake."

"Quite. And did you receive a report in due course?"

"I did not. Instead, I received a letter from Mr. Dickenson saying that he had decided not to accept my instructions."

"Did he say why?"

"He did not. However, later, in the course of investigating the matter myself, I went to the Royal Albert Dock, where I saw Chief Inspector Bryan. I asked him to let me inspect the diary and he produced it to me. Then in course of conversation, Mr. Bryan let slip a remark which I construed as indicating that he had discussed this case with Mr. Dickenson. I challenged him with this and he admitted it. I asked if it was he who persuaded the agent to decline my instructions and he agreed that he had advised Dickenson to this effect. It was plain to me from what Mr. Bryan said that he had known the details of the instructions I had given to Mr. Dickenson in professional confidence. I challenged Mr. Bryan with grave impropriety in this respect."

"Did he deny it?"

"He denied the impropriety, but not that he had learned the main lines of Mr. Willow's defence from a witness in this way."

"How did your conversation end?"

"By my telling him that I would insist on raising his improper conduct in court at this trial."

"Miss Drew—is there any further point that you now wish to give in evidence before you submit yourself to my learned friend's cross-examination?"

"There is not."

With a bow to the judge, Crane resumed his seat, wrapping himself within the folds of his gown as if to insulate himself from what was to come. It was as skilfully done as all Crane's moves. She had been presented so briefly, so informally, that one was left wondering what all the fuss was about. As Oliver Rickler rose and glanced at the notes on the stand before him, he reflected that perhaps it was really about remarkably little. Crane had, by a device which was distinctly unprofessional, merely made admissible a series of questions to George Bryan which had left that officer quite unshaken. Hardly a gain which justified laying one's whole professional future on the block. Of course, Crane might yet find a way to use the advantage he had gained—but just now, he had successfully made it seem like a storm in a tea-cup.

Still—it had presented Rickler with the interesting and important opportunity to cross-examine Erica Drew. And in the light of what he now knew about her, this was a task both delicate and significant. He had accepted without question Stratton's wish in conference the previous evening that he should use no more of what he now knew than was necessary to obtain from her a complete withdrawal of all the allegations of impropriety she had made. He kept his mind fixed on that target now.

He looked up for a few seconds, staring hard at the determined little figure in the box, roughly on the same level as himself above the well of the court which lay between them. Then he was off.

"You gave your name as Erica Drew."

"I did."

"That is not what you were christened, is it?"

"No."

"When did you change your name?"

"It is not illegal."

"I did not suggest it was, Miss Drew. It is significant only in that it shows how, by perfectly legal means, you have given the world a calculatedly wrong impression. In fact you were christened Gertrude Heather Drury, were you not?"

"I was."

The reply gave no sign of the hurt it must have caused her to know that someone had exposed one of her personal secrets.

"When did you change it?"

"I did not go through the formality of a deed poll, if that is what you are getting at."

"Miss Drew—you are devoting your attention to the motives *behind* what others are saying. If you will just take each question for what it is worth and answer it, we shall move along much more quickly. I know that it is legal to change a name without any formality. I ask you again. When did you renounce the name Gertrude Heather Drury and adopt the name Erica Drew?"

"After I left school and before I entered

into articles. It is hardly serious. Erica is merely Latin for Heather."

"I am aware of that, Miss Drew. The move was, I suggest, simply due to the fact that when you decided to earn your living, you felt that Gertrude Heather Drury would not catch the eye—the ear—not to mention the clients—as effectively as Erica Drew. Something like that?"

"If you wish."

"Not illegal. Not improper. But significant. A small alteration of facts so that things do not seem quite as they used to be. An alteration which, if it is found out, creates a natural need for others to examine with special care whatever you may do or say."

"It is no doubt your duty to be offensive."

"It is not my duty to be offensive, and particularly to a witness, as you very well know, Miss Drew. I may occasionally find it necessary to be so, but it is not my duty. You see—once more—something that seems very like what you say it is, but incorrect. How careful we must be, must we not? Again—you defined yourself as being 'the person having charge and conduct of this case'. I know that is true. But do you not think, upon reflection, that it is likely to mislead?"

"I do not."

"You do not? Well, Miss Erica Drew, I wonder how many people in this court will have assumed from that correct bit of legal jargon that you are a qualified solicitor. Whereas you are not, are you?"

"I am articled to a firm of solicitors. I have passed the Law Society Part I Examination. When I have passed Part II, generally known as 'The Final', I shall be a solicitor. I have never at any time held myself out to be a solicitor. That would be highly illegal."

"Quite. I merely say that by the wording you select, you may mislead a number of people into giving you the credit that normally attaches to a professional status. May we now put that right by agreeing that you are merely a law student?"

"I am technically not yet a solicitor but I soon will be. And you may allow me to inform you that there is no examination in Criminal Law in the Part II Examination —the subject comes only into Part I. I have therefore already achieved as high a qualification as the profession requires in that subject!"

Her voice had risen and now rang through the court, emphasised by the silence that Rickler allowed to follow it—one which the judge then quietly broke.

"Miss Drew—I am sure you appreciate that there is more to becoming a solicitor than passing exams. You may qualify educationally but that does not mean that the profession will admit you to practice. I mention the point not in order to criticise you but to correct what seemed to me to be a wrong impression in your mind."

The words were soft, the manner kindly, and both were accompanied by a charming smile. They had an instantly calming effect. The girl smiled and gave the suggestion of a bow.

"Your Lordship is of course absolutely right. I had not taken that into consideration. I apologise, my Lord."

The judge smiled his acceptance of the gesture and turned back to Rickler. "Shall we move on, Mr. Rickler?"

"Indeed, my Lord. Miss Drew, you have said that you considered Det. Chief

Inspector Bryan to have acted with grave impropriety in that he extracted from a witness what you had told that witness in professional confidence, and that he probably advised him to decline your instructions anyway. Do I put that fairly?"

"You do."

"I am obliged. I suggest, Miss Drew, that your view was wholly unjustified. Moreover—I suggest that if impropriety there was, it lay not on Mr. Bryan's part but on your own. And that suggestion it *is* my duty to make."

"Impropriety on *my* part?"

"On your part. Miss Drew—do you remember exactly what you wrote to Mr. Dickenson in your letter of instruction?"

"Not other than in general terms."

"Naturally. That is why I have the original here, so that you may refresh your memory. Indeed, I want you to look through it, to identify it as your original letter bearing your original signature at the bottom, and then I want you to read it out in full to the court. I could do so, but I think it would sound better coming from you—you may have the benefit of your own choice of inflection, for one thing. If

I read it out, you might feel that I stressed this word or that phrase unfairly. This is the letter which the usher will bring you to identify now."

It was among the papers in front of him —two pages stapled together. The usher stepped to Rickler's side, but below him in the well of the court, and took the document, crossing with it to the foot of the witness-box. There he held it up. Erica Drew reached over the ledge, her face a blank. She took the letter in complete silence. With every eye in the court upon her, she looked at it, noting the printed letter-heading, then her signature on the second page. Then she looked up and nodded.

"This is the letter I sent."

"Thank you, Miss Drew. And now will you please read it out to the court?"

"In full?"

"In full, Miss Drew. I do not want any later suggestions that anything was left out, save perhaps the printed firm heading and the date." There was a long pause. "We are waiting, Miss Drew."

"Very well. It is on the letter-headed notepaper of my firm in Loughton, and it reads as follows: 'Dear Sir, I am pleased to confirm my telephone conversation with you today. I am happy to accept the terms you quoted for your services. I should like you to accept my instructions as follows. I have been instructed by a Mr. Ian Willow, who is employed by the Port of London Authority as a Foreman at 'F' Shed, Royal Albert Dock. He is standing charged with being concerned in the theft of a large quantity of Scotch whisky in a container —one of the large kind that can be made to fit on to a long flat-bed lorry. The offence is alleged to have taken place on Thursday June 10th last. You may accept it from me that the necessary asportation took place, even though the intended removal of the whisky from the dock proved abortive. The full and sealed container had been delivered to 'F' Shed on Tuesday June 8th. It was for loading on to a ship at that Shed on the evening of the 10th. However, shortly before 2 p.m. on that day, an empty lorry arrived and the driver produced papers authorising its loading on to that lorry and its transfer at once to the West India Docks where it was for loading on to a different ship, bound for a different destination. It is a fact that these papers were forged, and very skilfully. They deceived my client, and also the policeman at 6 Gate. Being thus deceived, Mr. Willow, in good faith, supervised the loading of the container on to the lorry and authorised its departure, from 'F' Shed. In the event, the forgery came to light as the lorry was about to pass through the Gate and the lorry driver panicked and ran. He was immediately caught. Several men were arrested—in one case after a dramatic chase by policemen dressed as 'Hell's Angels'. There are at present six charged jointly. Committal (under s. 1, CJA, 1967) has taken place and I anticipate that a count of conspiracy will be added to the Indictment. So much for the background. It is suggested by the prosecution that the crime was organised by a well-known dockland gang who had previously engaged Mr. Willow as a secret operative. Mr. Willow was therefore interrogated at length by a Det. Chief Inspector George Bryan of the PLA Police. According to Mr. Bryan, whose evidence is corroborated by a colleague, Mr. Willow voluntarily surrendered for Mr. Bryan's inspection his personal diary. It is alleged that in this, Mr. Bryan discovered an entry of the name of one Harry Williams, now the first of the six defendants, followed by the alleged telephone number of Williams. My Client insists, and has insisted throughout, that he had no acquaintance with Williams before this case. It is obviously vital to my client that these suggestions should be eradicated from the prosecution's case. My client has never admitted the slightest guilt of this crime. He has a spotless criminal record. He has never before been interrogated. His state of mind may be imagined—he was in a state of unaccustomed high tension. I therefore wish you to assist me along the following lines. First, I wish you to try and secure evidence tending to show that after Mr. Willow had surrendered his diary as alleged, Mr. Bryan added the incriminating entry to a blank page, before returning the diary for inclusion among Mr. Willow's possessions. Secondly, I want you to investigate the line of defence that the diary was not Mr. Willow's at all, but that it was produced and having been prepared with the entry in advance it was 'planted' on my client so that it was included with the contents of his pockets. Thirdly (for I concede that to adduce admissible evidence of the second alternative would seem excessively difficult), other ideas come to mind. For example, I should like you to examine the possibility that Willow's genuine diary may have been switched by the police at some stage for that of somebody else—the diary of Burney, for instance, since it is clear that Burney knew Harry Williams and may have had a note of his phone number in his diary. Investigation of this line of defence would naturally involve an approach of some kind to Burney to find out if he had—or will say in court that he had—just such a small personal diary as Willow carried. It would also involve an approach to the PLA Police to examine the registered personal effects not only of Willow but of Burney—an operation which may take considerable skill and your earlier police experience. At best, it may be that there could be sworn to be two similar diaries, both fairly free of significant other entries. And it also occurs to me that while you are in contact with this little known

Force, you may be able to make a few enquiries in certain quarters as to whether in the past any allegations may have made in any cases against Mr. Bryan—or for that matter against any of his colleagues—of forging or planting evidence. Such allegations, even if not finally established, would give materially great credibility to the defence arguments in this case. I am in no way concerned with the exact nature of the evidence you obtain, nor of the methods used to obtain it, provided its effect is to clear Mr. Willow of this unjustified charge. Will you please attend to this matter with all speed and report to me as soon as your investigations are complete. I will happily arrange to see you if I can help. You should be ready to give evidence at the trial at the Old Bailey in due course. I look forward to hearing from you accordingly. Yours faithfully.' And it is signed by me."

She placed the letter on the ledge of the box before her and looked directly at Rickler. "If looks could kill...", he thought.

"That is what you wrote, Miss Drew."

"Dictated, yes it is."

"You stated the facts of the case clearly. You then instructed Mr. Dickenson to investigate the suggestion that the disputed entry was made in the diary of Mr. Bryan after he was handed it by Mr. Willow."

"I did."

"You then went on to instruct him to investigate an allegation that the diary was not Willow's at all but planted on him with the relevant entry already forged, and the diary's existence added to the record of possessions as if Willow had signed for it."

"I did."

"That second allegation never came from Mr. Willow at all, did it? It was 'dreamed up', if I may so put it, by you?"

"If you wish."

"Miss Drew—do you not consider yourself limited to investigate the accuracy of allegations made by your client?"

"I do not."

"Would you care to enlarge on that answer?"

"Sometimes one's client is the worst person to appraise what dirty tricks have been played on him by the police. An interrogation followed by an arrest can render the mind of a man with a clean record quite blank in several respects. The police always take advantage of this. Here, I considered that the second line of enquiry was at least as possible as the first one—the one suggested by Mr. Willow. It was certainly my idea, not his. But I was entitled to instruct Dickenson to follow it."

"Very well, Miss Drew. The jury will have noted your answer. The point, however interesting and revealing, is not really central to the case. Right or wrong though you may be, I accept the motives which governed your actions. But I can now turn to the last and most serious instruction to Mr. Dickenson. Read that paragraph again if you wish, and consider most carefully before you answer. Do you not agree that what you have written there cannot reasonably be interpreted as anything other than an instruction to provide you with evidence against the integrity of Mr. Bryan—*whether that evidence be true or false?*"

The silence as the court waited for her answer was almost tangible. Rickler had achieved emphasis as always without raising his voice—indeed, he had spoken the final phrase more quietly than the rest —by making a distinct pause, perfect in its length, before each single word of it. And now Erica Drew stood, her mind whirling, throwing up answer after answer, each more useless than the last. The question was unanswerable. It was checkmate.

Rickler knew it, too. He had planned it. He waited until the girl's head dropped forward. It was a visual concession. Not for the first time in his professional life, Oliver Rickler felt a right bastard. But he could not leave it there. She was in the box, after all, not in the dock. His target was withdrawal.

"Miss Drew—what I require is your agreement that your third instruction to Mr. Dickenson could only have been construed as meaning that you wanted evidence with which you could damage or destroy an honourable police officer in this court, whether that evidence was true or, if necessary, fabricated."

"That was not my intention."

"That was not my question!" Rickler's voice cut across her like a whip lash. It shook her visibly. "Assume if you wish that your motives were as pure as the driven snow. What I asked you, and what I will go on asking until you answer, is whether Mr. Dickenson could reasonably have understood anything other than that from your letter?"

From somewhere she drew defiance. She lifted her head and looked directly at Rickler across the court.

"I neither know nor care!"

"No. You never stopped to wonder, did you Miss Drew? You never paused to find out. You never hesitated at all. Well for a moment you are going to do so now. Here is a young ex-policeman, just started in business, no doubt anxious for all the custom he can get, receiving that letter. He has never fabricated evidence in his life, but he has doubtless seen it done—or knows how it can be done. And that part of your letter spoke to him of one thing only. It was an attempt by you to pervert the course of justice, don't you see?"

"It was nothing of the sort!"

"The point is immaterial. Must it not inevitably have appeared like that to Mr. Dickenson?"

Again she could not find an answer. Rickler paused and went on.

"Tell me, Miss Drew—just what do you think a reputable and honest young ex-policeman should do in such circumstances? Should he go bald-headed for a silly slip of a girl he's never even met? Or should he ring up his ex-colleagues at the Yard and report what he cannot but believe? He would have been entitled to do that. Perhaps he even had a duty to do that. But he does not. He rings up the chap in charge of the actual case down at the docks and he tells him what he's discovered. Consider, Miss Drew—if he did not do *at least* that, would he not be aiding and abetting this apparent attempt to pervert the course of justice? Was it not his absolute duty in law to do *at least* what he did when he read your letter?"

"But I was *not* attempting to pervert the course of justice!"

"Let us accept that. Let us credit—or debit—you with no more than a total lack of experience of criminal cases and a mental approach to the subject which smacks more of Perry Mason than of the Central Criminal Court. Do you not see that in the light of your letter Mr. Dickenson did the kindest, the mildest thing consistent with his duty as a citizen?"

"I do see that now."

"Good! Then we can advance a step further. When you came to the docks and saw Mr. Bryan, he knew from Mr. Dickenson that it *looked* as if you were trying to pervert the course of justice, although that was not in fact your intention. And what did Mr. Bryan do? Less, you may concede, than it was his duty to do. Very tactfully, he let you know that he was aware of what you had told Dickenson to do. You thought he slipped up. It has never occurred to you, I suppose, that his 'mistake' was a deliberate one? Instead of interrogating you as he could, and perhaps should, have done, do you not see that he chose instead to treat you as a kid out of her depth? Although you'd tried to ruin him, he chose to warn you off taking such a stupid course. Don't you see that now?"

"Yes."

"Excellent! One step more. When Mr. Dickenson telephoned Mr. Bryan about the matter, was it not wholly reasonable that he should ask this Chief Inspector—

a man of far greater experience than himself—whether he could properly decline your instructions *without explanation?* And was Mr. Bryan not correct to tell him that he could?"

"I see that now, yes."

"Miss Drew, I am really pleased to hear you say so. Because it was, like your name and professional status, something that you had never really considered. You did not realise that you were inducing in others by your words and actions conclusions that were wrong. I am glad because if you see that now, then it is unlikely to happen again. You see?"

She nodded without speaking. Rickler was speaking very quietly now, but with great intensity.

"Miss Drew—at this moment there stand on the record of this trial several allegations made by you, through Mr. Crane your counsel, as well as others which you have made yourself in the box, against Mr. Bryan and Mr. Dickenson. I have now to ask you if we may consider those allegations wholly and unreservedly withdrawn?"

Slowly her head lifted. Looking up at

her, Stratton expected to see tears in her eyes but there was no trace of any. From Rickler, she switched her regard to the judge.

"My Lord, I wish to withdraw unreservedly the allegations which I made in all innocence against Detective Chief Inspector Bryan and against Mr. Dickenson. I apologise to both of them. I also apologise to your Lordship and to this court for making the mistakes to which Mr. Rickler has drawn my attention."

The judge made a note. Then he spoke directly to her.

"I think we may all judge how you feel, Miss Drew. It is never easy to admit to having made a serious mistake, particularly in public. What you say has been officially noted. Your apology is accepted. You may now withdraw from the witness box and, if you wish, from this court. Mr. Crane will now be calling Mr. Willow to complete his evidence. But first, I propose to adjourn for a quarter of an hour. I think we can all do with a short pause."

28

THE coda of the English criminal trial is played in a curious temporal limbo—taking longer than those unfamiliar with it might expect, yet containing less sensation. Naturally the tremendous build-up of tension which reaches its climax with the return of the jury and is released by the verdict is almost bound to have an anti-climactic effect for all save those convicted, for whom it is released only by the sentence. For everyone else, it is a strange kind of no-man's-time.

For the acquitted, there is of course no coda at all. It had been Teddy Lane's fortune to be the last of the six to hear his fate. They had all told him he would be acquitted, but he knew that one can never be certain of anything with a jury, and as the stream of verdicts seeped closer and closer to his feet, it had not been easy for him.

"Williams?" "Guilty." "Burney?"

"Guilty." "Delafield?" "Guilty." "Rogers?" "Guilty." "Willow?" "Guilty." And then at last—

"Finally, Mr. Foreman, the case against Edward Lane. How say you—guilty or not guilty?"

For Teddy, time stopped and an eternity passed.

"*Not* guilty."

He did not even hear the Clerk's "Are those the verdicts of you all?", nor the Foreman's assent. He stood trembling violently in the corner of the dock while the Clerk passed a document up to the judge and everybody waited. At last the judge looked at him.

"Mr. Lane—by a verdict with which I entirely agree, the jury have acquitted you. You are discharged forthwith."

There was a tap on his shoulder. He turned. Just behind his left hip, the little door in the side wall of the dock was being held open by a smiling warder. He scuttled through it like a frightened rabbit—down the steps, through the swing doors and out into the dark lobby, into the marble hall beyond, down the stairs and away, hardly able to breathe with relief and mounting excitement and a stab of fear that it might not be true after all. It was 2.30 p.m. on Thursday.

Back in court, the five men sat twitching—anxious now only to know the worst. But much was to be done first. David Gunn rose from beside Stratton and crossed to the witness-box, a bundle of files under his arm. Smoothly he took the special form of oath. Then from the top file he took a sheaf of papers and began distributing them through the usher—top copy for the judge, carbons to the shorthand-writer, clerk and so forth. The lawyers had all been given their copies during the jury's absence and questions and answers asked and given informally. Thus, as Gunn set out on a potted biography of "Henry John Williams, 46 years of age, having been born in Stepney, London, on . . .", every word had been previously rehearsed. It was unhurried and, whether or not it was calculated to take the heat out of the situation, it did nothing else. Sentence was not the concern of the prosecution, nor the police. As Stratton repeatedly said—guilt was a heavy enough burden to bear—guilt or innocence.

Next followed the speeches in mitigation, starting with Peter Dennis for Williams, and ending with Crane, while Gunn resumed his seat beside Stratton. They were short. If a man pleads guilty, his counsel may let himself go with as much passion and as little accuracy as he likes, for a speech in mitigation cannot be challenged. But it is not easy to express remorse for doing something which, until minutes previously, he had strenuously denied doing at all.

At last the judge shuffled his papers and said a soft "Right!" to the clerk, who rose and recited the *allocutus*—that final oddity in the collection of curious conventions, which runs, "Have you anything to say why sentence should not be passed upon you?" If there had been anything worth saying, it had just been said by the barrister. Nothing the prisoner might add could affect the sentence which the judge had determined at the end of each mitigation speech. The pantomime closed with successive head-shakes from the five in the dock. Happily, Sir James Dover was not the man to make a meal out of the situation. What needed saying, he would say succinctly.

"Henry John Williams—with your record, you will not expect me to waste words on you. This was a cunningly organised crime which might have succeeded but for exceptional police skill and initiative. You were the planner-in-chief and the leader on the ground. You will go to prison for five years."

The warder touched Williams, who had expected no less. He turned without expression and disappeared down the stone steps to where, at the barred gate half way down, the cell warder awaited him.

"Paul Burney, you also are a professional criminal and a skilled operator. You knew just what you were doing and the stakes involved. The criminal world will be deprived of your specialised services for three years, which is the prison sentence I impose."

Burney was wheeled away. "Lucky" Delafield braced his pathetic frame and even gave the judge the semblance of a smile.

"Delafield—you are not only a failure in

life, you are a failure even as a criminal. As such, you attract a degree of sympathy which must, however, be rejected, for it is too easy to smile at the sight of an alibi blowing up in a liar's face. The trouble is that your sort always think that if a man is guilty he is permitted by the rules of the game to lie with impunity. We must try and eradicate this cardinal error. Your part in this operation was small, but your record is long, and I take your calculated perjury about the alibi into consideration. Two years' imprisonment."

The judge turned to Rogers as Lucky was wheeled away in his turn. "Terence Rogers—although you were in this carefully planned operation from the start, so that your panic was by no means as inexplicable as you claimed, your role was less than some of those involved. Despite your previous record I am persuaded that six months' imprisonment will on this occasion suffice for you."

With a nod of what might have been thanks, the lorry driver turned and disappeared below. Willow, now alone in the middle of the dock except for the two large warders behind him, seemed to diminish in size as the attention of everyone in court focused on him. The judge took a deep breath.

"Ian Willow—it has troubled me greatly what is the proper punishment for you. In a sense, you were the worst of all those in the dock, for you were a traitor to your employers and your colleagues. On the other hand, you have never been in trouble before criminally, and, as a greater judge than I once said, 'around you stand as silent witnesses each of the honest years of your life'. There is one thing I should perhaps make clear. I have had occasion to call into serious question some of the tactics involved in your defence. I have most scrupulously put all that aside in considering your sentence. Indeed, had they influenced me at all, they would have told in your favour rather than otherwise. I have considered whether I might even reconcile some non-custodial sentence with my duty. I am however afraid that although this was your first offence, the key part you played in this elaborate and cunning crime was of too great an importance to allow me to permit you your liberty. You will go to prison for twelve months."

For a moment, the big man's eyes closed and he swayed on his feet. Then, his face as blank as if it were carved of stone, he gave a suggestion of a bow before turning and walking to the steps. When he had disappeared from sight, the judge turned with a warm smile to the jury.

"Members of the jury, this has been a tiresome and difficult case. You are owed the thanks of your fellow citizens and of this court for the sustained attention you have shown and the unflinching way in which you did your duty. In token of that gratitude, I propose to recommend that each of you should be excused from further jury service for five years.

"Before I conclude, there are a few related matters with which I must deal. First, I convey my personal congratulations to the Port of London Authority in respect of their police force. Its efficiency could not have been bettered. In particular I publicly thank Det. Chief Inspector Bryan, who had to surmount not only the usual obstacles but serious and irresponsible attacks upon his personal integrity.

His conduct throughout has been admirable, the very essence of propriety and dignity. I would also like to commend the skill and initiative of PC Wilson, the motor-cycle officer who chased and caught the Jaguar car, and PC Jenkins, whose flying tackle of Rogers made me regret that the case was not being tried by my learned brother across the hall, Sir Carl Aarvold, the Recorder of London, who was once the greatest rugby three-quarter of his age and whose face, when I related the incident to him, was a study in evocation!

"Then with reluctance I have to add that, as I said during the case, it is my sad duty to have to send the papers with a report to the General Council of the Bar for them to consider the professional conduct of Mr. Crane, whom we had earlier all been so pleased to see returning to what I might call 'pastures old'. I make no further comment on this now, and wish strongly that I did not view what I must do as my bounden duty."

For a moment, he paused and looked down on the bowed head of the girl at the table in the well of the court.

"Finally, there is the question of Miss

Drew. After long and very painful reflection, I think it is necessary for certain aspects of this case to be drawn to the attention of the Law Society. I regret this extremely. But the standards of the legal profession must be maintained, or our whole judicial system will dissolve. What steps the Law Society take to ensure that this young lady will not be admitted as a solicitor unless they are sure that she is indeed a fit and proper person to be so admitted, is a matter entirely for them. I take this step in the hope that she will long abide by the brave public recognition of her earlier mistaken attitude in the witness-box, which made yesterday morning memorably sad for many of us. I do what I have to do in hope—hope for her professional future.

"I propose now to retire for twenty minutes."

29

SO the trial was over. Busy supervising the gathering up of the legal papers and documents, Stratton could not understand his curious feeling that all was not well.

As fast as PLA were clearing up, the prosecuting staff from Guildhall were setting their papers out ready for the start of a big fraud case which was expected to last ten days or more. He and Evan exchanged pleasantries with their City counterparts who were in the same state of pre-trial tension that they had suffered themselves, a little over a week before. He expected to feel tired—that was the normal release of the final tensions of the trial. But it should have been a satisfied tiredness, without this uneasy feeling that something, somewhere, was not well—that something ominous was casting its shadow before it.

David Gunn was equally busy arranging the collection by a police team of their files, reports, statements and so forth—stacking them into boxes and shifting the boxes out to the large police van waiting outside in Old Bailey. He seemed cheerful enough. Stratton looked at Evan and was interested to see a response to his private concern.

"Is that toe of yours twitching?" he asked quietly.

Evan's look was sharp. "Funnily enough, it is."

"So's mine—or so to speak," said Stratton. "Can't think why. Ought not to be. But if yours is, perhaps it's infectious!"

"We'll know soon enough," said Evan without any of his usual twinkle. "I'm worried—and I haven't a clue why."

He turned away to pick up the extra brief-case he always brought to the last day of a trial, to accommodate those papers which seemed to materialise during it. Stratton turned to Gunn.

"Everything all right your end, David?"

"Fine. Fine. By the time we've got rid of this lot, they'll be open, over at the 'Magpie'. We'll have a celebratory pint, eh?"

"Sure," said Stratton, feeling out on some ominous limb of his own. And at that moment, Evan saw or heard something. Stratton didn't quite see it and couldn't hear it, but he saw that Evan had turned to the side of the dock with a look on his face that showed dread.

Turning, Stratton saw the figure of Michael Black, the ex-PLA copper now on Harry Wager's squad of red-collar men. But Black's face, instead of being cheery and welcoming, particularly towards Gunn, whose personal team he had been on happily for some time, was looking concerned—even apprehensive.

"Hello Mike," said Stratton. "Good to see you. Evan mentioned you were around."

"Hello Mr. Stratton. Excuse me a minute, sir—there's a message for Mr. Gunn."

Gunn heard him and swung round. "Yes? Hello, Black—nice to see you. What is it?"

"This, guvnor," said Black, handing him a piece of folded paper. "I was there when it came, a few minutes ago. I knew I could find you."

Gunn took the note and opened it. For a second, he closed his eyes. Softly, under his breath, he murmured, "Jesus Christ!" Then he turned to Bryan. "Where's my car, George?"

"Just across the road, sir," said Bryan, catching the seriousness in his chief's tone.

"Right. I'll leave all this to you." He grabbed Stratton by the arm. "Come on, Charles. Tell you as we go!" He was already moving towards the court doors. Stratton had time only to catch Evan's eye as he went. Evan nodded, with no trace of a smile.

"Leave everything to me. See you back at the office."

Outside the court, David Gunn was half running along the hall. Down the main staircase they hurried—across the foyer below—out through the main doors, down the steps, across the pavement. Over the road they could see Gunn's black Ford. The police driver saw him coming and went to get out. Gunn waved him back in and snatched the rear door open.

"London Hospital—and quick! Come on!"

Stratton just managed to slam the door

shut behind him as the car moved off, just catching the traffic light ahead while it was still green and swinging right along Newgate Street. Once they were under way, Gunn turned for the first time to face Stratton.

"Sorry, Charles. Here—read that."

He thrust the note across. Stratton took it and read: "UNIDENTIFIED VICTIM OF MOTORING ACCIDENT ADMITTED LAST NIGHT WITH MULTIPLE INJURIES. LOCAL PC HAS VISITED. REPORTS MIGHT BE PLA MAN AND WILL STAY. SUGGEST YOU COME GREATEST URGENCY—CASUALTY DEPT, LONDON HOSPITAL. MP 'H'."

Stratton felt his stomach turn over. He looked at Gunn, who nodded.

"Yes, Charles. It could be Jack."

"I thought he was somewhere far off."

"He was. But he had several reasons for coming back. Don't know what. Told me he might. But he would take care of himself. It means they got on to him."

"How could they?"

"For the moment I can't move my brain

further than to find out if it is him. Time enough to answer those questions later."

"Fair enough. This bloke in hospital may not even be him. 'Motor accident' could mean someone driving, hitting a wall, for all we know."

"I know. But when H Division of the Met sent a man round, whether the victim was conscious or what I don't know, he reported back *something* that caused Leman Street to ring our HQ and tell us to get there fast."

"I know. I'm just trying not to lose hope."

"Of course. I'll tell you this. If it is Jack —and I feel in my bones it is—then whether he's alive or dead, I will not bloody rest until I find out how they got on to him!"

There was nothing Stratton could say to that. Miserably he sat back in his seat as their driver took another traffic light at amber and swerved to avoid a van.

From his seat on a wooden bench in the main front hall of Stepney's old and solid, if scruffy, London Hospital, Stratton could see the long corridor along which David

Gunn had hurried away with the young Met. constable in uniform who had been awaiting their arrival. He had felt it better to remain in support—available but not in the way. Again and again he tried not to think on the assumption—well, surely the probability—that the accident victim was the tall, thin, quiet man who had sat and sipped his lager so cheerfully in the Barbican flat, the night the gen came through. Giving it up finally, he reconciled himself to considering other probabilities, nearly as unpleasant. Assuming the casualty was Jack Denny, it was obvious that the Berry Gang had found out that someone had infiltrated their ranks. They would know at once that it was the tall, thin man—everyone else would have been well known to them. His sudden indisposition just before the container job would have been the confirmation they needed. But confirmation of *what?* It was more than someone letting them down. Someone had spoken to them at top level and said, in effect, "That bloke's a PLA copper." The rest followed. Then who told them?

It stood out a mile. Only a handful of people knew that Jack's identity had been openly stated in front of the judge in private. Only one of those few did not regard herself bound by the code of professional ethics. No barrister or solicitor could be thought for a moment as likely to effect such a total and deadly betrayal.

As these thoughts sank in, Stratton saw the swing doors open and David Gunn and the young PC emerged into the hall. He stood up as they approached him.

"Charles—this is PC Rowlands, of 'H' Division. Mr. Stratton is our solicitor."

Stratton and the young man exchanged nods.

"David—was it—?"

"Jack Denny—yes. He died just about the moment we arrived. He's in the mortuary now. I've made the formal identification. He never had a chance. The injuries were terrible. No doubt they had his digs staked out. Followed him. Caught him full on and smashed him against a wall. No hope of finding the car. No witnesses, but it's got the trademark of the Berry gang all over it. Christ, how that man must have suffered! But we'll discuss it all later. Not a hope in hell of pinning them of course."

"Naturally. What now, David?"

"Bit of clearing up, here. Rowlands and I will see to it all. Young lady doctor—very understanding. Her father was in our mob, a long time ago. I think I knew him. No—my car will run you back to Trap One and then come back and wait for me here. We'll be in touch. OK?"

"Sure. Thanks. Give me a ring whenever you've got time to talk at length and we'll arrange it. Nothing I can do at all to help, meanwhile?"

"Nothing at all, thanks. 'Bye now, Charles."

30

STRATTON was late.

The police car which brought them had got tangled up in a series of jams caused initially, it seemed, by a burst water main in Streatham. The driver had been as ingenious in his use of the "back doubles" as any expert could be, but London's arteries seemed to be as thrombose as he had ever known them, and it was twenty-three minutes to twelve when he and Evan came up the steps from Chancery Lane into the entrance hall of the Law Society.

Realising that the last thing he wanted to begin with was an apology, he had hoped that she might herself not be punctual for their 11.30 appointment. But there she was, sitting outside the Reading Room door, as smart and trim as ever, in the same black costume she had worn in the witness-box. As he crossed the hall to her, she could not resist a glance at her tiny wrist watch and a half smile which showed awareness of her advantage.

"Miss Drew, I am sorry I'm late. We've had a most difficult journey by car from Streatham—it really seemed to be one traffic jam after another. Never mind—we shall still have at least twenty minutes for our discussion."

He glanced over his shoulder at Evan who had been having a word with the Head Porter in his cubicle just inside the main door. "What's fixed, Evan?"

"Committee Room C. Up by the Council Chamber as you know. It's not in use at the moment. I've sent a message to the Secretary General that you're in the building but may be a wee bit late for your noon appointment. He seems to be in no difficulty."

"Good. Right—up in the lift, then. Miss Drew?"

She rose and walked beside him to the lift in the corner. He ushered her into it and followed. Evan came behind them and pressed the button. They rose in silence. At the second floor they walked up the steps to the right and into the Committee Room. He took off his black overcoat and put it with his bowler and brief-case on the chairs on his left, then led the way to the far end of the long table. He took the principal chair and she one with her back to the windows, next but one from his. Evan stayed at the end of the table nearest the door, his brief-case on the table in front of him. Stratton realised that up to this moment not one word had left her lips. But now she spoke first.

"You sent for me, Mr. Stratton."

"I did nothing of the sort, Miss Drew. That is another instance of your slightly altering the facts so as to give you some advantage. For the record—"

"Record? Don't tell me this room is 'bugged'!"

"A mere figure of speech. In order that we can avoid any misunderstanding, let me say that having received the papers and a report from Sir James Dover, the Secretary General has asked me to see him at noon, in order to amplify certain points. I told him I felt you should also be given an opportunity to attend with me so that you could make any reply or point you might wish, and hear from him what he has it in mind to do."

"I see. And is your Sancho Panza to be in on the act as usual?"

He glanced down the table at Evan whose profile might have been of stone.

"That was hardly worthy of you, Miss Drew. Mr. Baunton is here as my assistant mainly because you have proved yourself so gifted a manipulator of facts that I felt it would be stupid of me to occupy a room alone in your company."

"Aha! He's your chaperone! Well, bless my soul! I don't know whether to be insulted, amused or flattered! Are you really afraid that I will whip off my jacket, rip my blouse and scream 'Rape!'?"

"I will treat that remark with the contempt it deserves. To answer your earlier question, Mr. Baunton will not be accompanying me, or both of us, to see the Secretary General. Whether you choose to come or not is a matter of complete indifference to me. It is important only that you should have the opportunity."

"Well you wouldn't have arranged this chat half an hour before your appointment unless you had several things to say or to ask me. So for the moment I propose to reserve my decision whether or not to go and see the Secretary General with you."

"As you wish. Certainly there are things which have come to light since we last met which I think you ought to know."

"Such as?"

"Such as the fact that Mr. Baunton and I have arrived here today directly from Streatham, where we have been attending the funeral of a valued friend and colleague, Det. Sgt. Jack Denny. You needn't pretend you don't know who he is, since it is you who were responsible for his death."

The pencilled eyebrows rose.

"Perhaps it's as well this room isn't bugged! You wouldn't dare say that when there was anyone of consequence here other than me. Even a humble law student knows enough about the basic principles of defamation to be aware of that. But with your in-built circumlocution it really does surprise me. It's a new experience, too. I have never before been accused of murder to my face, even in private. In what way do you hold me 'personally responsible' for the death of a man whom I have never met killed in a hit-and-run accident in Stepney?"

"Jack Denny was not the victim of an accident, Miss Drew. He was the victim of murder by motor car."

"I do not even drive!"

"I do not suggest that you were at the wheel. If a charge were laid against you, it would not be that of murder but of conspiracy to murder."

"Oho—climbing down now, are we?"

"By no means. It was you who mentioned murder. I said only that you were personally responsible for Mr. Denny's death."

"Of course. I should have allowed for your passion for semantics. Forgive me. Then perhaps you will tell me in ordinary language exactly what it is that I am supposed to have done."

"Jack Denny was 'executed' by the Berry gang. They knew that he had to come back to London some time. No doubt they put a stake-out on his room in Stepney. He was killed because they had found out he was a policeman who had infiltrated the gang at its highest level. He had given his colleagues advance details not only about the container theft but of other jobs they were planning, not to mention other things they had done. They knew that something had gone seriously wrong when the whisky theft blew up in their faces. The traitor could only have been the tall, thin man who had been rushed to hospital just before the job was pulled. They didn't know exactly who and what he was, of course. Not at first. Jack Denny had taken every step over the last year to conceal his true identity. The degree to which he succeeded showed the measure of his success. Only a tiny handful of people knew the facts, Miss Drew."

"A handful that did not include me."

"Correct. But immediately before the trial of the gang started, there was a private meeting in the judge's room with all the counsel who were involved in the case."

"Plus yourself, I presume."

"Then you presume wrongly. That meeting was restricted solely to the members of the bar. Such occasions are infrequent but they can be arranged through 'the usual channels' in special circumstances. At that meeting, prosecuting counsel, under the seal of professional confidence, revealed that at the centre of the case was a police officer working under cover, who had infiltrated the gang. His identity and personal details were then disclosed. The direct effect of this meeting was that none of the counsel involved would seek to go behind the common phrase 'acting on information received' in open court."

"A neat professional carve-up, in other words!"

"Nothing of the sort. Merely the calling into operation of a professional code of honour, in order to protect someone who would otherwise be placed in considerable personal danger. As I said, the meeting was restricted solely to the bar. But in order to preclude any unintentional thrashing about by their instructing solicitors, each barrister is, by this same code, permitted to tell his instructing solicitor in person. If any is absent and represented in court by a clerk, then that clerk is not informed. Below the level of the qualified solicitor who is subject to his own professional code, there is no communication at all. So, when Mr. Rickler got up to open the case, each of the barristers knew the identity of Jack Denny and what he had achieved. And so did all the qualified instructing solicitors."

"I see. Which seems, Mr. Stratton, to let me clean out since, as your counsel very publicly stressed in open court, I am not a qualified solicitor."

"You are not, Miss Drew. But you treated yourself as one, and you were treated as one by everyone concerned in this case, until the truth emerged in court. It follows that you would have been informed by Mr. Crane about the meeting in the judge's room, under the seal of a professional confidence to which you alone were not subject."

"A convenient deduction, Mr. Stratton —exploiting the fact that you have already got poor Everett Crane on the run. For all the principles of fair play that you so pompously extol, you are not, evidently, above kicking a man when he's down!"

"Again you are quite wrong, Miss Drew."

"Am I really? Then ask yourself—why should it be me who blabbed to the Berry gang? Why could it not have been one of the other defence solicitors? Norden? Dickie Horton? They're the two who get the primary defence instructions in the gang's cases, as we both know. They've got far more direct contact with Berry in person than I have. But why shouldn't it be Elkins? Or Everett? Or your boozing companion Tomlinson? Of course you pick on me because you're out to get me—but you haven't any evidence. You couldn't prove that Crane let me in on the little secret."

"Wrong again, Miss Drew. I said earlier that there were certain facts you should be told before noon. One is that the day before yesterday, Mr. Crane went to see Sir James Dover. He had just learned of the death of Sgt. Denny. He told the judge that he had treated you as a qualified solicitor and had told you before the case began what had gone on at the meeting in the judge's room. He added that he was taking immediate steps to disbar himself professionally."

There was a long pause while she took this in. Then she looked him straight in the eye.

"And there it is, all cut and dried, you think? Well, I would remind you that there is such a thing as the admissibility of evidence, Mr. Stratton. You said earlier that you held me personally responsible for your chum's death. Well you couldn't even begin to prove anything against me and you know it!"

"You are right. I know it. If I could, you would not now be sitting in a Committee Room in the Law Society. You would be sitting in a cell, on remand. And any application you made for bail would be most vigorously opposed."

"I bet it would! By the way—would I find the hapless Crane in the cell with me as co-defendant? Or would he be expected to turn Queen's evidence and be principal witness for the prosecution?"

"Miss Drew, I've got more important things to do with my time than answer stupid hypothetical questions from you. But I would suggest that Mr. Crane, of whom you have taken such unscrupulous advantage—"

"Advantage? Me—taking advantage of that has-been? Are you serious? What do you imagine I've been doing to him—or with him—or for him? A little bit on the side, perhaps? You know, you've got a dirty mind, Charles Stratton, for all your vaunted purity!"

"I was thinking nothing of the sort. I had your special relationship in mind."

It brought her up sharply. For a long moment she stared with lowered brows at Stratton. Concentrated venom at length is not easy to withstand. Fortunately, neither is it easy to maintain—at least unsupported by words.

"Just exactly what do you mean by that?"

"Miss Drew—you really must learn not to under-estimate your opponents. Do you imagine that I have not taken the trouble to find out all about you? Don't you realise that I instructed Oliver Rickler to use in court only those bits about you which would ensure your withdrawal of the scurrilous allegations you'd made against George Bryan and young Dickenson? Did you think that was all we had managed to find out about you? *Did* you?"

"You're bluffing. What do you know about me?"

"Most things. I know, for instance, that

your mother was the daughter of a civil servant who lived in Ealing. I know that during the War she met an Infantry Lieutenant named Eric Drury, whom she married in October, 1943. I know that he, your father, was one of the first men on to the Normandy beaches on D Day, where he was killed within five minutes—a man of rare initiative and courage, as the citation of his posthumous Military Cross makes clear.

"I know that the news of his death had a dreadful effect on your mother, who was seven months pregnant, causing you to be born somewhat prematurely. I know that shortly after she had recovered, when you were out with her in your pram, a flying bomb destroyed the house and both your grandparents in it. I know that the shock of this, following on that of her widowhood and your birth, had a fatal effect on your mother.

"Fortunately your uncle, her only brother, who had been unfit for military service owing to a childhood accident which had left him with a limp, had by now become a successful barrister. He was happily married to a woman solicitor who was a partner in a commercial firm in the City. They brought you up as the child they never had themselves. You were naturally devoted to your aunt Judith, and one can easily understand the shock it was for you when she was accused of fraud in connection with a case with which she was professionally concerned. Whether out of guilt or not—probably not—she took a fatal overdose. Her name, as I need not remind you, was Crane. Before her marriage to your Uncle Everett, she was Judith Poulter."

He paused. She was staring at him blankly, incapable of speech. She looked as if she was not hearing what he was saying. Seeing no alternative, he continued.

"Tragically, your uncle took to alcohol for relief. You tried to look after him but in a year or two he had become a pathetic shadow of his former self—his practice virtually gone. Meanwhile, Judith Crane had a brother, a respectable, quiet conveyancing solicitor in Loughton. Sympathetically, he gave you your articles. No doubt it was your attempt to wean your uncle off the bottle and back to his former glory that drew you to the field of criminal law. The chance that a clerk in your office was related to Ian Willow gave you what looked like a splendid chance. You have never been slow to spot and to take your opportunities, Miss Drew. Unfortunately you made a series of grave errors of judgment in your handling of Willow's case —most of them due simply to lack of experience. Equally unfortunately, Everett Crane, who naturally felt he owed you a return for your efforts, did not have the strength of personality that he would once have used to over-rule you. About the case itself there is really no more to be said."

"You insufferable bastard!"

"When I first realised that the Secretary General would obviously ask me to supplement Sir James Dover's report about you, I made up my mind to suggest strongly that in the light of your background and personal history, a 'cooling off' period would probably suffice—an enforced delay in your being admitted as a solicitor for perhaps a year or two. But that was before Jack Denny was murdered —or shall we say executed, Miss Drew?— by those whose professional custom you are clearly angling for and who now owe you a return for the valuable information you gave them."

"And I'll get it! You haven't smashed the Berry gang, you know. They'll take a breather, but they'll be back in action one of these fine days. And next time their solicitor won't be Brooks of Stepney, and it won't be Dickie Horton. It will be Erica Drew, Mr. Stratton!"

"Wrong again, Miss Drew. Because whatever Sir James Dover has suggested in his report to the Secretary General, I am going to use every scrap of professional influence I have to make absolutely sure that Erica Drew will *never* be admitted as a solicitor. Not ever! It will be made clear to those concerned with such decisions that you have proved yourself totally incapable of that elementary standard of integrity that professional status demands."

At last something stung her savagely. Her expression changed to one of personal venom.

"Is that so?" she snarled. "Well, let me tell you a few things, Charles Stratton. You are a pompous prig. Sooner or later it may dawn on you and your type who are so keen to shut out anyone who may threaten to break down the protective walls you have erected that if you establish a system, you cannot then condemn those who conform to it strictly. Your predecessors could have made the criminal trial an enquiry into truth. They didn't. They chose to set up a contest—a contest which it is not merely the right but the duty of the defence to win without breaking so many of the rules that they get disqualified. Not to fight fairly—that's the prosecution's duty. My concern is to win. Not for myself, either—for my clients—and whether I believe them or not. It may be a rotten system—I don't care. It's the one your chaps set up. You want a contest. Right—then it's my job to lick the pants off you every single time I'm involved."

Stratton looked at her. The trouble was that, to a great extent, she was right. He knew it—and she knew that he knew it. He breathed in very slowly and deeply and spoke quietly and firmly.

"You have forgotten one factor, Miss Drew—one that throws your argument off balance and overturns your specious logic.

That factor is the code of ethics which governs all members of our profession—which is why it is a true profession. It over-rides all other considerations. It doesn't apply to your clients, but it does apply to every lawyer. That code is sacred. Without it, you are not only wrong—you are unfit to practise the law—to be a servant of justice."

Her lip curled. "Justice!" she spat.

"Yes, Miss Drew—justice. Our system is not the best that could be devised, I will grant you. But for better or for worse, it is the one that applies here in England, and it is the legal profession's function and its absolute duty to operate it. So, if justice is to stand any chance at all, let alone if it is to be properly served, professional standards must be maintained. There is no place in our profession for those who are not prepared to abide by its code of ethics. No place for you, Miss Drew. None at all. Not ever."

She was silent. It was as if a curtain had come down between herself and the world—herself and him, at any rate. He shrugged and looked at his watch.

"It is almost noon, Miss Drew. The

invitation to you to attend the Secretary General in his office downstairs remains open. Whether or not you wish to accept it is a matter entirely for you. As far as I am concerned, this meeting is at an end."

He turned his back on her and walked down the side of the long table to where Evan had now risen. Habit was too much for him. His eyebrows must have gone up minimally as he approached, for Evan's minimal wink was a response. He put his overcoat over his arm, picked up his briefcase and turned, to find that she had also moved down the room on the other side of the table and was now standing, silent, at the door, waiting for Evan to open it.

Along the corridor, they had to wait for the lift. None of them exchanged a glance, let alone a word. When it came, she stepped inside it ahead of them. They descended, still without looking at each other. It stopped with a slight bump and its door whooshed open. She stepped out.

"Well, Miss Drew?" he said.

She turned her back on him and took **three firm steps towards the main** entrance, then stopped. Over her shoulder, rather than directly to him, she spoke.

"This is not the last you will see of me, Mr. Stratton."

She snapped her head forward again and strode past the porter and out through the swing doors.

As he and Evan walked the other way, past the foot of the main staircase and up towards the corridor that leads to the Secretary General's suite of offices, Evan spoke quietly but clearly.

"I'll give her Sancho bloody Panza!"

Stratton smiled. "You've been called worse in your time."

In the pause that followed, Stratton did not have to look at the little man. He could feel the effect of that grin.

"You realise," said Mr. Baunton, "that it makes you Don Quixote?"

"Oh, every man has his particular windmills. But I am scarcely a knight. And certainly not a doleful one, I hope!"

"No. Not that, at any rate."

They reached the door of the suite.

"I don't know how long I'll be. Will you wait in the bar?"

"Probably. I'll be around, anyway—you can rely on that."

"I do, Evan. I always do," said Charles Stratton as he pushed the door open.

THE END

We hope this Large Print edition gives you the pleasure and enjoyment we ourselves experienced in its publication.

There are now more than 2,000 titles available in this ULVERSCROFT Large print Series. Ask to see a Selection at your nearest library.

The Publisher will be delighted to send you, free of charge, upon request a complete and up-to-date list of all titles available.

Ulverscroft Large Print Books Ltd.
The Green, Bradgate Road
Anstey
Leicestershire
LE7 7FU
England

GUIDE TO THE COLOUR CODING OF ULVERSCROFT BOOKS

Many of our readers have written to us expressing their appreciation for the way in which our colour coding has assisted them in selecting the Ulverscroft books of their choice. To remind everyone of our colour coding—this is as follows:

BLACK COVERS
Mysteries

★

BLUE COVERS
Romances

★

RED COVERS
Adventure Suspense and General Fiction

★

ORANGE COVERS
Westerns

★

GREEN COVERS
Non-Fiction

MYSTERY TITLES
in the
Ulverscroft Large Print Series

Henrietta Who?	*Catherine Aird*
Slight Mourning	*Catherine Aird*
The China Governess	*Margery Allingham*
Coroner's Pidgin	*Margery Allingham*
Crime at Black Dudley	*Margery Allingham*
Look to the Lady	*Margery Allingham*
More Work for the Undertaker	*Margery Allingham*
Death in the Channel	*J. R. L. Anderson*
Death in the City	*J. R. L. Anderson*
Death on the Rocks	*J. R. L. Anderson*
A Sprig of Sea Lavender	*J. R. L. Anderson*
Death of a Poison-Tongue	*Josephine Bell*
Murder Adrift	*George Bellairs*
Strangers Among the Dead	*George Bellairs*
The Case of the Abominable Snowman	*Nicholas Blake*
The Widow's Cruise	*Nicholas Blake*
The Brides of Friedberg	*Gwendoline Butler*
Murder By Proxy	*Harry Carmichael*
Post Mortem	*Harry Carmichael*
Suicide Clause	*Harry Carmichael*
After the Funeral	*Agatha Christie*
The Body in the Library	*Agatha Christie*

A Caribbean Mystery	*Agatha Christie*
Curtain	*Agatha Christie*
The Hound of Death	*Agatha Christie*
The Labours of Hercules	*Agatha Christie*
Murder on the Orient Express	*Agatha Christie*
The Mystery of the Blue Train	*Agatha Christie*
Parker Pyne Investigates	*Agatha Christie*
Peril at End House	*Agatha Christie*
Sleeping Murder	*Agatha Christie*
Sparkling Cyanide	*Agatha Christie*
They Came to Baghdad	*Agatha Christie*
Third Girl	*Agatha Christie*
The Thirteen Problems	*Agatha Christie*
The Black Spiders	*John Creasey*
Death in the Trees	*John Creasey*
The Mark of the Crescent	*John Creasey*
Quarrel with Murder	*John Creasey*
Two for Inspector West	*John Creasey*
His Last Bow	*Sir Arthur Conan Doyle*
The Valley of Fear	*Sir Arthur Conan Doyle*
Dead to the World	*Francis Durbridge*
My Wife Melissa	*Francis Durbridge*
Alive and Dead	*Elizabeth Ferrars*
Breath of Suspicion	*Elizabeth Ferrars*
Drowned Rat	*Elizabeth Ferrars*
Foot in the Grave	*Elizabeth Ferrars*

Murders Anonymous	Elizabeth Ferrars
Don't Whistle 'Macbeth'	David Fletcher
A Calculated Risk	Rae Foley
The Slippery Step	Rae Foley
This Woman Wanted	Rae Foley
Home to Roost	Andrew Garve
The Forgotten Story	Winston Graham
Take My Life	Winston Graham
At High Risk	Palma Harcourt
Dance for Diplomats	Palma Harcourt
Count-Down	Hartley Howard
The Appleby File	Michael Innes
A Connoisseur's Case	Michael Innes
Deadline for a Dream	Bill Knox
Death Department	Bill Knox
Hellspout	Bill Knox
The Taste of Proof	Bill Knox
The Affacombe Affair	Elizabeth Lemarchand
Let or Hindrance	Elizabeth Lemarchand
Unhappy Returns	Elizabeth Lemarchand
Waxwork	Peter Lovesey
Gideon's Drive	J. J. Marric
Gideon's Force	J. J. Marric
Gideon's Press	J. J. Marric
City of Gold and Shadows	Ellis Peters
Death to the Landlords!	Ellis Peters
Find a Crooked Sixpence	Estelle Thompson
A Mischief Past	Estelle Thompson

Three Women in the House	*Estelle Thompson*
Bushranger of the Skies	*Arthur Upfield*
Cake in the Hat Box	*Arthur Upfield*
Madman's Bend	*Arthur Upfield*
Tallant for Disaster	*Andrew York*
Tallant for Trouble	*Andrew York*
Cast for Death	*Margaret Yorke*

FICTION TITLES
in the
Ulverscroft Large Print Series

The Onedin Line: The High Seas
       Cyril Abraham
The Onedin Line: The Iron Ships
       Cyril Abraham
The Onedin Line: The Shipmaster
       Cyril Abraham
The Onedin Line: The Trade Winds
       Cyril Abraham
The Enemy   *Desmond Bagley*
Flyaway   *Desmond Bagley*
The Master Idol   *Anthony Burton*
The Navigators   *Anthony Burton*
A Place to Stand   *Anthony Burton*
The Doomsday Carrier   *Victor Canning*
The Cinder Path   *Catherine Cookson*
The Girl   *Catherine Cookson*
The Invisible Cord   *Catherine Cookson*
Life and Mary Ann   *Catherine Cookson*
Maggie Rowan   *Catherine Cookson*
Marriage and Mary Ann *Catherine Cookson*
Mary Ann's Angels   *Catherine Cookson*
All Over the Town   *R. F. Delderfield*
Jamaica Inn   *Daphne du Maurier*
My Cousin Rachel   *Daphne du Maurier*

Enquiry	*Dick Francis*
Flying Finish	*Dick Francis*
Forfeit	*Dick Francis*
High Stakes	*Dick Francis*
In The Frame	*Dick Francis*
Knock Down	*Dick Francis*
Risk	*Dick Francis*
Band of Brothers	*Ernest K. Gann*
Twilight For The Gods	*Ernest K. Gann*
Army of Shadows	*John Harris*
The Claws of Mercy	*John Harris*
Getaway	*John Harris*
Winter Quarry	*Paul Henissart*
East of Desolation	*Jack Higgins*
In the Hour Before Midnight	*Jack Higgins*
Night Judgement at Sinos	*Jack Higgins*
Wrath of the Lion	*Jack Higgins*
Air Bridge	*Hammond Innes*
A Cleft of Stars	*Geoffrey Jenkins*
A Grue of Ice	*Geoffrey Jenkins*
Beloved Exiles	*Agnes Newton Keith*
Passport to Peril	*James Leasor*
Goodbye California	*Alistair MacLean*
South By Java Head	*Alistair MacLean*
All Other Perils	*Robert MacLeod*
Dragonship	*Robert MacLeod*
A Killing in Malta	*Robert MacLeod*
A Property in Cyprus	*Robert MacLeod*

By Command of the Viceroy	Duncan MacNeil
The Deceivers	John Masters
Nightrunners of Bengal	John Masters
Emily of New Moon	L. M. Montgomery
The '44 Vintage	Anthony Price
High Water	Douglas Reeman
Rendezvous-South Atlantic	Douglas Reeman
Summer Lightning	Judith Richards
Louise	Sarah Shears
Louise's Daughters	Sarah Shears
Louise's Inheritance	Sarah Shears
Beyond the Black Stump	Nevil Shute
The Healer	Frank G. Slaughter
Sword and Scalpel	Frank G. Slaughter
Tomorrow's Miracle	Frank G. Slaughter
The Burden	Mary Westmacott
A Daughter's a Daughter	Mary Westmacott
Giant's Bread	Mary Westmacott
The Rose and the Yew Tree	Mary Westmacott
Every Man a King	Anne Worboys
The Serpent and the Staff	Frank Yerby

WESTERN TITLES
in the
Ulverscroft Large Print Series

Gone To Texas	*Forrest Carter*
Dakota Boomtown	*Frank Castle*
Hard Texas Trail	*Matt Chisholm*
Bigger Than Texas	*William R. Cox*
From Hide and Horn	*J. T. Edson*
Gunsmoke Thunder	*J. T. Edson*
The Peacemakers	*J. T. Edson*
Wagons to Backsight	*J. T. Edson*
Arizona Ames	*Zane Grey*
The Lost Wagon Train	*Zane Grey*
Nevada	*Zane Grey*
Rim of the Desert	*Ernest Haycox*
Borden Chantry	*Louis L'Amour*
Conagher	*Louis L'Amour*
The First Fast Draw *and* The Key-Lock Man	*Louis L'Amour*
Kiowa Trail *and* Killoe	*Louis L'Amour*
The Mountain Valley War	*Louis L'Amour*
The Sackett Brand *and* The Lonely Men	*Louis L'Amour*
Taggart	*Louis L'Amour*
Tucker	*Louis L'Amour*
Destination Danger	*Wm. Colt MacDonald*

Powder Smoke Feud *William MacLeod Raine*
Shane *Jack Schaefer*
A Handful of Men *Robert Wilder*